THE STRANGE CASE OF
DR. JEKYLL AND MR. HYDE

AND

KIDNAPPED

BY

ROBERT LOUIS STEVENSON

COURT BOOK COMPANY
NEW YORK :: :: N. Y.

Special Printing, May, 1941

 199

Printed in the United States of America
BY J. J. LITTLE & IVES COMPANY, NEW YORK

THE STRANGE CASE OF
DR. JEKYLL AND MR. HYDE

THE STRANGE CASE OF
DR. JEKYLL AND MR. HYDE.

STORY OF THE DOOR.

Mr. Utterson the lawyer was a man of a rugged countenance, that was never lighted by a smile; cold, scanty and em-
barrassed in discourse; backward in sentiment; lean, long,
dusty, dreary and yet somehow lovable. At friendly meetings,
and when the wine was to his taste, something eminently
human beaconed from his eye; something indeed which
never found its way into his talk, but which spoke not only
in these silent symbols of the after-dinner face, but more
often and loudly in the acts of his life. He was austere
with himself; drank gin when he was alone, to mortify a
taste for vintages; and though he enjoyed the theater, had
not crossed the doors of one for twenty years. But he had
an approved tolerance for others; sometimes wondering, almost with envy, at the high pressure of spirits involved
in their misdeeds; and in any extremity inclined to help rather
than to reprove. "I incline to Cain's heresy," he used to
say quaintly: "I let my brother go to the devil in his own
way." In this character, it was frequently his fortune to be
the last reputable acquaintance and the last good influence in
the lives of down-going men. And to such as these, so
long as they came about his chambers, he never marked a
shade of change in his demeanor.

No doubt the feat was easy to Mr. Utterson; for he
was undemonstrative at the best, and even his friendships
seemed to be founded in a similar catholicity of good-nature.
It is the mark of a modest man to accept his friendly circle
ready-made from the hands of opportunity; and that was the

lawyer's way. His friends were those of his own blood, or those whom he had known the longest; his affections, like ivy, were the growth of time, they implied no aptness in the object. Hence, no doubt, the bond that united him to Mr. Richard Enfield, his distant kinsman, the well-known man about town. It was a nut to crack for many, what these two could see in each other, or what subject they could find in common. It was reported by those who encountered them in their Sunday walks that they said nothing, looked singularly dull, and would hail with obvious relief the appearance of a friend. For all that, the two men put the greatest store by these excursions, counted them the chief jewel of each week, and not only set aside occasions of pleasure, but even resisted the calls of business, that they might enjoy them uninterrupted.

It chanced on one of these rambles that their way led them down a by-street in a busy quarter of London. The street was small and what is called quiet, but it drove a thriving trade on the weekdays. The inhabitants were all doing well, it seemed, and all emulously hoping to do better still, and laying out the surplus of their gains in coquetry; so that the shop fronts stood along that thoroughfare with an air of invitation, like rows of smiling saleswomen. Even on Sunday, when it veiled its more florid charms and lay comparatively empty of passage, the street shone out in contrast to its dingy neighborhood, like a fire in a forest; and with its freshly painted shutters, well-polished brasses, and general cleanliness and gayety of note, instantly caught and pleased the eye of the passenger.

Two doors from one corner, on the left hand going east, the line was broken by the entry of a court; and just at that point a certain sinister block of building thrust forward its gable on the street. It was two stories high; showed no window, nothing but a door on the lower story and a blind forehead of discolored wall on the upper; and bore in every feature the marks of prolonged and sordid negligence. The door, which was equipped with neither bell nor knocker, was blistered and distained. Tramps slouched into the recess and struck matches on the panels, children kept shop upon the steps; the schoolboy had tried his knife on the moldings;

and for close on a generation no one had appeared to drive away these random visitors or to repair their ravages.

Mr. Enfield and the lawyer were on the other side of the by-street; but when they came abreast of the entry the former lifted up his cane and pointed.

"Did you ever remark that door?" he asked; and when his companion had replied in the affirmative, "It is connected in my mind," added he, "with a very odd story."

"Indeed?" said Mr. Utterson, with a slight change of voice, "and what was that?"

"Well, it was this way," returned Mr. Enfield; "I was coming home from some place at the end of the world, about three o'clock of a black winter morning, and my way lay through a part of town where there was literally nothing to be seen but lamps. Street after street, and all the folks asleep—street after street, all lighted up as if for a procession and all as empty as a church—till at last I got into that state of mind when a man listens and listens and begins to long for the sight of a policeman. All at once I saw two figures: one a little man who was stumping along eastward at a good walk, and the other a girl of maybe eight or ten, who was running as hard as she was able down a cross street. Well, sir, the two ran into one another naturally enough at the corner; and then came the horrible part of things; for the man trampled calmly over the child's body and left her screaming on the ground. It sounds nothing to hear, but it was hellish to see. It wasn't like a man; it was like some damned Juggernaut. I gave a view halloa, took to my heels, collared my gentleman, and brought him back to where there was already quite a group about the screaming child. He was perfectly cool and made no resistance, but gave me one look, so ugly that it brought out the sweat on me like running. The people who had turned out were the girl's own family; and pretty soon the doctor, for whom she had been sent, put in his appearance. Well, the child was not much the worse, more frightened, according to the Sawbones; and there you might have supposed would be an end to it. But there was one curious circumstance. I had taken a loathing to my gentleman at first sight. So had the child's family, which was only natural. But the doctor's case was what struck me. He was the usual cut-and-dry apothecary, of no particular age and color, with a strong Edinburgh accent, and about as emotional as a bagpipe. Well, sir, he was like the rest of us; every time he looked at my prisoner I saw that Sawbones turn sick and white with the desire to kill him. I knew what was in his mind, just as he knew what was in mine; and killing being out of the question, we did the next best. We told the man we could and would make such a scandal out of this as should make his name stink from one end of London to the other. If he had any friends or any credit, we undertook that he should lose them. And all the time, as we were pitching it in red-hot, we were keeping the women off him as best we could, for they were as wild as harpies. I never saw a circle of such hateful faces; and there was the man in the middle, with a kind of black, sneering coolness—frightened, too, I could see that—but carrying it off, sir, really like Satan. 'If you choose to make capital out of this accident,' said he, 'I am naturally helpless. No gentleman but wishes to avoid a scene,' says he. 'Name your figure.' Well, we screwed him up to a hundred pounds for the child's family; he would have clearly liked to stick out; but there was something about the lot of us that meant mischief, and at last he struck. The next thing was to get the money; and where do you think he carried us but to that place with the door?—whipped out a key, went in, and presently came back with the matter of ten pounds in gold and a check for the balance on Coutts', drawn payable to bearer and signed with a name that I can't mention, though it's one of the points of my story, but it was a name at least very well known and often printed. The figure was stiff; but the signature was good for more than that, if it was only genuine. I took the liberty of pointing out to my gentleman that the whole business looked apocryphal, and that a man does not, in real life, walk into a cellar door at four in the morning and come out of it with another man's check for close upon a hundred pounds. But he was quite easy and sneering. 'Set your mind at rest,' says he, 'I will stay with you till the banks open and cash the check myself.' So we all set off, the doctor, and the child's father, and our friend and myself, and passed the rest of the night in my chambers; and next day, when we had breakfasted, went in a body to the bank. I gave in the check myself, and said I had every reason to believe it was a forgery. Not a bit of it. The check was genuine."

"Tut—tut," said Mr. Utterson.

"I see you feel as I do," said Mr. Enfield. "Yes, it's a bad story. For my man was a fellow that nobody could have to do with, a really damnable man; and the person that drew the check is the very pink of the proprieties, celebrated, too, and (what makes it worse) one of your fellows who do what they call good. Blackmail, I suppose; an honest man paying through the nose for some of the capers of his youth. Black Mail House is what I call that place with the door, in consequence. Though even that, you know, is far from explaining all," he added, and with the words fell into a vein of musing.

From this he was recalled by Mr. Utterson asking rather suddenly: "And you don't know if the drawer of the check lives there?"

"A likely place, isn't it?" returned Mr. Enfield. "But I happened to have noticed his address; he lives in some square or other."

"And you never asked about the—place with the door?" said Mr. Utterson.

"No, sir; I had a delicacy," was the reply. "I feel very strongly about putting questions; it partakes too much of the style of the day of judgment. You start a question, and it's like starting a stone. You sit quietly on the top of a hill; and away the stone goes, starting others; and presently some bland old bird (the last you would have thought of) is knocked on the head in his own back garden and the family have to change their name. No, sir, I make it a rule of mine: the more it looks like Queer Street, the less I ask."

"A very good rule, too," said the lawyer.

"But I have studied the place for myself," continued Mr. Enfield. "It seems scarcely a house. There is no other door, and nobody goes in or out of that one, but, once in a great while, the gentleman of my adventure. There are three windows looking on the court on the first floor; none below;

the windows are always shut, but they're clean. And then there is a chimney which is generally smoking; so somebody must live there. And yet it's not so sure; for the buildings are so packed together about that court that it's hard to say where one ends and another begins."

The pair walked on again for awhile in silence; and 'then, "Enfield," said Mr. Utterson, "that's a good rule of yours."

"Yes, I think it is," returned Enfield.

"But for all that," continued the lawyer, "there's one point I want to ask. I want to ask the name of that man who walked over the child."

"Well," said Mr. Enfield, "I can't see what harm it would do. It was a man of the name of Hyde."

"H'm," said Mr. Utterson. "What sort of a man is he to see?"

"He is not easy to describe. There is something wrong with his appearance; something displeasing, something downright detestable. I never saw a man I so disliked, and yet I scarcely know why. He must be deformed somewhere; he gives a strong feeling of deformity, although I couldn't specify the point. He's an extraordinary-looking man, and yet I really can name nothing out of the way. No, sir; I can make no hand of it; I can't describe him. And it's not want of memory; for I declare I can see him this moment."

Mr. Utterson again walked some way in silence and obviously under a weight of consideration. "You are sure he used a key?" he inquired at last.

"My dear sir—" began Enfield, surprised out of himself.

"Yes, I know," said Utterson; "I know it must seem strange. The fact is, if I do not ask you the name of the other party, it is because I know it already. You see, Richard, your tale has gone home. If you have been inexact in any point, you had better correct it."

"I think you might have warned me," returned the other with a touch of sullenness. "But I have been pedantically exact, as you call it. The fellow had a key; and what's more, he has it still. I saw him use it, not a week ago."

Mr. Utterson sighed deeply, but said never a word; and the young man presently resumed. "Here is another lesson to say nothing," said he. "I am ashamed of my long tongue. Let us make a bargain never to refer to this again."

"With all my heart," said the lawyer. "I shake hands on that, Richard."

SEARCH FOR MR. HYDE.

That evening Mr. Utterson came home to his bachelor house in somber spirits and sat down to dinner without relish. It was his custom of a Sunday, when this meal was over, to sit close by the fire, a volume of some dry divinity on his reading-desk, until the clock of the neighboring church rang out the hour of twelve, when he would go soberly and gratefully to bed. On this night, however, as soon as the cloth was taken away he took up a candle and went into his business-room. There he opened his safe, took from the most private part of it a document indorsed on the envelope as Dr. Jekyll's Will, and sat down with a clouded brow to study its contents. The will was holograph, for Mr. Utterson, though he took charge of it now that it was made, had refused to lend the least assistance in the making of it; it provided not only that, in case of the decease of Henry Jekyll, M.D., D.C.L., LL.D., F.R.S., etc., all his possessions were to pass into the hands of his "friend and benefactor Edward Hyde," but that in case of Dr. Jekyll's "disappearance or unexplained absence for any period exceeding three calendar months," the said Edward Hyde should step into the said Henry Jekyll's shoes without further delay and free from any burden or obligation, beyond the payment of a few small sums to the members of the doctor's household. This document had long been the lawyer's eyesore. It offended him both as a lawyer and as a lover of the sane and customary sides of life, to whom the fanciful was the immodest. And hitherto it was his ignorance of Mr. Hyde that had swelled his indignation; now, by a sudden turn, it was his knowledge. It was already bad enough when the name was but a name of which he could learn no more. It was worse when it began to be clothed upon with detestable attributes; and out of the shifting, insubstantial mists that had so long baffled his eye, there leaped up the sudden, definite presentment of a fiend.

"I thought it was madness," he said, as he replaced the obnoxious paper in the safe, "and now I begin to fear it is disgrace."

With that he blew out his candle, put on a greatcoat and set forth in the direction of Cavendish Square, that citadel of medicine, where his friend, the great Dr. Lanyon, had his house and received his crowding patients. "If any one knows, it will be Lanyon," he had thought.

The solemn butler knew and welcomed him; he was subjected to no stage of delay, but ushered direct from the door to the dining-room where Dr. Lanyon sat alone over his wine. This was a hearty, healthy, dapper, red-faced gentleman, with a shock of hair prematurely white, and a boisterous and decided manner. At sight of Mr. Utterson, he sprung up from his chair and welcomed him with both hands. The geniality, as was the way of the man, was somewhat theatrical to the eye; but it reposed on genuine feeling. For these two were old friends, old mates both at school and college, both thorough respecters of themselves and of each other, and, what does not always follow, men who thoroughly enjoyed each other's company.

After a little rambling talk the lawyer led up to the subject which so disagreeably preoccupied his mind.

"I suppose, Lanyon," said he, "you and I must be the two oldest friends that Henry Jekyll has?"

"I wish the friends were younger," chuckled Dr. Lanyon. "But I suppose we are. And what of that? I see little of him now."

"Indeed?" said Utterson. "I thought you had a bond of common interest."

"We had," was the reply. "But it is more than ten years since Henry Jekyll became too fanciful for me. He began to go wrong, wrong in mind; and though of course I continue to take an interest in him for old sake's sake, as they say, I see and I have seen devilish little of the man. Such unscientific balderdash," added the doctor, flushing suddenly purple, "would have estranged Damon and Pythias."

This little spirit of temper was somewhat of a relief to Mr. Utterson. "They have only differed on some point of science," he thought; and being a man of no scientific passions (except in the matter of conveyancing) he even added, "It is nothing worse than that!" He gave his friend a few seconds to recover his composure, and then approached the question he had come to put. "Did you ever come across a protégé of his—one Hyde?" he asked.

"Hyde?" repeated Lanyon. "No. Never heard of him. Since my time."

That was the amount of information that the lawyer carried back with him to the great, dark bed on which he tossed to and fro, until the small hours of the morning began to grow large. It was a night of little ease to his toiling mind, toiling in mere darkness, and besieged by questions.

Six o'clock struck on the bells of the church that was so conveniently near to Mr. Utterson's dwelling, and still he was digging at the problem. Hitherto it had touched him on the intellectual side alone; but now his imagination also was engaged or rather enslaved; and as he lay and tossed in the gross darkness of the night and the curtained room, Mr. Enfield's tale went by before his mind in a scroll of lighted pictures. He would be aware of the great field of lamps of a nocturnal city; then of the figure of a man walking swiftly; then of a child running from the doctor's; and then these met, and that human Juggernaut trod the child down and passed on regardless of her screams. Or else he would see a room in a rich house, where his friend lay asleep, dreaming and smiling at his dreams; and then the door of that room would be opened, the curtains of the bed plucked apart, the sleeper recalled, and lo! there would stand by his side a figure to whom power was given, and, even at that dead hour, he must rise and do its bidding. The figure in these two phases haunted the lawyer all night; and if at any time he dozed over, it was but to see it glide more stealthily through sleeping houses, or move the more swiftly and still the more swiftly, even to dizziness, through wider labyrinths of lamp-lighted city, and at every street corner crush a child and leave her screaming. And still the figure had no face by which he might know it; even in his dreams it had no face, or one that baffled him and melted before his eyes; and thus it was that there sprung up and grew apace in the lawyer's mind a singularly strong, almost an inordinate curiosity to behold the features of the real Mr. Hyde. If he could once set eyes on him, he thought the mystery would lighten and perhaps roll altogether away, as was the habit of mysterious things when well examined. He might see a reason for his friend's strange preference or bondage (call it which you please), and even for the startling clause of the will. At least it would be a face worth seeing: the face of a man who was without bowels or mercy; a face which had but to show itself to raise up, in the mind of the unimpressionable Enfield, a spirit of enduring hatred.

From that time forward Mr. Utterson began to haunt the door in the by-street of shops. In the morning before office hours, at noon, when business was plenty and time scarce, at night under the face of the fogged city moon, by all lights and at all hours of solitude or concourse, the lawyer was to be found on his chosen post.

"If he be Mr. Hyde," he thought, "I shall be Mr. Seek."

And at last his patience was rewarded. It was a fine, dry night; frost in the air; the streets as clean as a ball-room floor; the lamps, unshaken by any wind, drawing a regular pattern of light and shadow. By ten o'clock, when the shops were closed, the by street was very solitary and, in spite of the low growl of London from all round, very silent. Small sounds carried far; domestic sounds out of the houses were clearly audible on either side of the roadway, and the rumor of the approach of any passenger preceded him by a long time. Mr. Utterson had been some minutes at his post, when he was aware of an odd, light footstep drawing near. In the course of his nightly patrols he had long grown accustomed to the quaint effect with which the footfalls of a single person, while he is still a great way off, suddenly spring out distinct from the vast hum and clatter of the city. Yet his attention had never before been so sharply and decisively arrested, and it was with a strong, superstitious prevision of success that he withdrew into the entry of the court.

The steps drew swiftly nearer and swelled out suddenly louder as they turned the end of the street. The lawyer, looking forth from the entry, could soon see what manner of man he had to deal with. He was small and very plainly dressed, and the look of him, even at that distance, went somehow strongly against the watcher's inclination. But he made straight for the door, crossing the roadway to save time, and as he came he drew a key from his pocket like one approaching home.

Mr. Utterson stepped out and touched him on the shoulder as he passed. "Mr. Hyde, I think?"

Mr. Hyde shrunk back with a hissing intake of the breath. But his fear was only momentary, and though he did not look the lawyer in the face he answered coolly enough: "That is my name. What do you want?"

"I see you are going in," returned the lawyer. "I am an old friend of Dr. Jekyll's—Mr. Utterson, of Gaunt Street—you must have heard my name, and meeting you so conveniently I thought you might admit me."

"You will not find Dr. Jekyll; he is from home," replied Mr. Hyde, blowing in the key. And then suddenly, but still without looking up. "How did you know me?" he asked.

"On your side," said Mr. Utterson, "will you do me a favor?"

"With pleasure," replied the other. "What shall it be?"

"Will you let me see your face?" asked the lawyer.

Mr. Hyde appeared to hesitate, and then, as if upon some sudden reflection, fronted about with an air of defiance; and the pair stared at each other pretty fixedly for a few seconds. "Now I shall know you again," said Mr. Utterson. "It may be useful."

"Yes," returned Mr. Hyde, "it is as well we have met; and *a propos,* you should have my address." And he gave a number of a street in Soho.

"Good God!" thought Mr. Utterson, "can he, too, have been thinking of the will?" But he kept his feelings to himself and only grunted in acknowledgement of the address.

"And now," said the other, "how did you know me?"

"By description," was the reply.

"Whose description?"

"We have common friends," said Mr. Utterson.

"Common friends?" echoed Mr. Hyde, a little hoarsely. "Who are they?"

"Jekyll, for instance," said the lawyer.

"He never told you," cried Mr. Hyde, with a flush of anger. "I did not think you would have lied."

"Come," said Mr. Utterson, "that is not fitting language."

The other snarled aloud into a savage laugh; and the next moment, with extraordinary quickness, he had unlocked the door and disappeared into the house.

The lawyer stood awhile when Mr. Hyde had left him, the picture of disquietude. Then he began slowly to mount the street, pausing every step or two and putting his hand to his brow like a man in mental perplexity. The problem he was thus debating as he walked was one of a class that is rarely solved. Mr. Hyde was pale and dwarfish, he gave an impression of deformity without any namable malformation, he had a displeasing smile, he had borne himself to the lawyer with a sort of murderous mixture of timidity and boldness, and he spoke with a husky, whispering, and somewhat broken voice: all these were points against him, but not all of these together could explain the hitherto unknown disgust, loathing, and fear with which Mr. Utterson regarded him. "There must be something else," said the perplexed gentleman. "There *is* something more, if I could find a name for it. God bless me, the man seems hardly human! Something troglodytic, shall we say? or can it be the old story of Dr. Fell? or is it the mere radiance of a foul soul that thus transpires through, and transfigures its clay continent? The last, I think; for oh, my poor old Harry Jekyll, if ever I read Satan's signature on a face, it is on that of your new friend."

Round the corner from the by-street there was a square of ancient, handsome houses, now for the most part decayed from their high estate and let in flats and chambers to all sorts and conditions of men: map engravers, architects, shady lawyers, and the agents of obscure enterprises. One house, however, second from the corner, was still occupied entire; and at the door of this, which wore a great air of wealth and comfort, though it was now plunged in darkness except for the fanlight, Mr. Utterson stopped and knocked. A well-dressed, elderly servant opened the door.

"Is Dr. Jekyll at home, Poole?" asked the lawyer.

"I will see, Mr. Utterson," said Poole, admitting the visitor, as he spoke, into a large, low-roofed, comfortable hall, paved with flags, warmed (after the fashion of a country house) by a bright, open fire, and furnished with costly cabinets of oak. "Will you wait here by the fire, sir? or shall I give you a light in the dining-room?"

"Here, thank you," said the lawyer, and he drew near and leaned on the tall fender. This hall, in which he was now left alone, was a pet fancy of his friend the doctor's; and Utterson himself was wont to speak of it as the pleasantest room in London. But to-night there was a shudder in his blood; the face of Hyde sat heavy on his memory; he felt (what is rare with him) a nausea and distaste of life; and in the gloom of his spirits, he seemed to read a menace in the flickering of the firelight on the polished cabinets and the uneasy starting of the shadow on the roof. He was ashamed of his relief, when Poole presently returned to announce that Dr. Jekyll was gone out.

"I saw Mr. Hyde go in by the old dissecting-room door, Poole," he said. "Is that right, when Dr. Jekyll is from home?"

"Quite right, Mr. Utterson, sir," replied the servant. "Mr. Hyde has a key."

"Your master seems to repose a great deal of trust in that young man, Poole," resumed the other musingly.

"Yes, sir, he do, indeed," said Poole. "We have all orders to obey him."

"I do not think I ever met Mr. Hyde?" asked Utterson.

"Oh, dear, no, sir. He never *dines* here," replied the butler. "Indeed, we see very little of him on this side of the house; he mostly comes and goes by the laboratory."

"Well, good-night, Poole."

"Good-night, Mr. Utterson."

And the lawyer set out homeward with a very heavy heart. "Poor Harry Jekyll," he thought, "my mind misgives me he is in deep waters! He was wild when he was young—a long while ago, to be sure; but in the law of God there is no statute of limitations. Ay, it must be that, the ghost of some old sin, the cancer of some concealed disgrace: punishment coming, *pede claudo,* years after memory has forgotten, and self-love condoned the fault." And the lawyer,

scared by the thought, brooded awhile on his own past, groping in all the corners of memory, lest, by chance, some Jack-
in-the-Box of an old iniquity should leap to light there. His
past was fairly blameless; few men could read the rolls of
their life with less apprehension; yet he was humbled to
the dust by the many ill things he had done, and raised up
again into a sober and fearful gratitude by the many that
he had come so near to doing, yet avoided. And then, by a
return on his former subject, he conceived a spark of hope.
"This Master Hyde, if he were studied," thought he, "must
have secrets of his own—black secrets, by the look of him:
secrets compared to which poor Jekyll's worst would be like
sunshine. Things cannot continue as they are. It turns me
cold to think of this creature stealing like a thief to Harry's
bedside; poor Harry, what a wakening! And the danger of
it; for if this Hyde suspects the existence of the will, he
may grow impatient to inherit! Ay, I must put my shoulder
to the wheel, if Jekyll will but let me," he added, "if Jekyll
will only let me." For once more he saw before his mind's
eye, as clear as a transparency, the strange clauses of the will.

DR. JEKYLL WAS QUITE AT EASE.

A fortnight later, by excellent good fortune, the doctor
gave one of his pleasant dinners to some five or six old
cronies, all intelligent, reputable men, and all judges of good
wine; and Mr. Utterson so contrived that he remained behind after the others had departed. This was no new
arrangement, but a thing that had befallen many scores of
times. Where Utterson was liked, he was liked well. Hosts
loved to detain the dry lawyer, when the light-hearted and
the loose-tongued had already their foot on the threshold;
they liked to sit awhile in his unobtrusive company, prac-
ticing for solitude, sobering their minds in the man's rich
silence after the expense and strain of gayety. To this rule
Dr. Jekyll was no exception; and as he now sat on the opposite side of the fire—a large, well-made, smooth-faced man
of fifty, with something of a slyish cast, perhaps, but every
mark of capacity and kindness—you could see by his looks

that he cherished for Mr. Utterson a sincere and warm affection.

"I have been wanting to speak to you, Jekyll," began the latter. "You know that will of yours?"

A close observer might have gathered that the topic was distasteful; but the doctor carried it off gayly. "My poor Utterson," said he, "you are unfortunate in such a client. I never saw a man so distressed as you were by my will; unless it were that hide-bound pedant, Lanyon, at what he called my scientific heresies. Oh, I know he's a good fellow—you needn't frown—an excellent fellow, and I always mean to see more of him; but a hide-bound pedant for all that; an ignorant, blatant pedant. I was never more disappointed in any man than Lanyon."

"You know I never approved of it," pursued Utterson, ruthlessly disregarding the fresh topic.

"My will? Yes, certainly, I know that," said the doctor, a trifle sharply. "You have told me so."

"Well, I tell you so again," continued the lawyer. "I have been learning something of young Hyde."

The large handsome face of Dr. Jekyll grew pale to the very lips, and there came a blackness about his eyes. "I do not care to hear more," said he. "This is a matter I thought we had agreed to drop."

"What I heard was abominable," said Utterson.

"It can make no change. You do not understand my position," returned the doctor, with a certain incoherency of manner. "I am painfully situated, Utterson; my position is a very strange—a very strange one. It is one of those affairs that cannot be mended by talking."

"Jekyll," said Utterson, "you know me: I am a man to be trusted. Make a clean breast of this in confidence, and I make no doubt I can get you out of it."

"My good Utterson," said the doctor, "this is very good of you; this is downright good of you, and I cannot find words to thank you in. I believe you fully; I would trust you before any man alive, ay, before myself, if I could make the choice; but indeed it isn't what you fancy; it is not so bad as that; and just to put your good heart at rest, I will tell you one thing: the moment I choose, I can be rid of Mr.

Hyde. I give you my hand upon that; and I thank you again and again; and I will just add one little word, Utterson, that I'm sure you'll take in good part: this is a private matter, and I beg of you to let it sleep."

Utterson reflected a little, looking in the fire.

"I have no doubt you are perfectly right," he said at last, getting to his feet.

"Well, but since we have touched upon this business, and for the last time I hope," continued the doctor, "there is one point I should like you to understand. I have really a very great interest in poor Hyde. I know you have seen him; he told me so; and I fear he was rude. But I do sincerely take a great, a very great interest in that young man; and if I am taken away, Utterson, I wish you to promise me that you will bear with him and get his rights for him. I think you would, if you knew all; and it would be a weight off my mind if you would promise."

"I can't pretend that I shall ever like him," said the lawyer.

"I don't ask that," pleaded Jekyll, laying his hand upon the other's arm; "I only ask for justice; I only ask you to help him for my sake, when I am no longer here."

Utterson heaved an irrepressible sigh. "Well," said he, "I promise."

THE CAREW MURDER CASE.

Nearly a year later, in the month of October, 18—, London was startled by a crime of singular ferocity, and rendered all the more notable by the high position of the victim. The details were few and startling. A maid servant, living alone in a house not far from the river, had gone upstairs to bed about eleven. Although a fog rolled over the city in the small hours, the early part of the night was cloudless, and the lane, which the maid's window overlooked, was brilliantly lit by the full moon. It seems she was romantically given, for she sat down upon her box, which stood immediately under the window, and fell into a dream of musing. Never (she used to say, with streaming tears, when she narrated that experience), never had she felt more at peace with all men or thought more kindly of the world. And as she so sat she became aware of an aged and beautiful gentleman with white hair drawing near along the lane, and advancing to meet him another and very small gentleman, to whom at first she paid less attention. When they had come within speech (which was just under the maid's eyes) the older man bowed and accosted the other with a very pretty manner of politeness. It did not seem as if the subject of his address were of great importance; indeed, from his pointing, it sometimes appeared as if he were only inquiring his way, but the moon shone on his face as he spoke and the girl was pleased to watch it; it seemed to breathe such an innocent and old-world kindness of disposition, yet with something high, too, as of a well-founded self-content. Presently her eye wandered to the other, and she was surprised to recognize in him a certain Mr. Hyde, who had once visited her master and for whom she had conceived a dislike. He had in his hand a heavy cane, with which he was trifling, but he answered never a word and seemed to listen with an ill-contained impatience. And then all of a sudden he broke out in a great flame of anger, stamping with his foot, brandishing the cane and carrying on (as the maid described it) like a madman. The old gentleman took a step back, with the air of one very much surprised and a trifle hurt, and at that Mr. Hyde broke out of all bounds and clubbed him to the earth. And next moment, with ape-like fury, he was trampling his victim under foot and hailing down a storm of blows, under which the bones were audibly shattered and the body jumped upon the roadway. At the horror of these sights and sounds the maid fainted.

It was two o'clock when she came to herself and called for the police. The murderer was gone long ago, but there lay his victim in the middle of the lane, incredibly mangled. The stick with which the deed had been done, although it was of some rare and very tough and heavy wood, had broken in the middle under the stress of this insensate cruelty, and one splintered half had rolled in the neighboring gutter; the other, without doubt, had been carried away by the murderer. A purse and a gold watch were found upon the victim, but no cards or papers, except a sealed and stamped envelope, which he had been probably carrying to the post, and which bore the name and address of Mr. Utterson.

This was brought to the lawyer the next morning before he was out of bed, and he had no sooner seen it and been told the circumstances than he shot out a solemn lip. "I shall say nothing till I have seen the body," said he; "this may be very serious. Have the kindness to wait while I dress." And with the same grave countenance he hurried through his breakfast and drove to the police station, whither the body had been carried. As soon as he came into the cell he nodded.

"Yes," said he, "I recognize him. I am sorry to say that this is Sir Danvers Carew."

"Good God, sir," exclaimed the officer, "is it possible?" and the next moment his eyes lighted up with professional ambition. "This will make a deal of noise," he said. "And perhaps you can help us to the man." And he briefly narrated what the maid had seen, and showed the broken stick.

Mr. Utterson had already quailed at the name of Hyde, but when the stick was laid before him he could doubt no longer; broken and battered as it was, he recognized it for one that he had himself presented many years before to Henry Jekyll.

"Is this Mr. Hyde a person of small stature?" he inquired.

"Particularly small and particularly wicked-looking, is what the maid calls him," said the officer.

Mr. Utterson reflected; and then, raising his head, "If you will come with me in my cab," he said, "I think I can take you to his house."

It was by this time about nine in the morning, and the first fog of the season. A great chocolate-colored pall lowered over heaven, but the wind was continually charging and routing these embattled vapors; so that as the cab crawled from street to street, Mr. Utterson beheld a marvelous number of degrees and hues of twilight; for here it would be dark like the black end of evening; and there would be a glow of a rich, lurid brown, like the light of some strange conflagration; and here, for a moment, the fog would be quite broken up, and ╌ haggard shaft of daylight would glance in between the swirling wreaths. The dismal quarter of Soho seen under these changing glimpses, with its muddy ways, and slatternly passengers, and its lamps, which had never been extinguished or had been kindled afresh to combat this mournful reinvasion of darkness, seemed, in the lawyer's eyes, like a district of some city in a nightmare. The thoughts of his mind, besides, were of the gloomiest dye; and when he glanced at the companion of his drive he was conscious of some touch of that terror of the law and the law's officers which may at times assail the most honest.

As the cab drew up before the address indicated, the fog lifted a little and showed him a dingy street, a gin-palace, a low French eating-house, a shop for the retail of penny numbers and twopenny salads, many ragged children huddled in the doorways, and many women of many different nationalities passing out, key in hand, to have a morning glass; and the next moment the fog settled down again upon that part, as brown as umber, and cut him off from his blackguardly surroundings. This was the home of Henry Jekyll's favorite; of a man who was heir to quarter of a million sterling.

An ivory-faced and silvery-haired old woman opened the door. She had an evil face, smoothed by hypocrisy, but her manners were excellent. Yes, she said, this was Mr. Hyde's, but he was not at home; he had been in that night very late, but had gone away again in less than an hour; there was nothing strange in that; his habits were very irregular, and he was often absent; for instance, it was nearly two months since she had seen him till yesterday.

"Very well, then, we wish to see his rooms," said the lawyer; and when the woman began to declare it was impossible, "I had better tell you who this person is," he added. "This is Inspector Newcomen of Scotland Yard."

A flash of odious joy appeared upon the woman's face. "Ah!" said she, "he is in trouble! What has he done?"

Mr. Utterson and the inspector exchanged glances. "He don't seem a very popular character," observed the latter. "And now, my good woman, just let me and this gentleman have a look about us."

In the whole extent of the house, which but for the old woman remained otherwise empty, Mr. Hyde had only used a couple of rooms; but these were furnished with luxury and good taste. A closet was filled with wine; the plate was of silver, the napery elegant; a good picture hung upon the walls, a gift (as Utterson supposed) from Henry Jekyll, who was much of a connoisseur; and the carpets were of many plies and agreeable in color. At this moment, however, the rooms bore every mark of having been recently and hurriedly ransacked; clothes lay about the floor with their pockets inside out; lockfast drawers stood open; and on the hearth there lay a pile of gray ashes, as though many papers had been burned. From these embers the inspector disinterred the butt-end of a green check-book, which had resisted the action of the fire; the other half of the stick was found behind the door; and as this clinched his suspicions, the officer declared himself delighted. A visit to the bank, where several thousand pounds were found to be lying to the murderer's credit, completed his gratification.

"You may depend upon it, sir," he told Mr. Utterson: "I have him in my hand. He must have lost his head, or he never would have left the stick, or, above all, burned the check-book. Why, money's life to the man. We have nothing to do but wait for him at the bank, and get out the hand bills."

This last, however, was not so easy of accomplishment; for Mr. Hyde had numbered few familiars—even the master of the servant-maid had only seen him twice; his family could nowhere be traced; he had never been photographed; and the few who could describe him differed widely, as common observers will. Only on one point were they agreed; and that was the haunting sense of unexpressed deformity with which the fugitive impressed his beholders.

INCIDENT OF THE LETTER.

It was late in the afternoon when Mr. Utterson found his way to Dr. Jekyll's door, where he was at once admitted by Poole, and carried down by the kitchen offices and across a yard which had once been a garden, to the building which was indifferently known as the laboratory or the dissecting rooms. The doctor had bought the house from the heirs of a celebrated surgeon; and his own tastes being rather chemical than anatomical, had changed the destination of the block at the bottom of the garden. It was the first time that the lawyer had been received in that part of his friend's quarters; and he eyed the dingy, windowless structure with curiosity, and gazed round with a distasteful sense of strangeness as he crossed the theater, once crowded with eager students and now lying gaunt and silent, the tables laden with chemical apparatus, the floor strewn with crates and littered with packing straw, and the light falling dimly through the foggy cupola. At the further end a flight of stairs mounted to a door covered with red baize; and through this Mr. Utterson was at last received into the doctor's cabinet. It was a large room, fitted round with glass presses; furnished, among other things, with a cheval-glass and a business table, and looking out upon the court by three dusty windows barred with iron. The fire burned in the grate; a lamp was set lighted on the chimney shelf, for even in the houses the fog began to lie thickly; and there, close up to the warmth, sat Dr. Jekyll, looking deadly sick. He did not rise to meet his visitor, but held out a cold hand and bade him welcome in a changed voice.

"And now," said Mr. Utterson, as soon as Poole had left them, "you have heard the news?"

The doctor shuddered. "They were crying it in the square," he said. "I heard them in my dining-room."

"One word," said the lawyer. "Carew was my client, but so are you, and I want to know what I am doing. You have not been mad enough to hide this fellow?"

"Utterson, I swear to God," cried the doctor, "I swear to God I will never set eyes on him again. I bind my honor to you that I am done with him in this world. It is all at an end. And indeed he does not want my help; you do not know him as I do; he is safe, he is quite safe; mark my words, he will nevermore be heard of."

The lawyer listened gloomily; he did not like his friend's feverish manner. "You seem pretty sure of him," said he; "and for your sake, I hope you may be right. If it came to a trial, your name might appear."

"I am quite sure of him," replied Jekyll; "I have grounds for certainty that I cannot share with any one. But there is one thing on which you may advise me. I have—I have received a letter, and I am at a loss whether I should show it to the police. I should like to leave it in your hands, Utterson; you would judge wisely I am sure; I have so great a trust in you."

"You fear, I suppose, that it might lead to his detection?" asked the lawyer.

"No," said the other. "I cannot say that I care what becomes of Hyde; I am quite done with him. I was thinking of my own character, which this hateful business has rather exposed."

Utterson ruminated awhile; he was surprised at his friend's selfishness, and yet relieved by it. "Well," said he, at last, "let me see the letter."

The letter was written in an odd, upright hand, and signed "Edward Hyde;" and it signified, briefly enough, that the writer's benefactor, Dr. Jekyll, whom he had long so unworthily repaid for a thousand generosities, need labor under no alarm for his safety, as he had means of escape on which he placed a sure dependence. The lawyer liked this letter well enough; it put a better color on the intimacy than he had looked for; and he blamed himself for some of his past suspicions.

"Have you the envelope?" he asked.

"I burned it," replied Jekyll, "before I thought what I was about. But it bore no postmark. The note was handed in."

"Shall I keep this and sleep upon it?" asked Utterson.

"I wish you to judge for me entirely," was the reply. "I have lost confidence in myself."

"Well, I shall consider," returned the lawyer. "And now one word more: it was Hyde who dictated the terms in your will about that disappearance?"

The doctor seemed seized with a qualm of faintness; he shut his mouth tight and nodded.

"I knew it," said Utterson. "He meant to murder you. You have had a fine escape."

"I have had what is far more to the purpose," returned the doctor solemnly: "I have had a lesson—oh, God, Utterson, what a lesson I have had!" And he covered his face for a moment with his hands.

On his way out the lawyer stopped and had a word or

two with Poole. "By the by," said he, "there was a letter handed in to-day; what was the messenger like?" But Poole was positive nothing had come except by post; "and only circulars by that," he added.

This news sent off the visitor with his fears renewed. Plainly the letter had come by the laboratory door; possibly, indeed, it had been written in the cabinet; and if that were so, it must be differently judged, and handled with the more caution. The newsboys, as he went, were crying themselves hoarse along the foot-ways: "Special edition. Shocking murder of an M. P." That was the funeral oration of one friend and client; and he could not help a certain apprehension lest the good name of another should be sucked down in the eddy of the scandal. It was, at least, a ticklish decision that he had to make; and self-reliant as he was by habit, he began to cherish a longing for advice. It was not to be had directly; but perhaps, he thought, it might be fished for.

Presently after, he sat on one side of his own hearth, with Mr. Guest, his head clerk, upon the other, and midway between, at a nicely calculated distance from the fire, a bottle of a particular old wine that had long dwelt unsunned in the foundations of his house. The fog still slept on the wing above the drowned city, where the lamps glimmered like carbuncles; and through the muffle and smother of these fallen clouds, the procession of the town's life was still rolling in through the great arteries with a sound as of a mighty wind. But the room was gay with firelight. In the bottle the acids were long ago resolved; the imperial dye had softened with time, as the color grows richer in stained windows; and the glow of hot autumn afternoons on hillside vineyards was ready to be set free and to disperse the fogs of London. Insensibly the lawyer melted. There was no man from whom he kept fewer secrets than Mr. Guest; and he was not always sure that he kept as many as he meant. Guest had often been on business to the doctor's; he knew Poole; he could scarce have failed to hear of Mr. Hyde's familiarity about the house, he might draw conclusions: was it not as well, then, that he should see a letter which put that mystery to rights? and above all since Guest, being a great student and critic of handwriting, would consider the step natural and obliging? The clerk, besides, was a man of counsel; he would scarce read so strange a document without dropping a remark; and by that remark Mr. Utterson might shape his future course.

"This is a sad business about Sir Danvers," he said.

"Yes, sir, indeed. It has elicited a great deal of public feeling," returned Guest. "The man, of course, was mad."

"I should like to hear your views on that," replied Utterson. "I have a document here in his handwriting; it is between ourselves, for I scarce know what to do about it; it is an ugly business at the best. But there it is: quite in your way: a murderer's autograph."

Guest's eyes brightened, and he sat down at once and studied it with passion. "No, sir," he said; "not mad; but it is an odd hand."

"And by all accounts a very odd writer," added the lawyer.

Just then the servant entered with a note.

"Is that from Dr. Jekyll, sir?" inquired the clerk. "I thought I knew the writing. Anything private, Mr. Utterson?"

"Only an invitation to dinner. Why? do you want to see it?"

"One moment. I thank you, sir;" and the clerk laid the two sheets of paper alongside and sedulously compared their contents. "Thank you, sir," he said at last, returning both; "it's a very interesting autograph."

There was a pause, during which Mr. Utterson struggled with himself. "Why did you compare them, Guest?" he inquired suddenly.

"Well, sir," returned the clerk, "there's a rather singular resemblance; the two hands are in many points identical: only differently sloped."

"Rather quaint," said Utterson.

"It is, as you say, rather quaint," returned Guest.

"I wouldn't speak of this note, you know," said the master.

"No, sir," said the clerk. "I understand."

But no sooner was Mr. Utterson alone that night than he locked the note into his safe, where it reposed from that time forward. "What!" he thought. "Henry Jekyll forge for a murderer!" And his blood ran cold in his veins.

REMARKABLE INCIDENT OF DOCTOR LANYON.

Time ran on; thousands of pounds were offered in reward, for the death of Sir Danvers was resented as a public injury; but Mr. Hyde had disappeared out of the ken of the police as though he had never existed. Much of his past was unearthed, indeed, and all disreputable: tales came out of the man's cruelty, at once so callous and violent, of his vile life, of his strange associates, of the hatred that seemed to have surrounded his career; but of his present whereabouts, not a whisper. From the time he had left the house in Soho on the morning of the murder, he was simply blotted out; and gradually, as time grew on, Mr. Utterson began to recover from the hotness of his alarm, and to grow more at quiet with himself. The death of Sir Danvers was, to his way of thinking, more than paid for by the disappearance of Mr. Hyde. Now that that evil influence had been withdrawn a new life began for Dr. Jekyll. He came out of his seclusion, renewed relations with his friends, became once more their familiar guest and entertainer; and while he had always been known for charities, he was now no less distinguished for religion. He was busy, he was much in the open air, he did good; his face seemed to open and brighten, as if with an inward consciousness of service; and for more than two months the doctor was at peace.

On the 8th of January Utterson had dined at the doctor's with a small party; Lanyon had been there; and the face of the host had looked from one to the other as in the old days when the trio were inseparable friends. On the 12th, and again on the 14th, the door was shut against the lawyer. "The doctor was confined to the house," Poole said, "and saw no one." On the 15th he tried again, and was again refused; and having now been used for the last two months to see his friend almost daily, he found this return of solitude to weigh upon his spirits. The fifth night he had in

Guest to dine with him; and the sixth he betook himself to Dr. Lanyon's.

There at least he was not denied admittance; but when he came in he was shocked at the change that had taken place in the doctor's appearance. He had his death-warrant written legibly upon his face. The rosy man had grown pale; his flesh had fallen away; he was visibly balder and older; and yet it was not so much these tokens of a swift physical decay that arrested the lawyer's notice as a look in the eye and quality of manner that seemed to testify to some deep-seated terror of the mind. It was unlikely that the doctor should fear death; and yet that was what Utterson was tempted to suspect. "Yes," he thought: "he is a doctor; he must know his own state and that his days are counted; and the knowledge is more than he can bear." And yet when Utterson remarked on his ill-looks it was with an air of great firmness that Lanyon declared himself a doomed man.

"I have had a shock," he said, "and I shall never recover. It is a question of weeks. Well, life has been pleasant; I liked it; yes, sir, I used to like it. I sometimes think, if we knew all, we should be more glad to get away."

"Jekyll is ill, too," observed Utterson. "Have you seen him?"

But Lanyon's face changed, and he held up a trembling hand. "I wish to see or hear no more of Doctor Jekyll," he said in a loud, unsteady voice. "I am quite done with that person; and I beg that you will spare me any allusion to one whom I regard as dead."

"Tut-tut," said Mr. Utterson; and then after a considerable pause, "Can't I do anything?" he inquired. "We are three very old friends, Lanyon; we shall not live to make others."

"Nothing can be done," returned Lanyon; "ask himself."

"He will not see me," said the lawyer.

"I am not surprised at that," was the reply. "Some day, Utterson, after I am dead, you may perhaps come to learn the right and wrong of this. I cannot tell you. And in the meantime, if you can sit and talk with me of other things, for God's sake, stay and do so; but if you cannot keep clear of this accursed topic, then, in God's name, go, for I cannot bear it."

As soon as he got home Utterson sat down and wrote to Jekyll, complaining of his exclusion from the house, and asking the cause of this unhappy break with Lanyon; and the next day brought him a long answer, often very pathetically worded, and sometimes darkly mysterious in drift. The quarrel with Lanyon was incurable. "I do not blame our old friend," Jekyll wrote, "but I share his view that we must never meet. I mean from henceforth to lead a life of extreme seclusion; you must not be surprised, nor must you doubt my friendship, if my door is often shut, even to you. You must suffer me to go my own dark way. I have brought on myself a punishment and a danger that I cannot name. If I am the chief of sinners, I am the chief of sufferers also. I could not think that this earth contained a place for sufferings and terrors so unmanning; and you can do but one thing, Utterson, to lighten this destiny, and that is to respect my silence." Utterson was amazed; the dark influence of Hades had been withdrawn, the doctor had returned to his old tasks and amities; a week ago the prospect had smiled with every promise of a cheerful and an honored age; and now in a moment friendship and peace of mind, and the whole tenor of his life were wrecked. So great and unprepared a change pointed to madness; but in view of Lanyon's manner and words, there must lie for it some deeper ground.

A week afterward Dr. Lanyon took to his bed, and in something less than a fortnight he was dead. The night after the funeral, at which he had been sadly affected, Utterson locked the door of his business room, and sitting there by the light of a melancholy candle, drew out and set before him an envelope addressed by the hand and sealed with the seal of his dead friend. "PRIVATE: for the hands of G. J. UTTERSON ALONE, and in case of his predecease *to be destroyed unread,*" so it was emphatically superscribed; and the lawyer dreaded to behold the contents. "I have buried one friend to-day," he thought; "what if this should cost me another?" And then he condemned the fear as a disloyalty, and broke the seal. Within there was another inclosure, likewise sealed, and marked upon the cover as "not to be opened till the death or disappearance of Dr. Henry Jekyll." Utterson could not trust his eyes. Yes, it was disappearance; here again, as in the mad will which he had long ago restored to its author, here again were the idea of a disappearance and the name of Henry Jekyll bracketed. But in the will, that idea had sprung from the sinister suggestion of the man Hyde; it was set there with a purpose all too plain and horrible. Written by the hand of Lanyon, what should it mean? A great curiosity came on the trustee, to disregard the prohibition and dive at once to the bottom of these mysteries; but professional honor and faith to his dead friend were stringent obligations; and the packet slept in the inmost corner of his private safe.

It is one thing to mortify curiosity, another to conquer it; and it may be doubted if from that day forth Utterson desired the society of his surviving friend with the same eagerness. He thought of him kindly; but his thoughts were disquieted and fearful. He went to call indeed; but he was perhaps relieved to be denied admittance; perhaps in his heart he desired to speak with Poole upon the doorstep and surrounded by the air and sounds of the open city, rather than to be admitted into that house of voluntary bondage, and to sit and speak with its inscrutable recluse. Poole had, indeed, no very pleasant news to communicate. The doctor, it appeared, now more than ever confined himself to the cabinet over the laboratory, where he would sometimes even sleep; he was out of spirits, he had grown very silent, he did not read; it seemed as if he had something on his mind. Utterson became so used to the unvarying character of these reports that he fell off little by little in the frequency of his visits.

INCIDENT AT THE WINDOW.

It chanced on Sunday, when Mr. Utterson was on his usual walk with Mr. Enfield, that their way lay once again through the by-street; and that when they came in front of the door both stopped to gaze on it.

"Well," said Enfield, "that story's at an end at least. We shall never see more of Mr. Hyde."

"I hope not," said Utterson. "Did I ever tell you that I once saw him, and shared your feeling of repulsion?"

"It was impossible to do the one without the other," returned Enfield. "And by the way, what an ass you must have thought me, not to know that this was a back way to Dr. Jekyll's! It was partly your own fault that I found it out, even when I did."

"So you found it out, did you?" said Utterson. "But if that be so, we may step into the court and take a look at the windows. To tell you the truth, I am uneasy about poor Jekyll; and even outside, I feel as if the presence of a friend might do him good."

The court was very cool and a little damp, and full of premature twilight, although the sky, high up overhead, was still bright with sunset. The middle one of the three windows was halfway open; and sitting close beside it, taking the air with an infinite sadness of mien, like some disconsolate prisoner, Utterson saw Dr. Jekyll.

"What! Jekyll!" he cried. "I trust you are better."

"I am very low, Utterson," replied the doctor drearily, "very low. It will not last long, thank God."

"You stay too much indoors," said the lawyer. "You should be out, whipping up the circulation like Mr. Enfield and me. (This is my cousin—Mr. Enfield—Dr. Jekyll.) Come now; get your hat and take a quick turn with us."

"You are very good," sighed the other. "I should like to very much; but no, no, no, it is quite impossible; I dare not. But indeed, Utterson, I am very glad to see you; this is really a great pleasure; I would ask you and Mr. Enfield up, but the place is really not fit."

"Why, then," said the lawyer good-naturedly, "the best thing we can do is to stay down here and speak with you from where we are."

"That is just what I was about to venture to propose," returned the doctor with a smile. But the words were hardly uttered before the smile was struck out of his face and succeeded by an expression of such abject terror and despair as froze the very blood of the two gentlemen below. They saw it but for a glimpse, for the window was instantly thrust down; but that glimpse had been sufficient, and they turned and left the court without a word. In silence, too, they traversed the by-street; and it was not until they had come into a neighboring thoroughfare, where even upon a Sunday there were still some stirrings of life, that Mr. Utterson at last turned and looked at his companion. They were both pale; and there was an answering horror in their eyes.

"God forgive us, God forgive us," said Mr. Utterson.

But Mr. Enfield only nodded his head very seriously, and walked on once more in silence.

THE LAST NIGHT.

Mr. Utterson was sitting by his fireside one evening after dinner, when he was surprised to receive a visit from Poole.

"Bless me, Poole, what brings you here?" he cried; and then taking a second look at him, "What ails you?" he added, is the doctor ill?"

"Mr. Utterson," said the man, "there is something wrong."

"Take a seat, and here is a glass of wine for you," said the lawyer. "Now, take your time, and tell me plainly what you want."

"You know the doctor's ways, sir," replied Poole, "and how he shuts himself up. Well, he's shut up again in the cabinet; and I don't like it, sir—I wish I may die if I like it. Mr. Utterson, sir, I'm afraid."

"Now, my good man," said the lawyer, "be explicit. What are you afraid of?"

"I've been afraid for about a week," returned Poole, doggedly disregarding the question, "and I can bear it no more."

The man's appearance amply bore out his words; his manner was altered for the worse; and, except for the moment when he had first announced his terror, he had not once looked the lawyer in the face. Even now, he sat with the glass of wine untasted on his knee, and his eyes directed to a corner of the floor. "I can bear it no more," he repeated.

"Come," said the lawyer, "I see you have some good reason, Poole; I see there is something seriously amiss. Try to tell me what it is."

"I think there has been foul play," said Poole hoarsely.

"Foul play!" cried the lawyer, a good deal frightened and rather inclined to be irritated in consequence. "What foul play? What does the man mean?"

"I daren't say, sir," was the answer; "but will you come along with me and see for yourself?"

Mr. Utterson's only answer was to rise and get his hat and greatcoat; but he observed with wonder the greatness of the relief that appeared upon the butler's face, and, perhaps with no less, that the wine was still untasted when he set it down to follow.

It was a wild, cold, seasonable night of March, with a pale moon, lying on her back as though the wind had tilted her, and a flying wrack of the most diaphanous and lawny texture. The wind made talking difficult, and flecked the blood into the face. It seemed to have swept the streets unusually bare of passengers, besides; for Mr. Utterson thought he had never seen that part of London so deserted. He could have wished it otherwise; never in his life had he been conscious of so sharp a wish to see and touch his fellow-creatures; for struggle as he might, there was borne in upon his mind a crushing anticipation of calamity. The square, when they got there, was all full of wind and dust, and the thin trees in the garden were lashing themselves along the railing. Poole, who had kept all the way a pace or two ahead, now pulled up in the middle of the pavement and, in spite of the biting weather, took off his hat and mopped his brow with a red pocket-handkerchief. But for all the hurry of his coming, these were not the dews of exertion that he wiped away, but the moisture of some strangling anguish; for his face was white, and his voice, when he spoke, harsh and broken.

"Well, sir," he said, "here we are, and God grant there be nothing wrong."

"Amen, Poole," said the lawyer.

Thereupon the servant knocked in a very guarded manner; the door was opened on the chain; and a voice asked from within, "Is that you, Poole?"

"It's all right," said Poole. "Open the door."

The hall when they entered it was brightly lighted up,

the fire was built high, and about the hearth the whole of the servants, men and women, stood huddled together like a flock of sheep. At the sight of Mr. Utterson the household broke into hysterical whimpering, and the cook, crying out, "Bless God! it's Mr. Utterson!" ran forward as if to take him in her arms.

"What, what? Are you all here?" said the lawyer peevishly. "Very irregular, very unseemly; your master would be far from pleased."

"They're all afraid," said Poole.

Blank silence followed, no one protesting; only the maid lifted up her voice and now wept loudly.

"Hold your tongue!" Poole said to her, with a ferocity of accent that testified to his own jangled nerves; and indeed, when the girl had so suddenly raised the note of her lamentation, they had all started and turned toward the inner door with faces of dreadful expectation. "And now," continued the butler, addressing the knife-boy, "reach me a candle and we'll get this through hands at once." And then he begged Mr. Utterson to follow him and led the way to the back garden.

"Now, sir," said he, "you come as gently as you can. I want you to hear, and I don't want you to be heard. And see here, sir, if by any chance he was to ask you in, don't go."

Mr. Utterson's nerves, at this unlooked-for termination, gave a jerk that nearly threw him from his balance, but he recollected his courage and followed the butler into the laboratory building and through the surgical theater, with its lumber of crates and bottles, to the foot of the stair. Here Poole motioned him to stand on one side and listen, while he himself, setting down the candle and making a great and obvious call on his resolution, mounted the steps and knocked with a somewhat uncertain hand on the red baize of the cabinet door.

"Mr. Utterson, sir, asking to see you," he called, and even as he did so once more violently signed to the lawyer to give ear.

A voice answered from within: "Tell him I cannot see any one," it said complainingly.

"Thank you, sir," said Poole, with a note of something like triumph in his voice, and taking up his candle he led Mr. Utterson back across the yard and into the great kitchen, where the fire was out and the beetles were leaping on the floor.

"Sir," he said, looking Mr. Utterson in the eyes, "was that my master's voice?"

"It seems much changed," replied the lawyer, very pale, but giving look for look.

"Changed? Well, yes, I think so," said the butler. "Have I been twenty years in this man's house to be deceived about his voice? No, sir; master's made away with; he was made away with eight days ago when we heard him cry out upon the name of God, and *who's* in there instead of him and *why* it stays there is a thing that cries to Heaven, Mr. Utterson!"

"This is a very strange tale, Poole; this is rather a wild tale, my man," said Mr. Utterson, biting his finger. "Suppose it were as you suppose, supposing Dr. Jekyll to have been—well, murdered, what would induce the murderer to stay? That won't hold water; it doesn't commend itself to reason."

"Well, Mr. Utterson, you are a hard man to satisfy, but I'll do it yet," said Poole. "All this last week (you must know) him or it, or whatever it is that lives in that cabinet, has been crying night and day for some sort of medicine and cannot get it to his mind. It was sometimes his way —the master's, that is—to write his orders on a sheet of paper and throw it on the stair. We've had nothing else this week back—nothing but papers and a closed door, and the very meals left there to be smuggled in when nobody was looking. Well, sir, every day—ay, twice and thrice in the same day—there have been orders and complaints, and I have been sent flying to all the wholesale chemists in town. Every time I brought the stuff back there would be another paper telling me to return it because it was not pure and another order to a different firm. This drug is wanted bitter bad, sir, whatever for."

"Have you any of these papers?" asked Mr. Utterson.

Poole felt in his pocket, and handed out a crumpled note,

which the lawyer, bending nearer to the candle, carefully examined. Its contents ran thus: "Doctor Jekyll presents his compliments to Messrs. Maw. He assures them that their last sample is impure and quite useless for his present purpose. In the year 18—, Dr. J. purchased a somewhat large quantity from Messrs. M. He now begs them to search with the most sedulous care, and should any of the same quality be left, to forward it to him at once. Expense is no consideration. The importance of this to Dr. J. can hardly be exaggerated." So far the letter had run composedly enough, but here, with a sudden splutter of the pen, the writer's emotion had broken loose. "For God's sake," he had added, "find me some of the old."

"This is a strange note," said Mr. Utterson; and then sharply, "How do you come to have it open?"

"The man at Maw's was main angry, sir, and he threw it back to me like so much dirt," returned Poole.

"This is unquestionably the doctor's hand, do you know?" resumed the lawyer.

"I thought it looked like it," said the servant rather sulkily; and then, with another voice, "But what matters hand of write," he said. "I've seen him!"

"Seen him?" repeated Mr. Utterson. "Well?"

"That's it!" said Poole. "It was this way. I came suddenly into the theater from the garden. It seems he had slipped out to look for this drug or whatever it is; for the cabinet door was open, and there he was at the far end of the room digging among the crates. He looked up when I came in, gave a kind of cry, and whipped upstairs into the cabinet. It was but for one minute that I saw him, but the hair stood upon my head like quills. Sir, if that was my master, why had he a mask upon his face? If it was my master, why did he cry out like a rat, and run from me? I have served him long enough. And then—" the man paused and passed his hand over his face.

"These are all very strange circumstances," said Mr. Utterson, "but I think I begin to see daylight. Your master, Poole, is plainly seized with one of those maladies that both torture and deform the sufferer: hence, for aught I know, the alteration of his voice; hence the mask and the avoidance of his friends; hence his eagerness to find this drug, by means of which the poor soul retains some hope of ultimate recovery—God grant that he be not deceived! There is my explanation; it is sad enough, Poole, ay, and appalling to consider; but it is plain and natural, hangs well together and delivers us from all exorbitant alarms."

"Sir," said the butler, turning to a sort of mottled pallor, "that thing was not my master, and there's the truth. My master"—here he looked round him and began to whisper—"is a tall fine build of a man and this was more of a dwarf." Utterson attempted to protest. "Oh, sir," cried Poole, "do you think I do not know my master after twenty years? do you think I do not know where his head comes to in the cabinet door, where I saw him every morning of my life? No, sir, that thing in the mask was never Doctor Jekyll—God knows what it was, but it was never Doctor Jekyll; and it is the belief of my heart that there was murder done."

"Poole," replied the lawyer, "if you say that, it will become my duty to make certain. Much as I desire to spare your master's feeling, much as I am puzzled by this note which seems to prove him to be still alive, I shall consider it my duty to break in that door."

"Ah, Mr. Utterson, that's talking!" cried the butler.

"And now comes the second question," resumed Utterson: "Who is going to do it?"

"Why, you and me," was the undaunted reply.

"That's very well said," returned the lawyer; "and whatever comes of it, I shall make it my business to see you are no loser."

"There is an ax in the theater," continued Poole; "and you might take the kitchen poker for yourself."

The lawyer took that rude but weighty instrument into his hand, and balanced it. "Do you know, Poole," he said, looking up, "that you and I are about to place ourselves in a position of some peril?"

"You may say so, sir, indeed," returned the butler.

"It is well, then, that we should be frank," said the other. "We both think more than we have said; let us make a clean breast. This masked figure that you saw, did you recognize it?"

"Well, sir, it went so quick, and the creature was so doubled up, that I could hardly swear to that," was the answer. "But if you mean, was it Mr. Hyde?—why, yes, I think it was! You see, it was much of the same bigness; and it had the same quick, light way with it; and then who else could have got in by the laboratory door? You have not forgot, sir, that at the time of the murder he had still the key with him? But that's not all. I don't know, Mr. Utterson, if ever you met this Mr. Hyde?"

"Yes," said the lawyer, "I once spoke with him."

"Then you must know as well as the rest of us that there was something queer about that gentleman—something that gave a man a turn—I don't know rightly how to say it, sir, beyond this: that you felt it in your marrow kind of cold and thin."

"I own I felt something of what you describe," said Mr. Utterson.

"Quite so, sir," returned Poole. "Well, when that masked thing like a monkey jumped from among the chemicals and whipped into the cabinet, it went down my spine like ice. Oh, I know it's not evidence, Mr. Utterson; I'm book-learned enough for that; but a man has his feelings, and I give you my Bible word it was Mr. Hyde!"

"Ay, ay," said the lawyer. "My fears incline to the same point. Evil, I fear, founded—evil was sure to come—of that connection. Ay, truly, I believe you; I believe poor Harry is killed; and I believe his murderer (for what purpose God alone can tell) is still lurking in his victim's room. Well, let our name be vengeance. Call Bradshaw."

The footman came at the summons, very white and nervous.

"Pull yourself together, Bradshaw," said the lawyer. "This suspense, I know, is telling upon all of you; but it is now our intention to make an end of it. Poole, here, and I are going to force our way into the cabinet. If all is well, my shoulders are broad enough to bear the blame. Meanwhile, lest anything should really be amiss, or any malefactor seek to escape by the back, you and the boy must go round the corner with a pair of good sticks, and take your post at the laboratory door. We give you ten minutes to get to your stations."

As Bradshaw left, the lawyer looked at his watch. "And now, Poole, let us get to ours," he said; and taking the poker under his arm, led the way into the yard. The scud had banked over the moon, and it was now quite dark. The wind, which only broke in puffs and draughts into that deep well of building, tossed the light of the candle to and fro about their steps, until they came into the shelter of the theater, where they sat down silently to wait. London hummed solemnly all around; but nearer at hand, the stillness was only broken by the sounds of a footfall moving to and fro along the cabinet floor.

"So it will walk all day, sir," whispered Poole; "ay, and the better part of the night. Only when a new sample comes from the chemist, there's a bit of a break. Ah, it's an ill-conscience that's such an enemy to rest! Ah, sir, there's blood foully shed in every step of it! But hark again, a little closer—put your heart in your ears, Mr. Utterson, and tell me, is that the doctor's foot?"

The steps fell lightly and oddly, with a certain swing, for all they went so slowly; it was different indeed from the heavy, creaking tread of Henry Jekyll. Utterson sighed. "Is there never anything else?" he asked.

Poole nodded. "Once," he said, "Once I heard it weeping."

"Weeping? how that?" said the lawyer, conscious of a sudden thrill of horror.

"Weeping like a woman or a lost soul," said the butler. "I came away with that upon my heart, that I could have wept too."

But now the ten minutes drew to an end. Poole disinterred the ax from under a stack of packing straw; the candle was set upon the nearest table to light them to the attack; and they drew near with bated breath to where that patient foot was still going up and down, up and down, in the quiet of the night.

"Jekyll," cried Utterson, with a loud voice, "I demand to see you." He paused a moment, but there came no reply. "I give you fair warning, our suspicions are aroused, and I must and shall see you," he resumed; "if not by fair means, then by foul—if not of your consent, then by brute force."

"Utterson," said the voice, "for God's sake, have mercy!"

"Ah, that's not Jekyll's voice—it's Hyde's!" cried Utterson. "Down with the door, Poole."

Poole swung the ax over his shoulder; the blow shook the building, and the red baize door leaped against the lock and hinges. A dismal screech, as of mere animal terror, rang from the cabinet. Up went the ax again, and again the panels crashed and the frame bounded; four times the blow fell, but the wood was tough and the fittings were of excellent workmanship; and it was not until the fifth that the lock burst in sunder and the wreck of the door fell inward on the carpet.

The besiegers, appalled by their own riot and the stillness that had succeeded, stood back a little and peered in. There lay the cabinet before their eyes in the quiet lamplight, a good fire glowing and chattering on the hearth, the kettle singing its thin strain, a drawer or two open, papers neatly set forth on the business table, and nearer the fire, the things laid out for tea: the quietest room, you would have said, and, but for the glazed presses full of chemicals, the most commonplace that night in London.

Right in the midst there lay the body of a man sorely contorted and still twitching. They drew near on tiptoe, turned it on its back and beheld the face of Edward Hyde. He was dressed in clothes far too large for him, clothes of the doctor's bigness; the chords of his face still moved with a semblance of life, but life was quite gone: and by the crushed vial in his hand and the strong smell of kernels that hung upon the air, Utterson knew he was looking on the body of a self-destroyer.

"We have come too late," he said sternly, "whether to save or punish. Hyde is gone to his account; and it only remains for us to find the body of your master."

The far greater proportion of the building was occupied by the theater, which filled almost the whole ground-story and was lighted from above, and by the cabinet, which formed an upper story at one end and looked upon the court. A corridor joined the theater to the door on the by-street, and with this the cabinet communicated separately by a second flight of stairs. There were besides a few dark closets and a spacious cellar. All these they now thoroughly examined. Each closet needed but a glance, for all were empty, and all, by the dust that fell from their doors, had stood long unopened. The cellar, indeed, was filled with crazy lumber, mostly dating from the times of the surgeon who was Jekyll's predecessor; but even as they opened the door they were advertised of the uselessness of further search by the fall of a perfect mat of cobweb which had for years sealed up the entrance. Nowhere was there any trace of Henry Jekyll, dead or alive.

Poole stamped on the flags of the corridor. "He must be buried here," he said, hearkening to the sound.

"Or he may have fled," said Utterson, and he turned to examine the door in the by-street. It was locked; and lying near by on the flags they found the key, already stained with rust.

"This does not look like use," observed the lawyer.

"Use!" echoed Poole. "Do you not see, sir, it is broken? much as if a man had stamped on it."

"Ay," continued Utterson, "and the fractures, too, are rusty." The two men looked at each other with a scare. "This is beyond me, Poole," said the lawyer. "Let us go back to the cabinet."

They mounted the stair in silence, and still with an occasional awe-struck glance at the dead body, proceeded more thoroughly to examine the contents of the cabinet. At one table there were traces of chemical work, various measured heaps of some white salt being laid on glass saucers, as though for an experiment in which the unhappy man had been prevented.

"That is the same drug that I was always bringing him," said Poole; and even as he spoke, the kettle with a startling noise boiled over.

This brought them to the fireside, where the easy-chair was drawn cozily up, and the tea things stood ready to the sitter's elbow, the very sugar in the cup. There were several books on a shelf; one lay beside the tea things open, and Utterson was amazed to find it a copy of a pious work, for which Jekyll had several times expressed a great esteem, annotated, in his own hand, with startling blasphemies.

Next, in the course of their review of the chamber, the searchers came to the cheval glass, into whose depths they looked with an involuntary horror. But it was so turned as to show them nothing but the rosy glow playing on the roof, the fire sparkling in a hundred repetitions along the glazed front of the presses, and their own pale and fearful countenances stooping to look in.

"This glass have seen some strange things, sir," whispered Poole.

"And surely none stranger than itself," echoed the lawyer in the same tones. "For what did Jekyll"—he caught himself up at the word with a start, and then conquering the weakness—"what could Jekyll want with it?" he said.

"You may say that!" said Poole.

Next they turned to the business table. On the desk among the neat array of papers, a large envelope was uppermost, and bore, in the doctor's hand, the name of Mr. Utterson. The lawyer unsealed it, and several inclosures fell to the floor. The first was a will, drawn in the same eccentric terms as the one which he had returned six months before, to serve as a testament in case of death and as a deed of gift in case of disappearance; but in place of the name of Edward Hyde, the lawyer, with indescribable amazement, read the name of Gabriel John Utterson. He looked at Poole, and then back at the paper, and last of all at the dead malefactor stretched upon the carpet.

"My head goes round," he said. "He has been all these days in possession; he had no cause to like me; he must have raged to see himself displaced; and he has not destroyed this document."

He caught up the next paper; it was a brief note in the doctor's hand and dated at the top. "Oh, Poole!" the lawyer cried, "he was alive and here this day. He cannot have been disposed of in so short a space, he must be still alive, he must have fled! And then, why fled? and how? and in that case, can we venture to declare this suicide? Oh, we must be careful. I foresee that we may yet involve your master in some dire catastrophe."

"Why don't you read it, sir?" asked Poole.

"Because I fear," replied the lawyer solemnly; "God grant I have no cause for it!" And with that he brought the paper to his eyes and read as follows:

"MY DEAR UTTERSON: When this shall fall into your hands I shall have disappeared, under what circumstances I have not the penetration to foresee, but my instinct and all the circumstances of my nameless situation tell me that the end is sure and must be early. Go, then, and first read the narrative which Lanyon warned me he was to place in your hands; and if you care to hear more, turn to the confession of

"Your unworthy and unhappy friend,
"HENRY JEKYLL."

"There was a third inclosure?" asked Utterson.

"Here, sir," said Poole, and gave into his hands a considerable packet sealed in several places.

The lawyer put it in his pocket. "I would say nothing of this paper. If your master has fled, or is dead, we may at least save his credit. It is now ten; I must go home and read these documents in quiet; but I shall be back before midnight, when we shall send for the police."

They went out, locking the door of the theater behind them; and Utterson, once more leaving the servants gathered about the fire in the hall, trudged back to his office to read the two narratives in which this mystery was now to be explained.

DOCTOR LANYON'S NARRATIVE.

On the ninth of January, now four days ago, I received by the evening delivery a registered envelope, addressed in the hand of my colleague and old school-companion, Henry Jekyll. I was a good deal surprised by this; for we were by no means in the habit of correspondence; I had seen the man, dined with him, indeed, the night before; and I could imagine nothing in our intercourse that should justify formality of registration. The contents increased my wonder; for this is how the letter ran:

"10th December, 18—.

"DEAR LANYON: You are one of my oldest friends; and although we may have differed at times on scientific questions, I cannot remember, at least on my side, any break in our affection. There was never a day when if you had said to me, 'Jekyll, my life, my honor, my reason, depend upon you,' I would not have sacrificed my left hand to help you. Lanyon, my life, my honor, my reason, are all at your mercy; if you fail me to-night I am lost. You might suppose, after this preface, that I am going to ask you for something dishonorable to grant. Judge for yourself.

"I want you to postpone all other engagements for to-night —ay, even if you were summoned to the bedside of an emperor; to take a cab, unless your carriage should be actually at the door; and with this letter in your hand for consultation, to drive straight to my house. Poole, my butler, has his orders; you will find him waiting your arrival with a locksmith. The door of my cabinet is then to be forced: and you are to go in alone; to open the glazed press (letter E) on the left hand, breaking the lock if it be shut; and to draw out, *with all its contents as they stand,* the fourth drawer from the top or (which is the same thing) the third from the bottom. In my extreme distress of mind, I have a morbid fear of misdirecting you; but even if I am in error, you may know the right drawer by its contents: some powders, a vial and a paper book. This drawer I beg of you to carry back with you to Cavendish Square exactly as it stands.

"That is the first part of the service; now for the second. You should be back, if you set out at once on the receipt of this, long before midnight; but I will leave you that amount of margin, not only in the fear of one of those obstacles that can neither be prevented nor foreseen, but because an hour when your servants are in bed is to be preferred for what will then remain to do. At midnight, then, I have to ask you to be alone in your consulting-room, to admit with your own hand into the house a man who will present himself in my name, and to place in his hands the drawer that you will have brought with you from my cabinet. Then you will have played your part and earned my gratitude completely. Five minutes afterwards, if you insist upon an explanation, you will have understood that these arrangements are of capital importance, and that by the neglect of one of them, fantastic as they must appear, you might have charged your conscience with my death or the shipwreck of my reason.

"Confident as I am that you will not trifle with this appeal, my heart sinks and my hand trembles at the bare thought of such a possibility. Think of me at this hour, in a strange place, laboring under a blackness of distress that no fancy can exaggerate, and yet well aware that, if you will but punctually serve me, my troubles will roll away like a story that is told. Serve me, my dear Lanyon, and save

Your friend,

"H. J.

"P. S.—I had already sealed this up when a fresh terror struck upon my soul. It is possible that the post-office may fail me, and this letter not come into your hands until tomorrow morning. In that case, dear Lanyon, do my errand when it shall be most convenient for you in the course of the day; and once more expect my messenger at midnight. It may then already be too late; and if that night passes without event, you will know that you have seen the last of Henry Jekyll."

Upon the reading of this letter I made sure my colleague was insane; but till that was proved beyond the possibility of doubt I felt bound to do as he requested. The less I understood of this farrago, the less I was in a position to judge of its importance, and an appeal so worded could not be set aside without a grave responsibility. I rose accordingly from table, got into a hansom, and drove straight to Jekyll's house. The butler was awaiting my arrival; he had received by the same post as mine a registered letter of instruction, and had sent at once for a locksmith and a carpenter. The tradesmen came while we were yet speaking; and we moved in a body to old Dr. Denman's surgical theater (from which, as you are doubtless aware) Jekyll's private cabinet is most conveniently entered. The door was very strong, the lock excellent; the carpenter avowed he would have great trouble, and have to do much damage, if force were to be used, and the locksmith was near despair. But this last was a handy fellow, and after two hours' work the door stood open. The press marked E was unlocked; and I took out the drawer, had it filled up with straw and tied in a sheet, and returned with it to Cavendish Square.

Here I proceeded to examine its contents. The powders were neatly enough made up, but not with the nicety of

the dispensing chemist; so that it was plain they were of
Jekyll's private manufacture: and when I opened one of
the wrappers I found what seemed to me a simple crystalline
salt of a white color.   The vial, to which I next turned my
attention, might have been about half full of a blood-red
liquor, which was highly pungent to the sense of smell, and
seemed to me to contain phosphorus and some volatile ether.
At the other ingredients, I could make no guess.   The book
was an ordinary version book, and contained little but a
series of dates.   These covered a period of many years, but
I observed that the entries ceased nearly a year ago and quite
abruptly.   Here and there a brief remark was appended to
a date, usually no more than a single word: "double" oc-
curring perhaps six times in a total of several hundred entries; and once, very early in the list and followed by several marks of exclamation, "total failure!!!" All this, though
it whetted my curiosity, told me little that was definite.
Here were a vial of some tincture, a paper of some salt, and
the record of a series of experiments that had led (like too
many of Jekyll's investigations) to no end of practical use-
fulness.   How could the presence of these articles in my
house affect either the honor, the sanity, or the life of my
flighty colleague?   If his messenger could go to one place,
why could he not go to another?   And even granting some
impediment, why was this gentleman to be received by me
in secret?   The more I reflected, the more convinced I grew
that I was dealing with a case of cerebral disease; and though
I dismissed my servants to bed, I loaded an old revolver that
I might be found in some posture of self-defense.

Twelve o'clock had scarce rung out over London ere the
knocker sounded very gently on the door.   I went myself
at the summons, and found a small man crouching against
the pillars of the portico.

"Are you come from Dr. Jekyll?" I asked.

He told me "yes" by a constrained gesture, and when I
had bidden him enter he did not obey me without a searching
backward glance into the darkness of the square.   There
was a policeman not far off, advancing with his bull's-eye
open; and at the sight, I thought my visitor started and
made greater haste.

These particulars struck me, I confess, disagreeably; and as I followed him into the bright light of the consulting-room I kept my hand ready on my weapon. Here, at last, I had a chance of clearly seeing him. I had never set eyes on him before, so much was certain. He was small, as I have said; I was struck besides with the shocking expression of his face, with his remarkable combination of great muscular activity and great apparent debility of constitution, and —last but not least—with the odd, subjective disturbance caused by his neighborhood. This bore some resemblance to incipient rigor and was accompanied by a marked sinking of the pulse. At the time I set it down to some idiosyncratic, personal distaste, and merely wondered at the acuteness of the symptoms; but I have since had reason to believe the cause to lie much deeper in the nature of man, and to turn on some nobler hinge than the principle of hatred.

This person (who had thus, from the first moment of his entrance, struck in me what I can only describe as a dis-gustful curiosity) was dressed in a fashion that would have made an ordinary person laughable; his clothes, that is to say, although they were of rich and sober fabric, were enormously too large for him in every measurement—the trousers hanging on his legs and rolled up to keep them from the ground, the waist of the coat below his haunches, and the collar sprawling wide upon his shoulders. Strange to relate, this ludicrous accouterment was far from moving me to laughter. Rather, as there was something abnormal and misbegotten in the very essence of the creature that now faced me—something seizing, surprising, and revolting—this fresh disparity seemed but to fit in with and to reënforce it; so that to my interest in the man's nature and character there was added a curiosity as to his origin, his life, his fortune, and status in the world.

These observations, though they have taken so great a space to be set down in, were yet the work of a few seconds. My visitor was, indeed, on fire with somber excitement.

"Have you got it?" he cried. "Have you got it?" And so lively was his impatience that he even laid his hand upon my arm and sought to shake me.

I put him back, conscious at his touch of a certain icy

pang along my blood. "Come, sir," said I. "You forget that I have not yet the pleasure of your acquaintance. Be seated, if you please." And I showed him an example, and sat down myself in my customary seat and with as fair an imitation of my ordinary manner to a patient as the lateness of the hour, the nature of my preoccupations, and the horror I had of my visitor, would suffer me to muster.

"I beg your pardon, Doctor Lanyon," he replied, civilly enough. "What you say is very well founded; and my impatience has shown its heels to my politeness. I come here at the instance of your colleague, Doctor Henry Jekyll, on a piece of business of some moment; and I understood—" he paused and put his hand to his throat, and I could see, in spite of his collected manner, that he was wrestling against the approaches of the hysteria—"I understood, a drawer——"

But here I took pity on my visitor's suspense, and some perhaps on my own growing curiosity.

"There it is, sir," said I, pointing to the drawer, where it lay on the floor behind a table and still covered with the sheet.

He sprung to it, and then paused, and laid his hand upon his heart; I could hear his teeth grate with the convulsive action of his jaws; and his face was so ghastly to see that I grew alarmed both for his life and reason.

"Compose yourself," said I.

He turned a dreadful smile to me, and, as if with the decision of despair, plucked away the sheet. At sight of the contents he uttered one loud sob of such immense relief that I sat petrified. And the next moment, in a voice that was already fairly well under control, "Have you a graduated glass?" he asked.

I rose from my place with something of an effort and gave him what he asked.

He thanked me with a smiling nod, measured out a few minims of the red tincture and added one of the powders. The mixture, which was at first of a reddish hue, began, in proportion as the crystals melted, to brighten in color, to effervesce audibly, and to throw off small fumes of vapor. Suddenly and at the same moment, the ebullition ceased and the compound changed to a dark purple, which faded again more slowly to a watery green. My visitor, who had watched these metamorphoses with a keen eye, smiled, set down the glass upon the table, and then turned and looked upon me with an air of scrutiny.

"And now," said he, "to settle what remains. Will you be wise? will you be guided? will you suffer me to take this glass in my hand and to go forth from your house without further parley? or has the greed of curiosity too much command of you? Think before you answer, for it shall be done as you decide. As you decide, you shall be left as you were before, and neither richer nor wiser, unless the sense of service rendered to a man in mortal distress may be counted as a kind of riches of the soul. Or, if you shall so prefer to choose, a new province of knowledge and new avenues to fame and power shall be laid open to you, here in this room, upon the instant; and your sight shall be blasted by a prodigy to stagger the unbelief of Satan."

"Sir," said I, affecting a coolness that I was far from truly possessing, "you speak enigmas, and you will, perhaps, not wonder that I hear you with no very strong impression of belief. But I have gone too far in the way of inexplicable services to pause before I see the end."

"It is well," replied my visitor. "Lanyon, you remember your vows: what follows is under the seal of our profession. And now, you who have so long been bound to the most narrow and material views, you who have denied the virtue of transcendental medicine, you who have derided your superiors—behold!"

He put the glass to his lips, and drank at one gulp. A cry followed; he reeled, staggered, clutched at the table, and held on, staring with injected eyes, gasping with open mouth; and, as I looked, there came, I thought, a change; he seemed to swell; his face became suddenly black, and the features seemed to melt and alter—and the next moment I had sprung to my feet and leaped back against the wall, my arm raised to shield me from that prodigy, my mind submerged in terror.

"Oh, God!" I screamed, and "Oh, God!" again and again; for there before my eyes—pale and shaken, and half fainting, and groping before him with his hands, like a man restored from death—there stood Henry Jekyll!

What he told me in the next hour I cannot bring my mind to set on paper. I saw what I saw, I heard what I heard, and my soul sickened at it; and yet now, when that sight has faded from my eyes, I ask myself if I believe it, and I cannot answer. My life is shaken to its roots; sleep has left me; the deadliest terror sits by me at all hours of the day and night; I feel that my days are numbered, and that I must die; and yet I shall die incredulous. As for the moral turpitude that man unveiled to me, even with tears of penitence, I cannot, even in memory, dwell on it without a start of horror. I will say but one thing, Utterson, and that (if you can bring your mind to credit it) will be more than enough. The creature who crept into my house that night was, on Jekyll's own confession, known by the name of Hyde, and hunted for in every corner of the land as the murderer of Carew.

HASTIE LANYON.

HENRY JEKYLL'S FULL STATEMENT OF THE CASE.

I was born in the year 18— to a large fortune, endowed besides with excellent parts, inclined by nature to industry, fond of the respect of the wise and good among my fellow men, and thus, as might have been supposed, with every guarantee of an honorable and distinguished future. And indeed the worst of my faults was a certain impatient gayety of disposition, such as has made the happiness of many, but such as I found it hard to reconcile with my imperious desire to carry my head high, and wear a more than commonly grave countenance before the public. Hence it came about that I concealed my pleasures; and that when I reached years of reflection, and began to look round me and take stock of my progress and position in the world, I stood already committed to a profound duplicity of life. Many a man would have even blazoned such irregularities as I was guilty of; but from the high views that I had set before me,

I regarded and hid them with an almost morbid sense of shame. It was thus rather the exacting nature of my aspirations than any particular degradation in my faults that made me what I was, and with even a deeper trench than in the majority of men, severed in me those provinces of good and ill which divide and compound man's dual nature. In this case, I was driven to reflect deeply and inveterately on that hard law of life which lies at the root of religion and is one of the most plentiful springs of distress. Though so profound a double-dealer, I was in no sense a hypocrite; both sides of me were in dead earnest; I was no more myself when I laid aside restraint and plunged in shame than when I labored, in the eye of day, at the furtherance of knowledge or the relief of sorrow and suffering. And it chanced that the direction of my scientific studies, which led wholly toward the mystic and the transcendental, reacted and shed a strong light on this consciousness of the perennial war among my members. With every day, and from both sides of my intelligence, the moral and the intellectual, I thus drew steadily nearer to that truth, by whose partial discovery I have been doomed to such a dreadful shipwreck: that man is not truly one, but truly two. I say two, because the state of my own knowledge does not pass beyond that point. Others will follow, others will outstrip me on the same lines; and I hazard the guess that man will be ultimately known for a mere polity of multifarious, incongruous, and independent denizens. I, for my part, from the nature of my life, advanced infallibly in one direction, and in one direction only. It was on the moral side, and in my own person, that I learned to recognize the thorough and primitive duality of man; I saw that, of the two natures that contended in the field of my consciousness, even if I could rightly be said to be either, it was only because I was radically both; and from an early date, even before the course of my scientific discoveries had begun to suggest the most naked possibility of such a miracle, I had learned to dwell with pleasure, as a beloved day-dream, on the thought of the separation of these elements. If each, I told myself, could but be housed in separate identities, life would be relieved of all that was unbearable; the unjust might go his way, delivered from the aspirations and remorse of his more upright twin; and the just could walk steadfastly and securely on his upward path, doing the good things in which he found his pleasure, and no longer exposed to disgrace and penitence by the hands of this extraneous evil. It was the curse of mankind that these incongruous fagots were thus bound together—that in the agonized womb of consciousness, these polar twins should be continuously struggling. How, then, were they dissociated?

I was so far in my reflections when, as I have said, a side light began to shine upon the subject from the laboratory table. I began to perceive more deeply than it has ever yet been stated, the trembling immateriality, the mist-like transience, of this seemingly so solid body in which we walk attired. Certain agents I found to have the power to shake and to pluck back that fleshly vestment, even as a wind might toss the curtains of a pavilion. For two good reasons, I will not enter deeply into this scientific branch of my confession. First, because I have been made to learn that the doom and burden of our life is bound forever on man's shoulders, and when the attempt is made to cast it off it but returns upon us with more unfamiliar and more awful pressure. Second, because as my narrative will make, alas! too evident, my discoveries were incomplete. Enough, then, that I not only recognize my natural body for the mere aura and effulgence of certain of the powers that made up my spirit, but managed to compound a drug by which these powers should be dethroned from their supremacy, and a second form and countenance substituted none the less natural to me because they were the expression, and bore the stamp, of lower elements in my soul.

I hesitated long before I put this theory to the test of practice. I knew well that I risked death; for any drug that so potently controlled and shook the very fortress of identity might, by the least scruple of an overdose or at the least inopportunity in the moment of exhibition, utterly blot out that immaterial tabernacle which I looked to it to change. But the temptation of a discovery so singular and profound at last overcame the suggestions of alarm. I had long since prepared my tincture; I purchased at once, from a firm of wholesale chemists, a large quantity of a particular salt which I knew, from my experiments, to be the last ingredient required; and late one accursed night I compounded the elements, watched them boil and smoke together in the glass, and when the ebullition had subsided, with a strong glow of courage, drank off the potion.

The most racking pangs succeeded: a grinding in the bones, deadly nausea, and a horror of the spirit that cannot be exceeded at the hour of birth or death. Then these agonies began swiftly to subside, and I came to myself as if out of a great sickness. There was something strange in my sensations, something indescribably new, and, from its very novelty, incredibly sweet. I felt younger, lighter, happier in body; within I was conscious of a heady recklessness, a current of disordered sensual images running like a mill race in my fancy, a solution of the bonds of obligation, an unknown but not an innocent freedom of the soul. I knew myself, at the first breath of this new life, to be more wicked, tenfold more wicked, sold a slave to my original evil; and the thought, in that moment, braced and delighted me like wine. I stretched out my hands, exulting in the freshness of these sensations; and in the act, I was suddenly aware that I had lost in stature.

There was no mirror at that date in my room; that which stands beside me as I write was brought there later on and for the very purpose of these transformations. The night, however, was far gone into the morning—the morning, black as it was, was nearly ripe for the conception of the day— the inmates of my house were locked in the most rigorous hours of slumber; and I determined, flushed as I was with hope and triumph, to venture in my new shape as far as to my bedroom. I crossed the yard, wherein the constellations looked down upon me, I could have thought, with wonder, the first creature of that sort that their unsleeping vigilance had yet disclosed to them; I stole through the corridors, a stranger in my own house; and coming to my room, I saw for the first time the appearance of Edward Hyde.

I must here speak by theory alone, saying not that which I know, but that which I suppose to be most probable. The evil side of my nature, to which I had now transferred the stamping efficacy, was less robust and less developed than the good which I had just deposed. Again, in the course of my life, which had been, after all, nine-tenths a life of effort, virtue, and control, it had been much less exercised and much less exhausted. And hence, as I think, it came about that Edward Hyde was so much smaller, slighter, and younger than Henry Jekyll. Even as good shone upon the countenance of the one, evil was written broadly and plainly on the face of the other. Evil besides (which I must still believe to be the lethal side of man) had left on that body an imprint of deformity and decay. And yet when I looked upon that ugly idol in the glass, I was conscious of no repugnance, rather of a leap of welcome. This, too, was myself. It seemed natural and human. In my eyes it bore a livelier image of the spirit, it seemed more express and single than the imperfect and divine countenance I had been hitherto accustomed to call mine. And in so far I was doubtless right. I have observed that when I wore the semblance of Edward Hyde none could come near to me at first without a visible misgiving of the flesh. This, as I take it, was because all human beings, as we meet them, are commingled out of good and evil: and Edward Hyde, alone in the ranks of mankind, was pure evil.

I lingered but a moment at the mirror: the second and conclusive experiment had yet to be attempted; it yet remained to be seen if I had lost my identity beyond redemption and must flee before daylight from a house that was no longer mine; and hurrying back to my cabinet, I once more prepared and drank the cup, once more suffered the pangs of dissolution, and came to myself once more with the character, the stature, and the face of Henry Jekyll.

That night I had come to the fatal cross-roads. Had I approached my discovery in a more noble spirit, had I risked the experiment while under the empire of generous or pious aspirations, all must have been otherwise, and from these agonies of death and birth I had come forth an angel instead of a fiend. The drug had no discriminating action; it was neither diabolical nor divine; it but shook the doors of the prison-house of my disposition; and like the captives of

Philippi, that which stood within ran forth. At that time my virtue slumbered; my evil, kept awake by ambition, was alert and swift to seize the occasion; and the thing that was projected was Edward Hyde. Hence, although I had now two characters as well as two appearances, one was wholly evil, and the other was still the old Henry Jekyll, that incongruous compound of whose reformation and improvement I had already learned to despair. The movement was thus wholly toward the worse.

Even at that time I had not yet conquered my aversion to the dryness of a life of study. I would still be merrily disposed at times; and as my pleasures were (to say the least) undignified, and I was not only well known and highly considered, but growing toward the elderly man, this incoherency of my life was daily growing more unwelcome. It was on this side that my new power tempted me until I fell into slavery. I had but to drink the cup, to doff at once the body of the noted professor, and to assume, like a thick cloak, that of Edward Hyde. I smiled at the notion; it seemed to me at the time to be humorous; and I made my preparations with the most studious care. I took and furnished that house in Soho, to which Hyde was tracked by the police; and engaged as a housekeeper a creature whom I well knew to be silent and unscrupulous. On the other side, I announced to my servants that a Mr. Hyde (whom I described) was to have full liberty and power about my house in the square; and to parry mishaps, I even called and made myself a familiar object, in my second character. I next drew up that will to which you so much objected; so that if anything befell me in the person of Dr. Jekyll I could enter on that of Edward Hyde without pecuniary loss. And thus fortified, as I supposed, on every side, I began to profit by the strange immunities of my position.

Men have before hired bravoes to transact their crimes, while their own person and reputation sat under shelter. I was the first that ever did so for his pleasures. I was the first that could thus plod in the public eye with a load of genial respectability, and in a moment, like a schoolboy, strip off these lendings and spring headlong into the sea of liberty. But for me, in my impenetrable mantle, the safety was complete. Think of it—I did not even exist! Let me but escape into my laboratory door, give me but a second or two to mix and swallow the draught that I had always standing ready; and whatever he had done, Edward Hyde would pass away like the stain of breath upon a mirror; and there in his stead, quietly at home, trimming the midnight lamp in his study, a man who could afford to laugh at suspicion, would be Henry Jekyll.

The pleasures which I made haste to seek in my disguise were, as I have said, undignified; I would scarce use a harder term. But in the hands of Edward Hyde they soon began to turn toward the monstrous. When I would come back from these excursions I was often plunged into a kind of wonder at my vicarious depravity. This familiar that I called out of my own soul, and sent forth alone to do his good pleasure, was a being inherently malign and villainous; his every act and thought centered on self; drinking pleasure with bestial avidity from any degree of torture to another; relentless like a man of stone. Henry Jekyll stood at times aghast before the acts of Edward Hyde; but the situation was apart from ordinary laws, and insidiously relaxed the grasp of conscience. It was Hyde, after all, and Hyde alone, that was guilty. Jekyll was no worse; he woke again to his good qualities seemingly unimpaired; he would even make haste, where it was possible, to undo the evil done by Hyde. And thus his conscience slumbered.

Into the details of the infamy at which I thus connived (for even now I can scarce grant that I committed it) I have no design of entering; I mean but to point out the warnings and the successive steps with which my chastisement approached. I met with one accident which, as it brought on no consequence, I shall no more than mention. An act of cruelty to a child aroused against me the anger of a passer-by, whom I recognized the other day in the person of your kinsman; the doctor and the child's family joined him; there were moments when I feared for my life; and at last, in order to pacify their too just resentment, Edward Hyde had to bring them to the door and pay them in a check drawn in the name of Henry Jekyll. But this danger was easily eliminated from the future by opening an account at another bank in the name of Edward Hyde himself, and when, by sloping my own hand backward, I had supplied my double with a signature I thought I sat beyond the reach of fate.

Some two months before the murder of Sir Danvers I had been out for one of my adventures, had returned at a late hour and woke the next day in bed with somewhat odd sensations. It was in vain I looked about me, in vain I saw the decent furniture and tall proportions of my room in the square, in vain that I recognized the pattern of the bed-curtains and the design of the mahogany frame; something still kept insisting that I was not where I was, that I had not wakened where I seemed to be, but in the little room in Soho where I was accustomed to sleep in the body of Edward Hyde. I smiled to myself, and in my psychological way began lazily to inquire into the elements of this illusion, occasionally, even as I did so, dropping back into a comfortable morning doze. I was still so engaged when, in one of my more wakeful moments, my eyes fell upon my hand. Now, the hand of Henry Jekyll (as you have often remarked) was professional in shape and size: it was large, firm, white and comely. But the hand which I now saw, clearly enough, in the yellow light of a mid-London morning, lying half shut on the bedclothes, was lean, corded, knuckly, of a dusky pallor and thickly shaded with a swart growth of hair. It was the hand of Edward Hyde.

I must have stared upon it for near half a minute, sunk as I was in the mere stupidity of wonder, before terror woke up in my breast as sudden and startling as the crash of cymbals, and bounding from my bed I rushed to the mirror. At the sight that met my eyes my blood was changed into something exquisitely thin and icy. Yes, I had gone to bed Henry Jekyll, I had awakened Edward Hyde. How was this to be explained? I asked myself, and then, with another bound of terror—how was it to be remedied? It was well on in the morning; the servants were up; all my drugs were in the cabinet—a long journey down two pairs of stairs, through the back passage, across the open court and through the anatomical theater, from where I was then standing horror-struck. It might indeed be possible to cover my face,

but of what use was that when I was unable to conceal the
alteration in my stature? And then, with an overpowering
sweetness of relief, it came back upon my mind that the
servants were already used to the coming and going of my
second self. I had soon dressed, as well as I was able, in
clothes of my own size; had soon passed through the house,
where Bradshaw stared and drew back at seeing Mr. Hyde
at such an hour and in such a strange array, and ten minutes later Dr. Jekyll had returned to his own shape and was
sitting down, with a darkened brow, to make a feint of
breakfasting.

Small indeed was my appetite. This inexplicable incident,
this reversal of my previous experience, seemed, like the
Babylonian finger on the wall, to be spelling out the letters
of my judgment; and I began to reflect more seriously than
ever before on the issues and possibilities of my double
existence. That part of me which I had the power of
projecting had lately been much exercised and nourished;
it had seemed to me of late as though the body of Edward
Hyde had grown in stature, as though (when I wore that
form) I were conscious of a more generous tide of blood;
and I began to spy a danger that, if this were much prolonged, the balance of my nature might be permanently
overthrown, the power of voluntary change be forfeited, and
the character of Edward Hyde become irrevocably mine.
The power of the drug had not been always equally dis-
played. Once, very early in my career, it had totally failed
me; since then I had been obliged on more than one occasion to double, and once, with infinite risk of death, to treble
the amount; and these rare uncertainties had cast hitherto
the sole shadow on my contentment. Now, however, and in
the light of that morning's accident, I was led to remark
that whereas, in the beginning, the difficulty had been to
throw off the body of Jekyll, it had of late, gradually but
decidedly, transferred itself to the other side. All things
therefore seemed to point to this: that I was slowly losing
hold of my original and better self, and becoming slowly
incorporated with my second and worse.

Between these two, I now felt I had to choose. My two
natures had memory in common, but all other faculties were

most unequally shared between them. Jekyll (who was composite) now with the most sensitive apprehensions, now with a greedy gusto, projected and shared in the pleasures and adventures of Hyde; but Hyde was indifferent to Jekyll, or but remembered him as the mountain bandit remembers the cavern in which he conceals himself from pursuit. Jekyll had more than a father's interest; Hyde had more than a son's indifference. To cast in my lot with Jekyll was to die to those appetites which I had long secretly indulged and had of late begun to pamper. To cast it in with Hyde was to die to a thousand interests and aspirations, and to become, at a blow and forever, despised and friendless. The bargain might appear unequal; but there was still another consideration in the scales; for while Jekyll would suffer smartingly in the fires of abstinence, Hyde would not be even conscious of all that he had lost. Strange as my circumstances were, the terms of this debate are as old and commonplace as man; much the same inducements and alarms cast the die for any tempted and trembling sinner; and it fell out with me, as it falls with so vast a majority of my fellows, that I chose the better part and was found wanting in the strength to keep to it.

Yes, I preferred the elderly and discontented doctor, surrounded by friends and cherishing honest hopes; and bade a resolute farewell to the liberty, the comparative youth, the light step, leaping impulses and secret pleasures, that I had enjoyed in the disguise of Hyde. I made this choice perhaps with some unconscious reservation, for I neither gave up the house in Soho, nor destroyed the clothes of Edward Hyde, which still lay ready in my cabinet. For two months, however, I was true to my determination; for two months I led a life of such severity as I had never before attained to, and enjoyed the compensations of an approving conscience. But time began at last to obliterate the freshness of my alarm; the praises of conscience began to grow into a thing of course; I began to be tortured with throes and longings, as of Hyde struggling after freedom; and at last, in an hour of moral weakness, I once again compounded and swallowed the transforming draught.

I do not suppose that, when a drunkard reasons with

himself upon his vice, he is once out of five hundred times affected by the dangers that he runs through his brutish, physical insensibility; neither had I, long as I had considered my position, made enough allowance for the complete moral insensibility and insensate readiness to evil, which were the leading characters of Edward Hyde. Yet it was by these that I was punished. My devil had been long caged, he came out roaring. I was conscious, even when I took the draught, of a more unbridled, a more furious propensity to ill. It must have been this, I suppose, that stirred in my soul that tempest of impatience with which I listened to the civilities of my unhappy victim; I declare, at least, before God, no man morally sane could have been guilty of that crime upon so pitiful a provocation; and that I struck in no more reasonable spirit than that in which a sick child may break a plaything. But I had voluntarily stripped myself of all those balancing instincts, by which even the worst of us continues to walk with some degree of steadiness among temptations; and in my case, to be tempted, however slightly, was to fall.

Instantly the spirit of hell awoke in me and raged. With a transport of glee, I mauled the unresisting body, tasting delight from every blow; and it was not till weariness had begun to succeed that I was suddenly, in the top fit of my delirium, struck through the heart by a cold thrill of terror. A mist dispersed; I saw my life to be forfeit, and fled from the scene of these excesses, at once glorying and trembling, my lust of evil gratified and stimulated, my love of life screwed to the topmost peg. I ran to the house in Soho and (to make assurance doubly sure) destroyed my papers; thence I set out through the lamplit streets, in the same divided ecstasy of mind, gloating on my crime, lightheadedly devising others in the future, and yet still hastening and still hearkening in my wake for the steps of the avenger. Hyde had a song upon his lips as he compounded the draught, and as he drank it, pledged the dead man. The pangs of transformation had not done tearing him before Henry Jekyll, with streaming tears of gratitude and remorse, had fallen upon his knees and lifted his clasped hands to God. The veil of self-indulgence was rent from head to foot, I saw my life as a whole; I followed it up from the days of childhood, when I had walked with my father's hand, and through the self-denying toils of my professional life, to arrive again and again, with the same sense of unreality, at the damned horrors of the evening. I could have screamed aloud; I sought with tears and prayers to smother down the crowd of hideous images and sounds with which my memory swarmed against me; and still, between the petitions, the ugly face of my iniquity stared into my soul. As the acuteness of this remorse began to die away, it was succeeded by a sense of joy. The problem of my conduct was solved. Hyde was thenceforth impossible; whether I would or not, I was now confined to the better part of my existence; and oh, how I rejoiced to think it! with what willing humility I embraced anew the restrictions of natural life! with what sincere renunciation I locked the door by which I had so often gone and come, and ground the key under my heel!

The next day came the news that the murder had been overlooked, that the guilt of Hyde was patent to the world, and that the victim was a man high in public estimation. It was not only a crime, it had been a tragic folly. I think I was glad to know it; I think I was glad to have my better impulses thus buttressed and guarded by the terrors of the scaffold. Jekyll was now my city of refuge; let but Hyde peep out an instant, and the hands of all men would be raised to take and slay him.

I resolved in my future conduct to redeem the past; and I can say with honesty that my resolve was fruitful of some good. You know yourself how earnestly, in the last months of last year, I labored to relieve suffering; you know that much was done for others, and that the days passed quietly, almost happily, for myself. Nor can I truly say that I wearied of this beneficent and innocent life; I think instead that I daily enjoyed it more completely; but I was still cursed with my duality of purpose; and as the first edge of my penitence wore off the lower side of me, so long indulged, so recently chained down, began to growl for license. Not that I dreamed of resuscitating Hyde; the bare idea of that would startle me to frenzy; no, it was in my own

person that I was once more tempted to trifle with my conscience; and it was as an ordinary secret sinner that I at
last fell before the assaults of temptation.

There comes an end to all things; the most capacious
measure is filled at last; and this brief condescension to
my evil finally destroyed the balance of my soul. And yet I
was not alarmed; the fall seemed natural, like a return to
the old days before I had made my discovery. It was a fine,
clear, January day, wet under foot where the frost had
melted, but cloudless overhead; and the Regent's Park was
full of winter chirrupings and sweet with spring odors.
I sat in the sun on a bench; the animal within me licking
the chaps of memory; the spiritual side a little drowsed,
promising subsequent penitence, but not yet moved to begin.
After all, I reflected, I was like my neighbors; and then
I smiled, comparing myself with other men, comparing my
active good-will with the lazy cruelty of their neglect. And
at the very moment of that vainglorious thought a qualm
came over me, a horrid nausea and the most deadly shuddering. These passed away, and left me faint; and then as
in its turn the faintness subsided, I began to be aware of
a change in the temper of my thoughts, a greater boldness,
a contempt of danger, a solution of the bonds of obligation. I looked down; my clothes hung formlessly on my
shrunken limbs; the hand that lay on my knee was corded
and hairy. I was once more Edward Hyde. A moment
before I had been safe of all men's respect, wealthy, beloved—the cloth laying for me in the dining-room at home;
and now I was the common quarry of mankind, hunted,
houseless, a known murderer, thrall to the gallows.

My reason wavered, but it did not fail me utterly. I have
more than once observed that, in my second character, my
faculties seemed sharpened to a point and my spirits more
tensely elastic; thus it came about that, where Jekyll perhaps might have succumbed, Hyde rose to the importance
of the moment. My drugs were in one of the presses of
my cabinet; how was I to reach them? That was the problem that (crushing my temples in my hands) I set myself
to solve. The laboratory door I had closed. If I sought
to enter by the house my own servants would consign me

to the gallows. I saw I must employ another hand, and
thought of Lanyon. How was he to be reached? how persuaded? Supposing that I escaped capture in the streets,
how was I to make my way into his presence? and how
should I, an unknown and displeasing visitor, prevail on
the famous physician to rifle the study of his colleague, Dr.
Jekyll? Then I remembered that of my original character
one part remained to me; I could write my own hand; and
once I had conceived that kindling spark, the way that I
must follow became lighted up from end to end.

Thereupon, I arranged my clothes as best I could, and
summoning a passing hansom, drove to an hotel in Portland
Street, the name of which I chanced to remember. At my
appearance (which was indeed comical enough, however
tragic a fate these garments covered) the driver could not
conceal his mirth. I gnashed my teeth upon him with a
gust of devilish fury; and the smile withered from his face
—happily for him—yet more happily for myself, for in
another instant I had certainly dragged him from his perch.
At the inn, as I entered, I looked about me with so black
a countenance as made the attendants tremble; not a look
did they exchange in my presence; but obsequiously took
my orders, led me to a private room, and brought me where-
withal to write. Hyde in danger of his life was a creature
new to me; shaken with inordinate anger, strung to the
pitch of murder, lusting to inflict pain. Yet the creature
was astute; mastered his fury with a great effort of the
will; composed his two important letters, one to Lanyon
and one to Poole; and that he might receive actual evidence
of their being posted, sent them out with directions that
they should be registered.

Thenceforward, he sat all day over the fire in the private
room, gnawing his nails; there he dined, sitting alone with
his fears, the waiter visibly quailing before his eye; and
thence, when the night was fully come, he set forth in
the corner of a closed cab, and was driven to and fro about
the streets of the city. He, I say—I cannot say I. That
child of hell had nothing human; nothing lived in him but
fear and hatred. And when at last, thinking the driver
had begun to grow suspicious, he discharged the cab and

ventured on foot, attired in his misfitting clothes, an object marked out for observation, into the midst of the nocturnal passengers, these two base passions raged within him like a tempest. He walked fast, hunted by his fears, chattering to himself, skulking through the less frequented thoroughfares, counting the minutes that still divided him from midnight. Once a woman spoke to him, offering, I think, a box of lights. He smote her in the face, and she fled.

When I came to myself at Lanyon's the horror of my old friend perhaps affected me somewhat; I do not know; it was at least but a drop in the sea to the abhorrence with which I looked back upon these hours. A change had come over me. It was no longer the fear of the gallows, it was the horror of being Hyde that racked me. I received Lanyon's condemnation partly in a dream; it was partly in a dream that I came home to my own house and got into bed. I slept after the prostration of the day, with a stringent and profound slumber which not even the nightmares that wrung me could avail to break. I awoke in the morning shaken, weakened, but refreshed. I still hated and feared the thought of the brute that slept within me, and I had not of course forgotten the appalling dangers of the day before; but I was once more at home, in my own house and close to my drugs; and gratitude for my escape shone so strong in my soul that it almost rivaled the brightness of hope.

I was stepping leisurely across the court after breakfast, drinking the chill of the air with pleasure, when I was seized again with those indescribable sensations that heralded the change; and I had but the time to gain the shelter of my cabinet before I was once again raging and freezing with the passions of Hyde. It took on this occasion a double dose to recall me to myself; and alas! six hours after, as I sat looking sadly in the fire, the pangs returned, and the drug had to be readministered. In short, from that day forth it seemed only by a great effort, as of gymnastics, and only under the immediate stimulation of the drug, that I was able to wear the countenance of Jekyll. At all hours of the day and night I would be taken with the premonitory shudder; above all, if I slept, or even dozed for a moment in my chair, it was always as Hyde that I awakened. Under the strain of this continually impending doom and by the sleeplessness to which I now condemned myself, ay, even beyond what I had thought possible to man, I became, in my own person, a creature eaten up and emptied by fever, languidly weak both in body and mind, and solely occupied by one thought: the horror of my other self. But when I slept, or when the virtue of the medicine wore off, I would leap almost without transition (for the pangs of transformation grew daily less marked) into the possession of a fancy brimming with images of terror, a soul boiling with causeless hatreds, and a body that seemed not strong enough to contain the raging energies of life. The powers of Hyde seemed to have grown with the sickliness of Jekyll. And certainly the hate that now divided them was equal on each side. With Jekyll, it was a thing of vital instinct. He had now seen the full deformity of that creature that shared with him some of the phenomena of consciousness, and was co-heir with him to death; and beyond these links of community, which in themselves made the most poignant part of his distress, he thought of Hyde, for all his energy of life, as of something not only hellish but inorganic. This was the shocking thing; that the slime of the pit seemed to utter cries and voices; that the amorphous dust gesticulated and sinned; that what was dead, and had no shape, should usurp the offices of life. And this again, that that insurgent horror was knit to him closer than a wife, closer than an eye lay caged in his flesh, where he heard it mutter and felt it struggle to be born; and at every hour of weakness, and in the confidence of slumber, prevailed against him, and deposed him out of life. The hatred of Hyde for Jekyll was of a different order. His terror of the gallows drove him continually to commit temporary suicide, and return to his subordinate station of a part instead of a person; but he loathed the necessity, he loathed the despondency into which Jekyll was now fallen, and he resented the dislike with which he was himself regarded. Hence the ape-like tricks that he would play me, scrawling in my own hand blasphemies on the pages of my books, burning the letters and destroying the portrait of my father; and indeed, had it not been for his fear of death, he would long ago have ruined himself in order to involve me in the ruin. But his love of life is wonderful; I go further; I, who sicken and freeze at the mere thought of him, when I recall the abjection and passion of this attachment, and when I know how he fears my power to cut him off by suicide, I find it in my heart to pity him.

It is useless, and the time awfully fails me, to prolong this description; no one has ever suffered such torments, let that suffice; and yet even to these habit brought—no, not alleviation—but a certain callousness of soul, a certain acquiescence of despair; and my punishment might have gone on for years, but for the last calamity which has now fallen, and which has finally severed me from my own face and nature. My provision of the salt, which had never been renewed since the date of the first experiment, began to run low. I sent out for a fresh supply, and mixed the draught; the ebullition followed, and the first change of color, not the second; I drank it and it was without efficiency. You will learn from Poole how I have had London ransacked; it was in vain; and I am now persuaded that my first supply was impure, and that it was that unknown impurity which lent efficacy to the draught.

About a week has passed, and I am now finishing this statement under the influence of the last of the old powders. This, then, is the last time, short of a miracle, that Henry Jekyll can think his own thoughts or see his own face (now how sadly altered!) in the glass. Nor must I delay too long to bring my writing to an end; for if my narrative has hitherto escaped destruction, it has been by a combination of great prudence and great good luck. Should the throes of change take me in the act of writing it, Hyde will tear it in pieces; but if some time shall have elapsed after I have laid it by, his wonderful selfishness and circumscription to the moment will probably save it once again from the action of his ape-like spite. And indeed the doom that is closing on us both has already changed and crushed him. Half an hour from now, when I shall again and forever reindue that hated personality, I know how I shall sit shuddering and weeping in my chair, or continue, with the most strained and fear-struck ecstasy of listening, to pace up and down this room (my last earthly refuge) and give ear to every sound of menace. Will Hyde die upon the scaffold? or will he find courage to release himself at the last moment? God knows; I am careless; this is my true hour of death, and what is to follow concerns another than myself. Here then, as I lay down the pen and proceed to seal up my confession, I bring the life of that unhappy Henry Jekyll to an end.

THE END.

KIDNAPPED;

BEING

MEMOIRS OF THE ADVENTURES OF DAVID BAL-
FOUR ~~IN THE~~ YEAR 1751.

I SE ... OF SHAWS.

... certain
... 1751,
... of

h...
val...
die a...

Mr. ... waiting
for me by ... me if I
had breakfas... nothing, he
took my hand ... kindly under
his arm.

"Well, Davie, la... go with you as far
as the ford, to set yo...

And we began to walk... silence.

"Are ye sorry to leav... ...endean?" said he, after a
while.

"Why, sir," said I, "if I knew where I was going, or
what was likely to become of me, I would tell you candidly.
Essendean is a good place indeed, and I have been very

67

happy there; but then I have never been anywhere else. My father and mother, since they are both dead, I shall be no nearer to in Essendean than in the Kingdom of Hungary; and to speak truth, if I thought I had a chance to better myself where I was going, I would go with a good will."

"Ay?" said Mr. Campbell. "Very well, Davie. Then it behooves me to tell your fortune; or so far as I may. When your mother was gone, and your father (the worthy, Christian man) began to sicken for his end, he gave me in charge a certain letter, which he said was your inheritance. 'So soon,' says he, 'as I am gone, and the house is redd up and the gear disposed of' (all which, Davie, hath been done) 'give my boy this letter into his hand, and start him off to the house of Shaws, not far from Cramond. That is the place I came from,' he said, 'and it's where it befits that my boy should return. He is a steady lad,' your father said, 'and a canny goer; and I doubt not he will come safe, and be well liked where he goes.'"

"The house of Shaws!" I cried. "What had my poor father to do with the house of Shaws?"

"Nay," said Mr. Campbell, "who can tell that for a surety? But the name of that family, Davie boy, is the name you bear—Balfours of Shaws: an ancient, honest reputable house, peradventure in these latter days decayed. Your father, too, was a man of learning as befitted his position; no man more plausibly conducted school; nor had he the manner or the speech of a common dominie; but (as ye will yourself remember) I took aye a pleasure to have him to the manse to meet the gentry; and those of my own house, Campbell of Kilrennet, Campbell of Dunswire, Campbell of Minch, and others, all well-kenned gentlemen, had pleasure in his society. Lastly, to put all the elements of this affair before you, here is the testamentary letter itself, superscribed by the own hand of our departed brother."

He gave me the letter, which was addressed in these words: "To the hands of Ebenezer Balfour, Esquire, of Shaws, in his house of Shaws, these will be delivered by my son, David Balfour." My heart was beating hard at this great prospect now suddenly opening before a lad of sixteen years of age, the son of a poor country dominie in the Forest of Ettrick.

"Mr. Campbell," I stammered, "and if you were in my shoes, would you go?"

"Of a surety," said the minister, "that would I, and without pause. A pretty lad like you should get to Cramond (which is near in by Edinburgh) in two days of walk. If the worst came to the worst, and your high relations (as I cannot but suppose them to be somewhat of your blood) should put you to the door, ye can but walk the two days back again and risp at the manse door. But I would rather hope that ye shall be well received, as your poor father forecast for you, and for anything that I ken, come to be a great man in time. And here, David laddie," he resumed, "it lies near upon my conscience to improve this parting, and set you on the right guard against the dangers of the world."

Here he cast about for a comfortable seat, lighted on a big boulder under a birch by the trackside, sat down upon it with a very long, serious upper lip, and the sun now shining in upon us between two peaks, put his pocket handkerchief over his cocked hat to shelter him. There, then, with uplifted forefinger, he first put me on my guard against a considerable number of heresies, to which I had no temptation, and urged upon me to be instant in my prayers and reading of the Bible. That done, he drew a picture of the great house that I was bound to, and how I should conduct myself with its inhabitants.

"Be soople, Davie, in things immaterial," said he. "Bear ye this in mind, that, though gentle born, ye have had a country rearing. Dinnae shame us, Davie, dinnae shame us! In yon great, muckle house, with all these domestics, upper and under, show yourself as nice, as circumspect, as quick at the conception, and as slow of speech as any. As for the laird—remember he's the laird; I say no more: honor to whom honor. It's a pleasure to obey a laird; or should be, to the young."

"Well, sir," said I, "it may be; and I'll promise you I'll try to make it so."

"Why, very well said," replied Mr. Campbell, heartily. "And now to come to the material, or (to make a quibble) to the immaterial. I have here a little packet which contains four things." He tugged it, as he spoke, and with some difficulty, from the skirt pocket of his coat. "Of these four things, the first is your legal due: the little pickle money for your father's books and plenishing, which I have bought (as I have explained from the first, in the design of re-selling at a profit to the incoming dominie. The other three are gifties that Mrs. Campbell and myself would be blithe of your acceptance. The first, which is round, will likely please ye best at the first off-go; but, O Davie laddie, it's but a drop of water in the sea; it'll help you but a step, and vanish like the morning. The second, which is flat and square and written upon, will stand by you through life, like a good staff for the road, and a good pillow to your head in sickness. And as for the last, which is cubical, that'll see you, it's my prayerful wish, into a better land."

With that he got upon his feet, took off his hat, and prayed a little while aloud, and in affecting terms, for a young man setting out into the world; then suddenly took me in his arms and embraced me very hard; then held me at arm's length, looking at me with his face all working with sorrow; and then whipped about, and crying good-bye to me, set off backward by the way that we had come at a sort of jogging run. It might have been laughable to another; but I was in no mind to laugh. I watched him as long as he was in sight; and he never stopped hurrying, nor once looked back. Then it came in upon my mind that this was all his sorrow at my departure; and my conscience smote me hard and fast, because I, for my part, was overjoyed to get away out of that quiet country-side, and go to a great, busy house, among rich and respected gentlefolk of my own name and blood.

"Davie, Davie," I thought, "was ever seen such black ingratitude! Can you forget old favors and old friends at the mere whistle of a name? Fy, fy; think shame!"

And I sat down on the boulder the good man had just left, and opened the parcel to see the nature of my gifts. That which he had called cubical, I had never had much doubt of; sure enough it was a little Bible, to carry in a plaid-neuk. That which he had called round, I found to be a shilling piece; and the third, which was to help me so wonderfully both in health and sickness all the days of my life, was a little piece of coarse yellow paper, written upon thus in red ink:

"To Make Lilly of the Valley Water.—Take the flowers of lilly of the valley and distil them in sack, and drink a spoonuful or two as there is occasion. It restores speech to those that have the dumb palsey. It is good against the Gout; it comforts the heart and strengthens the memory; and the flowers, put into a Glasse, close stopt, and set into ane hill of ants for a month, then take it out, and you will find a liquor which comes from the flowers, which keep in a vial; it is good, ill or well, and whether man or woman."

And then, in the minister's own hand, was added:

"Likewise for sprains, rub it in; and for the cholic, a great spooneful in the hour."

To be sure, I laughed over this; but it was rather tremulous laughter; and I was glad to get my bundle on my staff's end and set out over the ford and up the hill upon the further side; till, just as I came on the green drove-road running wide through the heather, I took my last look of Kirk Essendean, the trees about the manse, and the big rowans in the kirkyard where my father and my mother lay.

CHAPTER II.

I COME TO MY JOURNEY'S END.

On the forenoon of the second day, coming to the top of a hill, I saw all the country fall away before me down to the sea; and in the midst of this descent, on a long ridge, the city of Edinburgh smoking like a kiln. There was a flag upon the castle, and ships moving or lying anchored in the firth; both of which, for as far away as they were, I could distinguish clearly; and both brought my country heart into my mouth.

A little farther on, and I was told I was in Cramond parish, and began to substitute in my inquiries the name of the house of Shaws. It was a word that seemed to surprise those of whom I sought my way. At first I thought the plainness of my appearance, in my country habit, and that all dusty from the road, consorted ill with the greatness of the place to which I was bound. But after two, or maybe three, had given me the same look and the same answer, I began to take it in my head there was something strange about the Shaws itself.

The better to set this fear at rest, I changed the form of my inquiries; and spying an honest fellow coming along a lane on the shaft of his cart, I asked him if he had ever heard tell of a house they called the house of Shaws.

He stopped his cart and looked at me, like the others.

"Ay," said he. "What for?"

"It's a great house?" I asked.

"Doubtless," says he. "The house is a big, muckle house."

"Ay," said I, "but the folk that are in it?"

"Folk?" cries he. "Are ye daft? There's nae folk there —to call folk."

"What?" says I; "not Mr. Ebenezer?"

"O, ay," says the man; "there's the laird, to be sure, if it's him you're wanting. What'll like be your business, mannie?"

"I was led to think that I would get a situation," I said, looking as modest as I could.

"What?" cries the carter, in so sharp a note that his very horse started; and then, "Well, mannie," he added, "it's nane of my affairs; but ye seem a decent-spoken lad; and if ye'll take a word from me, ye'll keep clear of the Shaws."

The next person I came across was a dapper little man in a beautiful white wig, whom I saw to be a barber on his rounds: and knowing well that barbers were great gossips, I asked him plainly what sort of a man was Mr. Balfour of the Shaws.

"Hoot, hoot, hoot," said the barber, "nae kind of a man, nae kind of a man at all;" and began to ask me very shrewdly what my business was; but I was more than a match for him at that, and he went on to his next customer no wiser than he came.

I cannot well describe the blow this dealt to my illusions. The more indistinct the accusations were, the less I liked them, for they left the wider field to fancy. What kind of a great house was this, that all the parish should start and stare to be asked the way to it? or what sort of a gentleman, that his ill-fame should be thus current on the wayside? If an hour's walking would have brought me back to Essendean, I had left my adventure then and there, and returned to Mr. Campbell's. But when I had come so far away already, mere shame would not suffer me to desist till I had put the matter to the touch of proof; I was bound, out of mere self-respect, to carry it through; and little as I liked the sound of what I heard, and slow as I began to travel, I still kept asking my way and still kept advancing.

It was drawing on to sundown when I met a stout, dark, sour-looking woman coming trudging down a hill; and she, when I had put my usual question, turned sharp about, accompanied me back to the summit she had just left, and pointed to a great bulk of building standing very bare upon a green in the bottom of the next valley. The country was pleasant round about, running in low hills, pleasantly watered and wooded, and the crops, to my eyes, wonderfully good; but the house itself appeared to be a kind of ruin; no road led up to it; no smoke arose from any of the chimneys; nor was there any semblance of a garden. My heart sank. "That!" I cried.

The woman's face lit up with a malignant anger. "That is the house of Shaws!" she cried. "Blood built it; blood stopped the building of it; blood shall bring it down. See here!" she cried again—"I spit upon the ground, and crack my thumb at it! Black be its fall! If ye see the laird, tell him what ye hear; tell him this makes the twelve hunner and nineteen time that Jennet Clouston has called down the curse on him and his house, byre and stable, man, guest, and master, wife, miss, or bairn—black, black be their fall!"

And the woman, whose voice had risen to a kind of eldritch sing-song, turned with a skip, and was gone. I stood where she left me, with my hair on end. In these days folks still believed in witches and trembled at a curse; and this one, falling so pat, like a wayside omen, to arrest me ere I carried out my purpose, took the pith out of my legs.

I sat me down and stared at the house of Shaws. The more I looked, the pleasanter that country-side appeared; being all set with hawthorn bushes full of flowers; the fields dotted with sheep; a fine flight of rooks in the sky; and every sign of a kind soil and climate; and yet the barrack in the midst of it went sore against my fancy.

Country folk went by from the fields as I sat there on the side of the ditch, but I lacked the spirit to give them a good-e'en. At last the sun went down, and then, right up against the yellow sky, I saw a scroll of smoke go mounting, not much thicker, as it seemed to me, than the smoke of a candle; but still there it was, and meant a fire, and warmth, and cookery, and some living inhabitant that must have lit it; and this comforted my heart wonderfully—more, I feel sure, than a whole flask of the lily of the valley water that Mrs. Campbell set so great a store by.

So I set forward by a little faint track in the grass that led in my direction. It was very faint indeed to be the only way to a place of habitation; yet I saw no other. Presently it brought me to stone uprights, with an unroofed lodge beside them, and coats of arms upon the top. A main entrance, it was plainly meant to be, but never finished; instead of gates of wrought iron, a pair of hurdles were tied across with a straw rope; and as there were no park walls, nor any sign of avenue, the track that I was following passed on the right hand of the pillars, and went wandering on toward the house.

The nearer I got to that, the drearier it appeared. It seemed like the one wing of a house that had never been finished. What should have been the inner end stood open on the upper floors, and showed against the sky with steps and stairs of uncompleted masonry. Many of the windows were unglazed, and bats flew in and out like doves out of a dove-cote.

The night had begun to fall as I got close; and in three of the lower windows, which were very high up, and narrow, and well barred, the changing light of a little fire began to glimmer.

Was this the palace I had been coming to? Was it within these walls that I was to seek new friends and begin great fortunes? Why, in my father's house on Essen-Waterside, the fire and the bright lights would show a mile away, and the door open to a beggar's knock.

I came forward cautiously, and giving ear as I came, heard

some one rattling with dishes, and a little dry, eager cough
that came in fits; but there was no sound of speech, and not
a dog barked.

The door, as well as I could see it in the dim light, was a
great piece of wood all studded with nails; and I lifted my
hand with a faint heart under my jacket, and knocked once.
Then I stood and waited. The house had fallen into a dead
silence; a whole minute passed away, and nothing stirred
but the bats overhead. I knocked again, and hearkened
again. By this time my ears had grown so accustomed to
the quiet, that I could hear the ticking of the clock inside
as it slowly counted out the seconds; but whoever was
in that house kept deadly still, and must have held his
breath.

I was in two minds whether to run away; but anger got
the upper hand, and I began instead to rain kicks and buffets
on the door, and to shout out aloud for Mr. Balfour. I was
in full career, when I heard the cough right overhead, and
jumping back and looking up, beheld a man's head in a tall
nightcap, and the bell mouth of a blunderbuss, at one of the
first story windows.

"It's loaded," said a voice.

"I have come here with a letter," I said, "to Mr. Ebenezer
Balfour of Shaws. Is he here?"

"From whom is it?" asked the man with the blunderbuss.

"That is neither here nor there," said I, for I was growing
very wroth.

"Well," was the reply, "ye can put it down upon the doorstep, and be off with ye."

"I will do no such thing," I cried. "I will deliver it into
Mr. Balfour's hands, as it was meant I should. It is a letter
of introduction."

"A what?" cried the voice, sharply.

I repeated what I had said.

"Who are ye, yourself?" was the next question, after a
considerable pause.

"I am not ashamed of my name," said I. "They call me
David Balfour."

At that, I made sure the man started, for I heard the
blunderbuss rattle on the window-sill; and it was after quite

a long pause, and with a curious change of voice, that the next question followed:

"Is your father dead?"

I was so much surprised at this, that I could find no voice to answer, but stood staring.

"Ay," the man resumed, "he'll be dead, no doubt; and that'll be what brings ye chapping to my door." Another pause, and then, defiantly, "Well, man," he said, "I'll let ye in;" and he disappeared from the window.

CHAPTER III.

I MAKE ACQUAINTANCE OF MY UNCLE.

Presently there came a great rattling of chains and bolts, and the door was cautiously opened, and shut to again behind me as soon as I had passed.

"Go into the kitchen and touch naething," said the voice; and while the person of the house set himself to replacing the defenses of the door, I groped my way forward and entered the kitchen.

The fire had burned up fairly bright, and showed me the barest room I think I ever put my eyes on. Half-a-dozen dishes stood upon the shelves; the table was laid for supper with a bowl of porridge, a horn spoon, and a cup of small beer. Besides what I have named, there was not another thing in that great, stone-vaulted, empty chamber, but lock-fast chests arranged along the wall and a corner cupboard with a padlock.

As soon as the last chain was up the man rejoined me. He was a mean, stooping, narrow-shouldered, clay-faced creature; and his age might have been anything between fifty and seventy. His nightcap was of flannel, and so was the nightgown that he wore, instead of coat and waistcoat, over his ragged shirt. He was long unshaved; but what most distressed and even daunted me, he would neither take his eyes away from me nor look me fairly in the face. What he was, whether by trade or birth, was more than I could fathom; but he seemed most like an old, unprofitable serving-man, who should have been left in charge of that big house upon board wages.

"Are ye sharp-set?" he asked, glancing at about the level of my knee. "Ye can eat that drop parritch."

I said I feared it was his own supper.

"O," said he, "I can do fine wanting it. I'll take the ale though, for it moistens my cough." He drank the cup about half out, still keeping an eye upon me as he drank; and then suddenly held out his hand. "Let's see the letter," said he.

I told him the letter was for Mr. Balfour; not for him.

"And who do ye think I am?" says he. "Give me Alexander's letter!"

"You know my father's name?"

"It would be strange if I didnae," he returned, "for he was my born brother; and little as ye seem to like either me or my house, or my good parritch, I'm your born uncle, Davie my man, and you my born nephew. So give us the letter, and sit down and fill your kyte."

If I had been some years younger, what with shame, weariness, and disappointment, I believe I had burst into tears. As it was, I could find no words, neither black nor white, but handed him the letter, and sat down to the porridge with as little appetite for meat as ever a young man had.

Meanwhile, my uncle, stooping over the fire, turned the letter over and over in his hands.

"Do ye ken what's in it?" he asked suddenly.

"You see for yourself, sir," said I, "that the seal has not been broken."

"Ay," said he, "but what brought you here?"

"To give the letter," said I.

"No," says he, cunningly, "but ye'll have had some hopes, nae doubt?"

"I confess, sir," said I, "when I was told that I had kinsfolk well-to-do, I did indeed indulge the hope that they might help me in my life. But I am no beggar; I look for no favors at your hands, and I want none that are not freely given. For as poor as I appear, I have friends of my own that will be blithe to help me."

"Hoot-hoot!" said Uncle Ebenezer, "dinnae fly up in the

snuff at me. We'll agree fine yet. And, Davie my man, if you're done with that bit parritch, I could just take a sup of it myself. Ay," he continued, as soon as he had ousted me from the stool and spoon, "they're fine, halesome food— they're grand food, parritch." He murmured a little grace to himself and fell to. "Your father was very fond of his meat, I mind; he was a hearty, if not a great eater; but as for me, I could never do mair than pyke at food." He took a pull at the small beer, which probably reminded him of hospitable duties; for his next speech ran thus: "If ye're dry, ye'll find water behind the door."

To this I returned no answer, standing stiffly on my two feet, and looking down upon my uncle with a mighty angry heart. He, on his part, continued to eat like a man under some pressure of time, and to throw out little darting glances now at my shoes and now at my homespun stockings. Once only, when he had ventured to look a little higher, our eyes met; and no thief taken with a hand in a man's pocket could have shown more lively signals of distress. This set me in a muse, whether his timidity arose from too long a disuse of any human company; and whether perhaps, upon a little trial, it might pass off, and my uncle change into an altogether different man. From this I was awakened by his sharp voice.

"Your father's been long dead?" he asked.

"Three weeks, sir," said I.

"He was a secret man, Alexander; a secret, silent man," he continued. "He never said muckle when he was young. He'll never have spoken muckle of me?"

"I never knew, sir, till you told it me yourself, that he had any brother."

"Dear me, dear me!" said Ebenezer. "Nor yet of Shaws, I daresay?"

"Not so much as the name, sir," said I.

"To think o' that!" said he. "A strange nature of a man!" For all that, he seemed singularly satisfied, but whether with himself, or me, or with this conduct of my fathers, was more than I could read. Certainly, however, he seemed to be outgrowing that distaste, or ill-will, that he had conceived at first against my person; for presently he jumped up, came across the room behind me, and hit me a smack upon the shoulder. "We'll agree fine yet!" he cried. "I'm just as glad I let you in. And now come awa' to your bed."

To my surprise, he lit no lamp or candle, but set forth into the dark passage, groped his way, breathing deeply, up a flight of steps, and paused before a door, which he unlocked. I was close upon his heels, having stumbled after him as best I might; and he bade me go in, for that was my chamber. I did as he bid, but paused after a few steps, and begged a light to go to bed with.

"Hoot-toot!" said Uncle Ebenezer, "there's a fine moon."

"Neither moon nor star, sir, and dark as a pit," said I. "I cannae see the bed."

"Hoot-toot, hoot-toot!" said he. "Lights in a house is a thing I dinnae agree with. I'm unco feared of fires. Good-night to ye, Davie my man." And before I had time to add a further protest, he pulled the door to, and I heard him lock me in from the outside.

I did not know whether to laugh or cry. The room was as cold as a well, and the bed, when I had found my way to it, as damp as a peat-hag; but by good fortune I had caught up my bundle and my plaid, and rolling myself in the latter, I lay down upon the floor under the lee of the big bedstead, and fell speedily asleep.

With the first peep of day I opened my eyes, to find myself in a great chamber, hung with stamped leather, furnished with fine embroidered furniture, and lit by three fair windows. Ten years ago, or perhaps twenty, it must have been as pleasant a room to lie down or to awake in as a man could wish; but damp, dirt, disuse, and the mice and spiders had done their worst since then. Many of the window-panes, besides, were broken; and indeed this was so common a feature in that house, that I believe my uncle must at some time have stood a siege from his indignant neighbors— perhaps with Jennet Clouston at their head.

Meanwhile the sun was shining outside; and being very cold in that miserable room, I knocked and shouted till my jailer came and let me out. He carried me to the back of the house, where was a draw-well, and told me to "wash my face there, if I wanted;" and when that was done, I made the best of my own way back to the kitchen, where he had lit the fire and was making the porridge. The table was laid with two bowls and two horn spoons, but the same single measure of small beer. Perhaps my eye rested on this particular with some surprise, and perhaps my uncle observed it; for he spoke up as if in answer to my thought, asking me if I would like to drink ale—for so he called it.

I told him such was my habit, but not to put himself about.

"Na, na," said he; "I'll deny you nothing in reason."

He fetched another cup from the shelf; and then, to my great surprise, instead of drawing more beer, he poured an accurate half from one cup to the other. There was a kind of nobleness in this that took my breath away; if my uncle was certainly a miser, he was one of that thorough breed that goes near to make the vice respectable.

When we had made an end of our meal, my uncle Ebenezer unlocked a drawer, and drew out of it a clay pipe and a lump of tobacco, from which he cut one fill before he locked it up again. Then he sat down in the sun at one of the windows and silently smoked. From time to time his eyes came coasting round to me, and he shot out one of his questions. Once it was, "And your mother?" and when I had told him that she, too, was dead, "Ay, she was a bonnie lassie!" Then after another long pause, "Whae were these friends o' yours?"

I told him they were different gentlemen of the name of Campbell; though, indeed, there was only one, and that the minister, that had ever taken the least note of me; but I began to think my uncle made too light of my position, and finding myself all alone with him, I did not wish him to suppose me helpless.

He seemed to turn this over in his mind; and then, "Davie my man," said he, "ye've come to the right bit when ye came to your Uncle Ebenezer. I've a great notion of the family, and I mean to do the right by you; but while I'm taking a bit think to mysel' of what's the best thing to put you to—whether the law, or the meenistry, or maybe the army, whilk is what boys are fondest of—I wouldnae like the Balfours to be humbled before a wheen Hieland Campbells, and I'll ask you to keep your tongue within your teeth. Nae letters;

nae messages; no kind of word to onybody; or else—there's my door."

"Uncle Ebenezer," said I, "I've no manner of reason to suppose you mean anything but well by me. For all that, I would have you to know that I have a pride of my own. It was by no will of mine that I came seeking you; and if you show me your door again, I'll take you at the word."

He seemed grievously put out. "Hoots-toots," said he, "ca' cannie, man—ca' cannie! Bide a day or two. I'm nae warlock, to find a fortune for you in the bottom of a parritch bowl; but just you give me a day or two, and say naething to naebody, and as sure as sure, I'll do the right by you."

"Very well," said I, "enough said. If you want to help me, there's no doubt but I'll be glad of it, and none but I'll be grateful."

It seemed to me (too soon, I daresay) that I was getting the upper hand of my uncle; and I began next to say that I must have the bed and bedclothes aired and put to sun-dry; for nothing would make me sleep in such a pickle.

"Is this my house or yours?" said he, in his keen voice, and then all of a sudden broke off. "Na, na," said he, "I dinnae mean that. What's mine is yours, Davie my man, and what's yours is mine. Blood's thicker than water; and there's naebody but you and me that ought the name." And then on he rambled about the family, and its ancient greatness, and his father that began to enlarge the house, and himself that stopped the building as a sinful waste; and this put it in my head to give him Jennet Clouston's message.

"The limmer!" he cried. "Twelve hunner and fifteen— that's every day since I had the limmer rowpit! Dod, David, I'll have her roasted on red peats before I'm by with it! A witch—a proclaimed witch! I'll aff and see the session clerk."

And with that he opened a chest, and got out a very old and well-preserved blue coat and waistcoat, and a good enough beaver hat, both without lace. These he threw on anyway, and taking a staff from the cupboard, locked all up again, and was for setting out, when a thought arrested him.

"I cannae leave you by yoursel' in the house," said he. "I'll have to lock you out."

The blood came into my face. "If you lock me out," I said, "it'll be the last you see of me in friendship."

He turned very pale, and sucked his mouth in. "This is no the way," he said, looking wickedly at a corner of the floor—"this is no the way to win my favor, David."

"Sir," says I, "with a proper reverence for your age and our common blood, I do not value your favor at a boddle's purchase. I was brought up to have a good conceit of myself; and if you were all the uncle, and all the family, I had in the world ten times over, I wouldn't buy your liking at such prices."

Uncle Ebenezer went and looked out of the window for a while. I could see him all trembling and twitching, like a man with palsy. But when he turned round, he had a smile upon his face.

"Well, well," said he, "we must bear and forbear. I'll no go; that's all that's to be said of it."

"Uncle Ebenezer," said I, "I can make nothing out of this. You use me like a thief; you hate to have me in this house; you let me see it, every word and every minute; it's not possible that you can like me; and as for me, I've spoken to you as I never thought to speak to any man. Why do you seek to keep me, then? Let me gang back—let me gang back to the friends I have, and that like me!"

"Na, na; na, na," he said, very earnestly. "I like you fine; we'll agree fine yet; and for the honor of the house I could-nae let you leave the way ye came. Bide here quiet, there's a good lad; just you bide here quiet a bittie, and ye'll find that we agree."

"Well, sir," said I, after I had thought the matter out in silence, "I'll stay a while. It's more just I should be helped by my own blood than strangers; and if we don't agree, I'll do my best it shall be through no fault of mine."

CHAPTER IV.

I RUN A GREAT DANGER IN THE HOUSE OF SHAWS.

For a day that was begun so ill, the day passed fairly well. We had the porridge cold again at noon, and hot porridge at night: porridge and small beer was my uncle's diet. He spoke but little, and that in the same way as before, shooting a question at me after a long silence; and when I sought to lead him in talk about my future, slipped out of it again. In a room next door to the kitchen, where he suffered me to go, I found a great number of books, both Latin and English, in which I took great pleasure all the afternoon. Indeed the time passed so lightly in this good company, that I began to be almost reconciled to my residence at Shaws; and nothing but the sight of my uncle, and his eyes playing hide and seek with mine, revived the force of my distrust.

One thing I discovered, which put me in some doubt. This was an entry on the fly-leaf of a chapbook (one of Patrick Walker's) plainly written by my father's hand and thus conceived: "To my brother Ebenezer on his fifth birthday." Now, what puzzled me was this: That as my father was of course the younger brother, he must either have made some strange error, or he must have written, before he was yet five, an excellent, clear, manly hand of writing.

I tried to get this out of my head; but though I took down many interesting authors, old and new, history, poetry, and story-book, this notion of my father's hand of writing stuck to me; and when at length I went back into the kitchen, and sat down once more to porridge and small beer, the first thing I said to Uncle Ebenezer was to ask him if my father had not been very quick at his book.

"Alexander? No him!" was the reply. "I was far quicker mysel'; I was a clever chappie when I was young. Why, I could read as soon as he could."

This puzzled me yet more; and a thought coming into my head, I asked if he and my father had been twins.

He jumped upon his stool, and the horn spoon fell out of his hand upon the floor. "What gars ye ask that?" he said, and caught me by the breast of the jacket, and looked this time straight into my eyes; his own, which were little and light, and bright like a bird's, blinking and winking strangely.

"What do you mean?" I asked, very calmly, for I was far stronger than he, and not easily frightened. "Take your hand from my jacket. This is no way to behave."

My uncle seemed to make a great effort upon himself. "Dod, man David," he said, "ye shouldnae speak to me about your father. That's where the mistake is." He sat a while and shook, blinking in his plate: "He was all the brother that ever I had," he added, but with no heart in his voice; and then he caught up his spoon and fell to supper again, but still shaking.

Now this last passage, this laying of hands upon my person and sudden profession of love for my dead father, went so clean beyond my comprehension that it put me into both fear and hope. On the one hand, I began to think my uncle was perhaps insane and might be dangerous; on the other, there came up into my mind (quite unbidden by me and even discouraged) a story like some ballad I had heard folk singing, of a poor lad that was a rightful heir and a wicked kinsman that tried to keep him from his own. For why should my uncle play a part with a relative that came, almost a beggar, to his door, unless in his heart he had some cause to fear him?

With this notion, all unacknowledged, but nevertheless getting firmly settled in my head, I now began to imitate his covert looks; so that we sat at table like a cat and a mouse, each stealthily observing the other. Not another word had he to say to me, black or white, but was busy turning something secretly over in his mind; and the longer we sat and the more I looked at him, the more certain I became that the something was unfriendly to myself.

When he had cleared the platter, he got out a single pipeful of tobacco, just as in the morning, turned round a stool into the chimney corner, and sat a while smoking, with his back to me.

"Davie," he said, at length, "I've been thinking;" then he paused, and said it again. "There's a wee bit siller that I half promised ye before ye were born," he continued; "prom-

ised it to your father. O, naething legal, ye understand;
just gentlemen daffing at their wine. Well, I keepit that bit
money separate—it was a great expense, but a promise is a
promise—and it has grown by now to be a maitter of just
precisely—just exactly"—and here he paused and stumbled—
"of just exactly forty pounds!" This last he rapped out with
a sidelong glance over his shoulder; and the next moment
added, almost with a scream, "Scots!"

The pound Scots being the same thing as an English shilling, the difference made by this second thought was considerable; I could see, besides, that the whole story was a lie,
invented with some end which it puzzled me to guess; and I
made no attempt to conceal the tone of raillery in which I
answered:

"O, think again, sir! Pounds sterling, I believe!"

"That's what I said," returned my uncle; "pounds sterling! And if you'll step out-by to the door a minute, just to
see what kind of a night it is, I'll get it out to ye and call
ye in again."

I did his will, smiling to myself in my contempt that he
should think I was so easily to be deceived. It was a dark
night, with a few stars low down; and as I stood just outside
the door, I heard a hollow moaning of wind far off among
the hills. I said to myself there was something thundery
and changeful in the weather, and little knew of what a vast
importance that should prove to me before the evening passed.

When I was called in again, my uncle counted out into my
hand seven and thirty golden guinea pieces; the rest was in
his hands, in small gold and silver; but his heart failed him
there, and he crammed the change into his pocket.

"There," said he, "that'll show you! I'm a queer man,
and strange wi' strangers; but my word is my bond, and
there's the proof of it."

Now, my uncle seemed so miserly that I was struck dumb
by this sudden generosity, and could find no words in which
to thank him.

"No a word!" said he. "Nae thanks; I want nae thanks.
I do my duty; I'm no saying that everybody would have
done it; but for my part (though I'm a careful body, too)
it's a pleasure to me to do the right by my brother's son;

and it's a pleasure to me to think that now we'll agree as such near friends should."

I spoke him in return as handsomely as I was able; but all the while I was wondering what would come next, and why he had parted with his precious guineas; for as to the reason he had given, a baby would have refused it.

Presently, he looked toward me sideways:

"And see here," says he, "tit for tat."

I told him I was ready to prove my gratitude in any reasonable degree, and then waited, looking for some monstrous demand. And yet, when at last he plucked up courage to speak, it was only to tell me (very properly, as I thought) that he was growing old and a little broken, and that he would expect me to help him with the house and the bit garden.

I answered, and expressed my readiness to serve.

"Well," he said, "let's begin." He pulled out of his pocket a rusty key. "There," says he, "there's the key of the stair-tower at the far end of the house. Ye can only win into it from the outside, for that part of the house is no finished. Gang ye in there, and up the stairs, and bring me down the chest that's at the top. There's papers in it," he added.

"Can I have a light, sir?" said I.

"Na," said he, very cunningly. "Nae lights in my house."

"Very well, sir," said I. "Are the stairs good?"

"They're grand," said he; and then as I was going, "Keep to the wall," he added; "there's nae banisters. But the stairs are grand underfoot."

Out I went into the night. The wind was still moaning in the distance, though never a breath of it came near the house of Shaws. It had fallen blacker than ever; and I was glad to feel along the wall, till I came the length of the stair-tower door at the far end of the unfinished wing. I had got the key into the keyhole and had just turned it, when all upon a sudden, without sound of wind or thunder, the whole sky was lighted up with wild fire and went black again. I had to put my hand over my eyes to get back to the color of the darkness; and indeed I was already half-blinded when I stepped into the tower.

It was so dark inside, it seemed a body could scarce

breathe; but I pushed out with foot and hand, and presently struck the wall with the one, and the lowermost round of the stair with the other. The wall, by the touch, was of fine hewn stone; the steps too, though somewhat steep and narrow, were of polished mason-work, and regular and solid underfoot. Minding my uncle's word about the banisters, I kept close to the tower side, and felt my way up in the pitch darkness with a beating heart.

The house of Shaws stood some five full stories high, not counting lofts. Well, as I advanced, it seemed to me the stair grew airier and a thought more lightsome; and I was wondering what might be the cause of this change, when a second blink of the summer lightning came and went. If I did not cry out, it was because fear had me by the throat; and if I did not fall, it was more by Heaven's mercy than my own strength. It was not only that the flash shone in on every side through breaches in the wall, so that I seemed to be clambering aloft upon an open scaffold, but the same passing brightness showed me the steps were of unequal length, and that one of my feet rested that moment within two inches of the well.

This was the grand stair! I thought! and with the thought, a gust of a kind of angry courage came into my heart. My uncle had sent me here, certainly to run great risks, perhaps to die. I swore I would settle that "perhaps," if I should break my neck for it; got me down upon my hands and knees; and as slowly as a snail, feeling before me every inch, and testing the solidity of every stone, I continued to ascend the stair. The darkness, by contrast with the flash, appeared to have redoubled; nor was that all; for my ears were now troubled and my mind confounded by a great stir of bats in the top part of the tower, and the foul beasts, flying downward, sometimes beat about my face and body.

The tower, I should have said, was square; and in every corner the step was made of a great stone of a different shape, to join the flights. Well, I had come close to one of these turns, when, feeling forward as usual, my hand slipped upon an edge and found nothing but emptiness beyond it. The stair had been carried no higher: to set a stranger mounting it in the darkness was to send him straight to his death;

and (although, thanks to the lightning and my own precautions, I was safe enough) the mere thought of the peril in which I might have stood, and the dreadful height I might have fallen from, brought out the sweat upon my body and relaxed my joints.

But I knew what I wanted now, and turned and groped my way down again, with a wonderful anger in my heart. About half-way down, the wind sprang up in a clap and shook the tower, and died again; the rain followed; and before I had reached the ground level, it fell in buckets. I put out my head into the storm, and looked along toward the kitchen. The door, which I had shut behind me when I left, now stood open, and shed a little glimmer of light; and I thought I could see a figure standing in the rain, quite still, like a man hearkening. And then there came a blinding flash, which showed me my uncle plainly, just where I had fancied him to stand; and hard upon the heels of it, a great tow-row of thunder.

Now, whether my uncle thought the crash to be the sound of my fall, or whether he heard in it God's voice denouncing murder, I will leave you to guess. Certain it is, at least, that he was seized on by a kind of panic fear, and that he ran into the house and left the door open behind him. I followed as softly as I could, and coming unheard into the kitchen, stood and watched him.

He had found time to open the corner cupboard and bring out a great case bottle of aqua vitae, and now sat with his back toward me at the table. Ever and again he would be seized with a fit of deadly shuddering and groan aloud, and carrying the bottle to his lips, drink down the raw spirits by the mouthful.

I stepped forward, came close behind him where he sat, and suddenly clapping my two hands down upon his shoulders —"Ah!" cried I.

My uncle gave a kind of broken cry like a sheep's bleat, flung up his arms, and tumbled to the floor like a dead man. I was somewhat shocked at this; but I had myself to look to first of all, and did not hesitate to let him lie as he had fallen. The keys were hanging in the cupboard; and it was my design to furnish myself with arms before my uncle should come again to his senses and the power of devising evil. In the cupboard were a few bottles, some apparently of medicine; a great many bills and other papers, which I should willingly enough have rummaged, had I had the time; and a few necessaries, that were nothing to my purpose. Thence I turned to the chests. The first was full of meal; the second of money-bags and papers tied into sheaves; in the third, with many other things (and these for the most part clothes) I found a rusty, ugly looking Highland dirk without the scabbard. This, then, I concealed inside my waistcoat, and turned to my uncle.

He lay as he had fallen, all huddled, with one knee up and one arm sprawling abroad; his face had a strange color of blue, and he seemed to have ceased breathing. Fear came on me that he was dead; then I got water and dashed it in his face; and with that he seemed to come a little to himself, working his mouth and fluttering his eyelids. At last he looked up and saw me, and there came into his eyes a terror that was not of this world.

"Come, come," said I, "sit up."

"Are ye alive?" he sobbed. "O man, are ye alive?"

"That I am," said I. "Small thanks to you!"

He had begun to seek for his breath with deep sighs. "The blue phial," said he—"in the aumry—the blue phial." His breath came slower still.

I ran to the cupboard, and, sure enough, found there a blue phial of medicine, with the dose written on it on a paper, and this I administered to him with what speed I might.

"It's the trouble," said he, reviving a little; "I have a trouble, Davie. It's the heart."

I set him on a chair and looked at him. It is true I felt some pity for a man that looked so sick, but I was full besides of righteous anger; and I numbered over before him the points on which I wanted explanation: why he lied to me at every word; why he feared that I should leave him; why he disliked it to be hinted that he and my father were twins —"Is that because it is true?" I asked; why he had given me money to which I was convinced I had no claim; and, last of all, why he had tried to kill me. He heard me all

through in silence; and then, in a broken voice, begged me
to let him go to bed.

"I'll tell ye the morn," he said; "as sure as death I will."

And so weak was he that I could do nothing but consent.
I locked him into his room, however, and pocketed the key;
and then returning to the kitchen, made up such a blaze as
had not shone there for many a long year, and wrapping
myself in my plaid, lay down upon the chests and fell asleep.

CHAPTER V.

I GO TO THE QUEEN'S FERRY.

Much rain fell in the night; and the next morning there
blew a bitter wintry wind out of the northwest, driving
scattered clouds. For all that, and before the sun began to
peep or the last of the stars had vanished, I made my way
to the side of the burn, and had a plunge in a deep whirling
pool. All aglow from my bath, I sat down once more beside
the fire, which I replenished, and began gravely to consider
my position.

There was now no doubt about my uncle's enmity; there
was no doubt I carried my life in my hand, and he would
leave no stone unturned that he might compass my destruction. But I was young and spirited, and like most lads that
have been country-bred, I had a great opinion of my shrewd-
ness. I had come to his door no better than a beggar and
little more than a child; he had met me with treachery and
violence; it would be a fine consummation to take the upper
hand, and drive him like a herd of sheep.

I sat there nursing my knee and smiling at the fire; and
I saw myself in fancy smell out his secrets one after another, and grow to be that man's king and ruler. The warlock of Essendean, they say, had made a mirror in which men
could read the future; it must have been of other stuff than
burning coal; for in all the shapes and pictures that I sat and
gazed at, there was never a ship, never a seaman with a hairy

cap, never a big bludgeon for my silly head, or the least sign of all those tribulations that were ripe to fall on me.

Presently, all swollen with conceit, I went upstairs and gave my prisoner his liberty. He gave me good-morning civilly; and I gave the same to him, smiling down upon him from the heights of my sufficiency. Soon we were set to breakfast, as it might have been the day before.

"Well, sir," said I, with a jeering tone, "have you nothing more to say to me?" And then, as he made no articulate reply, "It will be time, I think, to understand each other," I continued. "You took me for a country Johnnie Raw, with no more mother-wit or courage than a porridge-stick. I took you for a good man, or no worse than others at least. It seems we were both wrong. What cause you have to fear me, to cheat me, and to attempt my life——"

He murmured something about a jest, and that he liked a bit of fun; and then, seeing me smile, changed his tone, and assured me he would make all clear as soon as we had breakfasted. I saw by his face that he had no lie ready for me, though he was hard at work preparing one; and I think I was about to tell him so, when we were interrupted by a knocking at the door.

Bidding my uncle sit where he was, I went to open it, and found on the doorstep a half-grown boy in sea-clothes. He had no sooner seen me than he began to dance some steps of the sea-hornpipe (which I had never before heard of, far less seen) snapping his fingers in the air and footing it right cleverly. For all that, he was blue with the cold; and there was something in his face, a look between tears and laughter, that was highly pathetic and consorted ill with his gayety of manner.

"What cheer, mate?" says he, with a cracked voice.

I asked him soberly to name his pleasure.

"O, pleasure!" says he; and then began to sing:

> "For it's my delight, of a shiny night
> In the season of the year."

"Well," said I, "if you have no pleasure at all, I will even be so unmannerly as shut you out."

"Stay, brother!" he cried. "Have you no fun about you? or do you want to get me thrashed? I've brought a letter from old Heasy-oasy to Mr. Belflower." He showed me a letter as he spoke. "And I say, mate," he added, "I'm mortal hungry."

"Well," said I, "come into the house, and you shall have a bite if I go empty for it."

With that I brought him in and set him down to my own place, where he fell-to greedily on the remains of breakfast, winking to me between whiles, and making many faces, which I think the poor soul considered manly. Meanwhile, my uncle had read the letter and sat thinking; then, suddenly, he got to his feet with a great air of liveliness, and pulled me apart into the furthest corner of the room.

"Read that," said he, and put the letter in my hand.

Here it is, lying before me as I write:

"The Hawes Inn, at the Queen's Ferry.

"Sir,—I lie here with my hawser up and down, and send my cabin-boy to informe. If you have any further commands for over-seas, to-day will be the last occasion, as the wind will serve us well out of the firth. I will not seek to deny that I have had crosses with your Agent, Mr. Rankeillor; of which, if not speedily redd up, you may looke to see some losses follow. I have drawn a bill upon you, as per margin, and am, sir, your most obedt., humble servant.
　　　　　　　　　　　　　　　　　　　"Elias Hoseason."

"You see, Davie," resumed my uncle, as soon as he saw that I had done, "I have a venture with this man Hoseason, the captain of a trading brig, the *Covenant*, of Dysart. Now, if you and me was to walk over with yon lad, I could see the captain at the Hawes, or maybe on board the *Covenant*, if there was papers to be signed; and so far from a loss of time, we can jog on to the lawyer, Mr. Rankeillor's. After a' that's come and gone, ye would be unwilling to believe me upon my naked word; but ye'll can believe Rankeillor. He's factor to half the gentry in these parts; an auld man, forby; highly respeckit; and he kenned your father."

I stood awhile and thought. I was going to some place of shipping, which was doubtless populous, and where my

uncle durst attempt no violence, and, indeed, even the society
of the cabin-boy so far protected me. Once there, I believed
I could force on the visit to the lawyer, even if my uncle
were now insincere in proposing it; and perhaps, in the bottom of my heart, I wished a nearer view of the sea and ships.
You are to remember I had lived all my life in the inland
hills, and just two days before had my first sight of the firth
lying like a blue floor, and the sailed ships moving on the
face of it, no bigger than toys. One thing with another, I
made up my mind.

"Very well," says I, "let us go to the ferry."

My uncle got into his hat and coat, and buckled an old
rusty cutlass on; and then we trod the fire out, locked the
door, and set forth upon our walk.

The wind, being in that cold quarter, the northwest, blew
nearly in our faces as we went. It was the month of June; the
grass was all white with daisies and the trees with blossom;
but, to judge by our blue nails and aching wrists, the time
might have been winter and the whiteness a December frost.

Uncle Ebenezer trudged in the ditch, jogging from side to
side like an old ploughman coming home from work. He
never said a word the whole way; and I was thrown for talk
on the cabin-boy. He told me his name was Ransome, and
that he had followed the sea since he was nine, but could not
say how old he was, as he had lost his reckoning. He showed
me tattoo marks, baring his breast in the teeth of the wind
and in spite of my remonstrances, for I thought it was enough
to kill him; he swore horribly whenever he remembered, but
more like a silly schoolboy than a man; and boasted of many
wild and bad things that he had done; stealthy thefts, false
accusations, ay, and even murder; but all with such a dearth
of likelihood in the details, and such a weak and crazy swagger in the delivery, as disposed me rather to pity than to
believe him.

I asked him of the brig (which he declared was the finest
ship that sailed) and of Captain Hoseason, in whose praise
he was equally loud. Heasy-oasy (for so he still named the
skipper) was a man, by his account, that minded for nothing
either in heaven or earth; one that, as people said, would
"crack on all sail into the day of judgment;" rough, fierce,

unscrupulous, and brutal; and all this my poor cabin-boy had
taught himself to admire as something seamanlike and manly.
He would only admit one flaw in his idol. "He ain't no seaman," he admitted. "That's Mr. Shuan that navigates the
brig; he's the finest seaman in the trade, only for drink; and
I tell you I believe it! Why, look 'ere;" and turning down
his stocking, he showed me a great, raw, red wound that
made my blood run cold. "He done that—Mr. Shuan done
it," he said, with an air of pride.

"What!" I cried, "do you take such savage usage at his
hands? Why, you are no slave to be so handled!"

"No," said the poor moon-calf, changing his tune at once,
"and so he'll find! See 'ere;" and he showed me a great
case-knife, which he told me was stolen.

"O," says he, "let me see him try; I dare him to; I'll do
for him! O, he ain't the first!" And he confirmed it with
a poor, silly, ugly oath.

I have never felt such a pity for any one in this wide world
as I felt for that half-witted creature; and it began to come
over me that the brig *Covenant* (for all her pious name)
was little better than a hell upon the seas.

"Have you no friends?" said I.

He said he had a father in some English seaport, I forget
which. "He was a fine man, too," he said; "but he's dead."

"In Heaven's name," cried I, "can you find no reputable
life on shore?"

"O, no!" says he, winking and looking very sly; "they
would put me to a trade. I know a trick worth two of that,
I do!"

I asked him what trade could be so dreadful as the one he
followed, where he ran the continual peril of his life, not
alone from wind and sea, but by the horrid cruelty of those
who were his masters. He said it was very true; and then
began to praise the life, and tell what a pleasure it was to
get on shore with money in his pocket, and spend it like a
man, and buy apples, and swagger, and surprise what he
called stick-in-the-mud boys. "And then it's not all as bad
as that," says he; "there's worse off than me: there's the
twenty-pounders. O, laws! you should see them taking on.
Why, I've seen a man as old as you, I dessay"—(to him I

seemed old)—"ah, and he had a beard, too—well, and as soon as we cleaned out of the river, and he had the drug out of his head—my! how he cried and carried on! I made a fine fool of him, I tell you! And then there's little uns, too: O, little by me! I tell you, I keep them in order. When we carry little uns, I have a rope's end of my own to wollop 'em." And so he ran on, until it came in on me that what he meant by twenty-pounders were those unhappy criminals who were sent over-seas to slavery in North America, or the still more unhappy innocents who were kidnapped or trepanned (as the word went) for private interests or vengeance.

Just then we came to the top of the hill, and looked down on the ferry and the hope. The Firth of Forth (as is very well known) narrows at this point to the width of a good-sized river, which makes a convenient ferry going north, and turns the upper reach into a land-locked haven for all manner of ships. Right in the midst of the narrows lies an islet with some ruins; on the south shore they have built a pier for the service of the ferry; and at the end of the pier, on the other side of the road, and backed against a pretty garden of holly-trees and hawthorns, I could see the building which they call the Hawes Inn.

The town of Queensferry lies farther west, and the neighborhood of the inn looked pretty lonely at that time of day, for the boat had just gone north with passengers. A skiff, however, lay beside the pier, with some seamen sleeping on the thwarts; this, as Ransome told me, was the brig's boat waiting for the captain; and about half a mile off, and all alone in the anchorage, he showed me the *Covenant* herself. There was a sea-going bustle on board; yards were swinging into place; and as the wind blew from that quarter, I could hear the song of the sailors as they pulled upon the ropes. After all I had listened to upon the way, I looked at that ship with an extreme abhorrence; and from the bottom of my heart I pitied all poor souls that were condemned to sail in her.

We had all three pulled up on the brow of the hill; and now I marched across the road and addressed my uncle. "I think it right to tell you, sir," says I, "there's nothing that will bring me on board that *Covenant*."

He seemed to waken from a dream. "Eh?" he said. "What's that?"

I told him over again.

"Well, well," he said, "we'll have to please ye, I suppose. But what are we standing here for? It's perishing cold, and if I'm no mistaken they're busking the *Covenant* for sea."

CHAPTER VI.

WHAT BEFELL AT THE QUEEN'S FERRY.

As soon as we came to the inn, Ransome led us up the stair to a small room, with a bed in it, and heated like an oven by a great fire of coal. At a table hard by the chimney, a tall, dark, sober-looking man sat writing. In spite of the heat of the room, he wore a thick sea-jacket, buttoned to the neck, and a tall hairy cap drawn down over his ears; yet I never saw any man, not even a judge upon the bench, look cooler, or more studious and self-possessed, than this ship captain.

He got to his feet at once, and coming forward, offered his large hand to Ebenezer. "I am proud to see you, Mr. Balfour," said he, in a fine deep voice, "and glad that ye are here in time. The wind's fair, and the tide upon the turn; we'll see the old coalbucket burning on the Isle of May before to-night."

"Captain Hoseason," returned my uncle, "you keep your room unco' hot."

"It's a habit I have, Mr. Balfour," said the skipper. "I'm a cold-rife man by my nature; I have a cold blood, sir. There's neither fur, nor flannel—no, sir, nor hot rum, will warm up what they call the temperature. Sir, it's the same with most men that have been carbonadoed, as they call it, in the tropic seas."

"Well, well, captain," replied my uncle, "we must all be the way we're made."

But it chanced that this fancy of the captain's had a great share in my misfortune. For though I had promised myself not to let my kinsman out of sight, I was both so impatient for a nearer look of the sea, and so sickened by the closeness of the room, that when he told me to "run downstairs and play myself awhile," I was fool enough to take him at his word.

Away I went, therefore, leaving the two men sitting down to a bottle and a great mass of papers; and crossing the road in front of the inn, walked down upon the beach. With the wind in that quarter, only little wavelets, not much bigger than I had seen upon a lake, beat upon the shore. But the weeds were new to me—some green, some brown and long, and some with little bladders that crackled between my fingers. Even so far up the firth, the smell of the sea water was exceedingly salt and stirring the *Covenant,* besides, was beginning to shake out her sails, which hung upon the yards in clusters; and the spirit of all that I beheld put me in thoughts of far voyages and foreign places.

I looked, too, at the seamen with the skiff—big brown fellows, some in shirts, some with jackets, some with colored handkerchiefs about their throats, one with a brace of pistols stuck into his pockets, two or three with knotty bludgeons, and all with their case-knives. I passed the time of day with one that looked less desperate than his fellows, and asked him of the sailing of the brig. He said they would get under way as soon as the ebb set, and expressed his gladness to be out of a port where there were no taverns and fiddlers; but all with such horrifying oaths, that I made haste to get away from him.

This threw me back on Ransome, who seemed the least wicked of that gang, and who soon came out of the inn and ran to me, crying for a bowl of punch. I told him I would give him no such thing, for neither he nor I was of age for such indulgences. "But a glass of ale you may have, and welcome," said I. He moped and mowed at me, and called me names; but he was glad to get the ale, for all that; and presently we were set down at a table in the front room of the inn, and both eating and drinking with a good appetite.

Here it occurred to me that, as the landlord was a man of that country, I might do well to make a friend of him. I offered him a share, as was much the custom in these days;

but he was far too great a man to sit with such poor customers as Ransome and myself, and he was leaving the room,
when I called him back to ask if he knew Mr. Rankeillor.

"Hoot, ay," says he, "and a very honest man. And, O,
by-the-bye," says he, "was it you that came in with Ebenezer?" And when I had told him yes, "Ye'll be no friend
of his?" he asked, meaning, in the Scotch way, that I would
be no relative.

I told him no, none.

"I thought not," said he; "and yet ye have a kind of look
of Mr. Alexander."

I said it seemed that Ebenezer was ill-seen in the country.

"Nae doubt," said the landlord. "He's a wicked auld man,
and there's many would like to see him grinning in a rope:
Jennet Clouston and mony mair that he has harried out of
house and hame. And yet he was ance a fine young fellow,
too. But that was before the report gaed abroad about Mr.
Alexander; that was like the death of him."

"And what was it?" I asked.

"Ou, just that he had killed him," said the landlord. "Did
ye never hear that?"

"And what would he kill him for?" said I.

"And what for, but just to get the place," said he.

"The place?" said I. "The Shaws?"

"Nae other place that I ken," said he.

"Ay, man?" said I. "Is that so? Was my—was Alexander the eldest son?"

"'Deed was he," said the landlord. "What else would he
have killed him for?"

And with that he went away, as he had been impatient to
do from the beginning.

Of course, I had guessed it a long while ago; but it is one
thing to guess, another to know; and I sat stunned with my
good fortune, and could scarce grow to believe that the same
poor lad who had trudged in the dust from Ettrick Forest not
two days ago, was now one of the rich of the earth, and had
a house and broad lands, and if he but knew how to ride,
might mount his horse to-morrow. All these pleasant things,
and a thousand others, crowded into my mind, as I sat staring
before me out of the inn window, and paying no heed to what

I saw; only I remember that my eye lighted on Captain Hoseason down on the pier among his seamen, and speaking with some authority. And presently he came marching back toward the house, with no mark of a sailor's clumsiness, but carrying his fine, tall figure with a manly bearing, and still with the same sober, grave expression on his face. I wondered if it was possible that Ransome's stories could be true, and half disbelieved them; they fitted so ill with the man's looks. But indeed, he was neither so good as I supposed him, nor quite so bad as Ransome did; for, in fact, he was two men, and left the better one behind as soon as he set foot on board his vessel.

The next thing, I heard my uncle calling me, and found the pair in the road together. It was the captain who addressed me, and that with an air (very flattering to a young lad) of grave equality.

"Sir," said he, "Mr. Balfour tells me great things of you; and for my own part, I like your looks. I wish I was for longer here, that we might make the better friends; but we'll make the most of what we have. Ye shall come on board my brig for half-an-hour, till the ebb sets, and drink a bowl with me."

Now, I longed to see the inside of a ship more than words can tell; but I was not going to put myself in jeopardy, and I told him my uncle and I had an appointment with a lawyer.

"Ay, ay," said he, "he passed me word of that. But, ye see, the boat'll set ye ashore at the town pier, and that's but a penny stonecast from Rankeillor's house." And here he suddenly leaned down and whispered in my ear: "Take care of the old fox; he means mischief. Come aboard till I can get a word with ye." And then, passing his arm through mine, he continued aloud, as he set off toward his boat: "But come, what can I bring ye from the Carolinas? Any friend of Mr. Balfour's can command. A roll of tobacco? Indian featherwork? a skin of a wild beast? a stone pipe? the mocking-bird that mews for all the world like a cat? the cardinal bird that is as red as blood?—take your pick and say your pleasure."

By this time we were at the boat-side, and he was handing me in. I did not dream of hanging back; I thought (the poor fool!) that I had found a good friend and helper, and I was rejoiced to see the ship. As soon as we were all set in our places, the boat was thrust off from the pier and began to move over the waters; and what with my pleasure in this new movement and my surprise at our low position, and the appearance of the shores, and the growing bigness of the brig as we drew near to it, I could hardly understand what the captain said, and must have answered him at random.

As soon as we were alongside (where I sat fairly gaping at the ship's height, the strong humming of the tide against its sides, and the pleasant cries of the seamen at their work) Hoseason, declaring that he and I must be the first on board, ordered a tackle to be sent down from the main-yard. In this I was whipped into the air and set down again on the deck, where the captain stood ready waiting for me, and instantly slipped back his arm under mine. There I stood some while, a little dizzy with the unsteadiness of all around me, perhaps a little afraid, and yet vastly pleased with these strange sights; the captain meanwhile pointing out the strangest, and telling me their names and uses.

"But where is my uncle?" said I, suddenly.

"Ay," said Hoseason, with a sudden grimness, "that's the point."

I felt I was lost. With all my strength, I plucked myself clear of him and ran to the bulwarks. Sure enough, there was the boat pulling for the town, with my uncle sitting in the stern. I gave a piercing cry—"Help, help! Murder!"—so that both sides of the anchorage rang with it, and my uncle turned round where he was sitting, and showed me a face full of cruelty and terror.

It was the last I saw. Already strong hands had been plucking me back from the ship's side; and now a thunderbolt seemed to strike me; I saw a great flash of fire, and fell senseless.

CHAPTER VII.

I GO TO SEA IN THE BRIG "COVENANT" OF DYSART.

I came to myself in darkness, in great pain, bound hand and foot, and deafened by many unfamiliar noises. There sounded in my ears a roaring of water as of a huge mill-dam; the thrashing of heavy sprays, the thundering of the sails, and the shrill cries of the seamen. The whole world now heaved giddily up, and now rushed giddily downward; and so sick and hurt was I in body, and my mind so much confounded, that it took me a long while, chasing my thoughts up and down, and ever stunned again by a fresh stab of pain, to realize that I must be lying somewhere bound in the belly of that unlucky ship, and that the wind must have strength-ened to a gale. With the clear perception of my plight, there fell upon me a blackness of despair, a horror of remorse at my own folly, and a passion of anger at my uncle, that once more bereft me of my senses.

When I returned again to life, the same uproar, the same confused and violent movements, shook and deafened me; and presently, to my other pains and distresses, there was added the sickness of an unused landsman on the sea. In that time of my adventurous youth, I suffered many hard-ships; but none that was so crushing to my mind and body, or lit by so few hopes, as these first hours on board the brig.

I heard a gun fire, and supposed the storm had proved too strong for us, and we were firing signals of distress. The thought of deliverance, even by death in the deep sea, was welcome to me. Yet it was no such matter; but (as I was afterward told) a common habit of the captain's, which I here set down to show that even the worst man may have his kindlier sides. We were then passing, it appeared, within some miles of Dysart, where the brig was built, and where old Mrs. Hoseason, the captain's mother, had come some years before to live; and whether outward or inward bound, the *Covenant* was never suffered to go by that place by day without a gun fired and colors shown.

I had no measure of time; day and night were alike in that

ill-smelling cavern of the ship's bowels, where I lay; and the
misery of my situation drew out the hours to double. How
long, therefore, I lay waiting to hear the ship split upon some
rock, or to feel her reel head foremost into the depths of the
sea, I have not the means of computation. But sleep at length
stole from me the consciousness of sorrow.

I was wakened by the light of a hand-lantern shining in
my face. A small man of about thirty, with green eyes and
a tangle of fair hair, stood looking down at me.

"Well," said he, "how goes it?"

I answered by a sob; and my visitor then felt my pulse
and temples, and set himself to wash and dress the wound
upon my scalp.

"Ay," said he, "a sore stroke. What, man? Cheer up!
The world's no done; you've made a bad start of it, but
you'll make a better. Have you had any meat?"

I said I could not look at it; and thereupon he gave me
some brandy and water in a tin pannikin, and left me once
more to myself.

The next time he came to see me, I was lying betwixt sleep
and waking, my eyes wide open in the darkness, the sickness
quite departed, but succeeded by a horrid giddiness and
swimming that was almost worse to bear. I ached, besides,
in every limb, and the cords that bound me seemed to be of
fire. The smell of the hole in which I lay seemed to have
become a part of me; and during the long interval since his
last visit, I had suffered tortures of fear, now from the
scurrying of the ship's rats that sometimes pattered on my
very face, and now from the dismal imaginings that haunt
the bed of fever.

The glimmer of the lantern, as a trap opened, shone in like
the heaven's sunlight; and though it only showed me the
strong, dark beams of the ship that was my prison, I could
have cried aloud for gladness. The man with the green eyes
was the first to descend the ladder, and I noticed that he
came somewhat unsteadily. He was followed by the captain.
Neither said a word; but the first set to and examined me,
and dressed my wound as before, while Hoseason looked me
in my face with an odd, black look.

"Now, sir, you see for yourself," said the first: "a high

fever, no appetite, no light, no meat: you see for yourself what that means."

"I am no conjurer, Mr. Riach," said the captain.

"Give me leave, sir," said Riach; "you've a good head upon your shoulders, and a good Scotch tongue to ask with; but I will leave you no manner of excuse: I want that boy taken out of this hole and put in the forecastle."

"What ye may want, sir, is a matter of concern to nobody but yoursel'," returned the captain; "but I can tell ye that which is to be. Here he is; here he shall bide."

"Admitting that you have been paid in a proportion," said the other, "I will crave leave humbly to say that I have not. Paid I am, and none too much, to be the second officer of this old tub; and you ken very well if I do my very best to earn it. But I was paid for nothing more."

"If ye could hold back your hand from the tin-pan, Mr. Riach, I would have no complaint to make of ye," returned the skipper; "and instead of asking riddles, I make bold to say that ye would keep your breath to cool your porridge. We'll be required on deck," he added, in a sharper note, and set one foot upon the ladder.

But Mr. Riach caught him by the sleeve.

"Admitting that you have been paid to do a murder——" he began.

Hoseason turned upon him with a flash.

"What's that?" he cried. "What kind of talk is that?"

"It seems it is the talk that you can understand," said Mr. Riach, looking him steadily in the face.

"Mr. Riach, I have sailed with ye three cruises," replied the captain. "In all that time, ye should have learned to know me: I'm a stiff man, and a dour man; but for what ye say now—fy, fy!—it comes from a bad heart and a black conscience. If ye say the lad will die——"

"Ay, will he!" said Mr. Riach.

"Well, sir, is not that enough?" said Hoseason. "Flit him where you please!"

Thereupon the captain ascended the ladder; and I, who had lain silent throughout this strange conversation, beheld Mr. Riach turn after him and bow as low as to his knees in what was plainly a spirit of derision. Even in my then state of sickness, I perceived two things: that the mate was touched with liquor, as the captain hinted, and that (drunk or sober) he was like to prove a valuable friend.

Five minutes afterward my bonds were cut, I was hoisted on a man's back, carried up to the forecastle, and laid in a bunk on some sea-blankets; where the first thing that I did was to lose my senses.

It was a blessed thing indeed to open my eyes again upon the daylight, and to find myself in the society of men. The forecastle was a roomy place enough, set all about with berths, in which the men of the watch below were seated smoking, or lying down asleep. The day being calm and the wind fair, the scuttle was open, and not only the good daylight, but from time to time (as the ship rolled) a dusty beam of sunlight shone in, and dazzled and delighted me. I had no sooner moved, moreover, than one of the men brought me a drink of something healing which Mr. Riach had prepared, and bade me lie still and I should soon be well again. There were no bones broken, he exclaimed: "A clour on the head was naething. Man," said he, "it was me that gave it ye!"

Here I lay for the space of many days a close prisoner, and not only got my health again, but came to know my companions. They were a rough lot indeed, as sailors mostly are; being men rooted out of all the kindly parts of life, and condemned to toss together on the rough seas, with masters no less cruel. There were some among them that had sailed with the pirates and seen things it would be a shame even to speak of; some were men that had run from the king's ships, and went with a halter round their necks, of which they made no secret; and all, as the saying goes, were "at a word and a blow," with their best friends. Yet I had not been many days shut up with them before I began to be ashamed of my first judgment, when I had drawn away from them at the Ferry pier, as though they had been unclean beasts. No class of man is altogether bad; but each has its own faults and virtues; and these shipmates of mine were no exception to the rule. Rough they were, sure enough; and bad, I suppose; but they had many virtues. They were kind when it occurred to them, simple even beyond the simplicity of a country lad like me, and had some glimmerings of honesty.

There was one man of maybe forty, that would sit on my berthside for hours, and tell me of his wife and child. He was a fisher that had lost his boat, and thus been driven to the deep-sea voyaging. Well, it is years ago now; but I have never forgotten him. His wife (who was "young by him," as he often told me) waited in vain to see her man return; he would never again make the fire for her in the morning, nor yet keep the bairn when she was sick. Indeed, many of these poor fellows (as the event proved) were upon their last cruise; the deep seas and cannibal fish received them; and it is a thankless business to speak ill of the dead.

Among other good deeds that they did, they returned my money which had been shared among them; and though it was about a third short, I was very glad to get it, and hoped great good from it in the land I was going to. The ship was bound for the Carolinas; and you must not suppose that I was going to that place merely as an exile. The trade was even then much depressed; since that, and with the rebellion of the colonies and the formation of the United States, it has, of course, come to an end; but in these days of my youth, white men were still sold into slavery on the plantations, and that was the destiny to which my wicked uncle had condemned me.

The cabin-boy Ransome (from whom I had first heard of these atrocities) came in at times from the round-house, where he berthed and served, now nursing a bruised limb in silent agony, now raving against the cruelty of Mr. Shuan. It made my heart bleed; but the men had a great respect for the chief mate, who was, as they said, "the only seaman of the whole jing-bang, and none such a bad man when he was sober." Indeed, I found there was a strange peculiarity about our two mates: that Mr. Riach was sullen, unkind, and harsh when he was sober, and Mr. Shuan would not hurt a fly except when he was drinking. I asked about the captain; but I was told drink made no difference upon that man of iron.

I did my best in the small time allowed me to make something like a man, or rather I should say something like a boy, of the poor creature, Ransome. But his mind was scarce truly human. He could remember nothing of the time before he came to sea; only that his father had made clocks, and had a starling in the parlor, which could whistle "The North Countrie"; all else had been blotted out in these years of hardship and cruelties. He had a strange notion of the dry land, picked up from sailors' stories: that it was a place where lads were put to some kind of slavery called a trade, and where apprentices were continually lashed and clapped into foul prisons. In a town, he thought every second person a decoy, and every third house a place in which seamen would be drugged and murdered. To be sure, I could tell him how kindly I had myself been used upon that dry land he was so much afraid of, and how well fed and carefully taught both by my friends and my parents: and if he had been recently hurt, he would weep bitterly and swear to run away; but if he was in his usual crackbrain humor or (still more) if he had had a glass of spirits in the round-house, he would deride the notion.

It was Mr. Riach (Heaven forgive him!) who gave the boy drink; and it was, doubtless, kindly meant; but besides that it was ruin to his health; it was the pitifullest thing in life to see this unhappy, unfriended creature staggering, and dancing, and talking he knew not what. Some of the men laughed, but not all; others would grow as black as thunder (thinking, perhaps, of their own childhood or their own children) and bid him stop that nonsense, and think what he was doing. As for me, I felt ashamed to look at him, and the poor child still comes about me in my dreams.

All this time, you should know, the *Covenant* was meeting continual head-winds and tumbling up and down against head-seas, so that the scuttle was almost constantly shut, and the forecastle lighted only by a swinging lantern on a beam. There was constant labor for all hands; the sails had to be made and shortened every hour; the strain told on the men's temper; there was a growl of quarreling all day long from berth to berth; and as I was never allowed to set my foot on deck, you can picture to yourself how weary of my life I grew to be, and how impatient for a change.

And a change I was to get, as you shall hear; but I must

first tell of a conversation I had with Mr. Riach, which put a little heart in me to bear my troubles. Getting him in a favorable stage of drink (for indeed he never looked near me when he was sober) I pledged him to secrecy, and told him my whole story.

He declared it was like a ballad; that he would do his best to help me; that I should have paper, pen, and ink, and write one line to Mr. Campbell and another to Mr. Rankeillor; and that if I had told the truth, ten to one he would be able (with their help) to pull me through and set me in my rights.

"And in the meantime," says he, "keep your heart up. You're not the only one, I'll tell you that. There's many a man hoeing tobacco over-seas that should be mounting his horse at his own door at home; many and many! And life is all a variorum, at the best. Look at me: I'm a laird's son and more than half a doctor, and here I am, man-Jack to Hoseason!"

I thought it would be civil to ask him for his story.

He whistled loud.

"Never had one," said he. "I liked fun, that's all." And he skipped out of the forecastle.

CHAPTER VIII.

THE ROUND-HOUSE.

One night, about twelve o'clock, a man of Mr. Riach's watch (which was on deck) came down for his jacket; and instantly there began to go a whisper about the forecastle that "Shuan had done for him at last." There was no need of a name; we all knew who was meant; but we had scarce time to get the idea rightly in our heads, far less to speak of it, when the scuttle was again flung open, and Captain Hoseason came down the ladder. He looked sharply round the bunks in the tossing light of the lantern; and then, walking straight up to me, he addressed me, to my surprise, in tones of kindness.

"My man," said he, "we want you to serve in the round-

house.   You and Ransome are to change berths.   Run
away aft with ye."

Even as he spoke, two seamen appeared in the scuttle,
carrying Ransome in their arms; and the ship at that moment giving a great sheer into the sea, and the lantern
swinging, the light fell direct on the boy's face.   It was as
white as wax, and had a look upon it like a dreadful smile.
The blood in me ran cold, and I drew in my breath as if
I had been struck.

"Run away aft; run away aft with ye!" cried Hoseason.

And at that I brushed by the sailors and the boy (who
neither spoke nor moved) and ran up the ladder on deck.

The brig was sheering swiftly and giddily through a long,
cresting swell.   She was on the starboard tack, and on the
left hand, under the arched foot of the foresail, I could see
the sunset still quite bright.   This, at such an hour of the
night, surprised me greatly; but I was too ignorant to draw
the true conclusion—that we were going north-about round
Scotland, and were now on the high sea between the Orkney
and the Shetland Islands, having avoided the dangerous
currents of the Pentland Firth.   For my part, who had been
so long shut in the dark and knew nothing of head-winds,
I thought we might be halfway or more across the Atlantic.
And indeed (beyond that I wondered a little at the lateness
of the sunset light) I gave no heed to it, and pushed on
across the decks, running between the seas, catching at
ropes, and only saved from going overboard by one of the
hands on deck, who had been always kind to me.

The round-house, for which I was bound and where I was
now to sleep and serve, stood some six feet above the decks,
and considering the size of the brig, was of good dimensions.
Inside were a fixed table and bench, and two berths, one for
the captain and the other for the two mates, turn and turn
about.   It was all fitted with lockers from top to bottom, so
as to stow away the officers' belongings and a part of the
ship's stores; there was a second store-room underneath,
which you entered by a hatchway in the middle of the deck;
indeed, all the best of the meat and drink and the whole of
the powder were collected in this place; and all the firearms,
except the two pieces of brass ordnance, were set in a rack

in the aftermost wall of the round-house. The most of the cutlasses were in another place.

A small window with a shutter on each side, and a skylight in the roof, gave it light by day; and after dark, there was a lamp always burning. It was burning when I entered, not brightly, but enough to show Mr. Shuan sitting at the table, with the brandy bottle and a tin pannikin in front of him. He was a tall man, strongly made and very black; and he stared before him on the table like one stupid.

He took no notice of my coming in; nor did he move when the captain followed and leant on the berth beside me, looking darkly at the mate. I stood in great fear of Hoseason, and had my reasons for it; but something told me I need not be afraid of him just then; and I whispered in his ear, "How is he?" He shook his head like one that does not know and does not wish to think, and his face was very stern.

Presently Mr. Riach came in. He gave the captain a glance that meant the boy was dead as plain as speaking, and took his place like the rest of us; so that we all three stood without a word, staring down at Mr. Shuan, and Mr. Shuan (on his side) sat without a word, looking hard upon the table.

All of a sudden he put out his hand to take the bottle; and at that Mr. Riach started forward and caught it away from him, rather by surprise than violence, crying out, with an oath, that there had been too much of this work altogether, and that a judgment would fall upon the ship. And as he spoke (the weather sliding-doors standing open) he tossed the bottle into the sea.

Mr. Shuan was on his feet in a trice; he still looked dazed, but he meant murder, ay, and would have done it, for the second time that night, had not the captain stepped in between him and his victim.

"Sit down!" roars the captain. "Ye sot and swine, do ye know what ye've done? Ye've murdered the boy!"

Mr. Shuan seemed to understand; for he sat down again and put up his hand to his brow.

"Well," he said, "he brought me a dirty pannikin!"

At that word, the captain and I and Mr. Riach all looked

at each other for a second with a kind of frightened look; and then Hoseason walked up to his chief officer, took him by the shoulder, led him across to his bunk, and bade him lie down and go to sleep, as you might speak to a bad child. The murderer cried a little, but he took off his sea-boots and obeyed.

"Ah!" cried Mr. Riach, with a dreadful voice, "ye should have interfered long syne. It's too late now."

"Mr. Riach," said the captain, "this night's work must never be kennt in Dysart. The boy went overboard, sir; that's what the story is; and I would give five pounds out of my pocket if it was true!" He turned to the table. "What made ye throw the good bottle away?" he added. "There was nae sense in that, sir. Here, David, draw me another. They're in the bottom locker;" and he tossed me a key. "Ye'll need a glass yourself, sir," he added, to Riach. "Yon was an ugly thing to see."

So the pair sat down and hob-a-nobbed; and while they did so, the murderer, who had been lying and whimpering in his berth, raised himself upon his elbow and looked at them and at me.

That was the first night of my new duties; and in the course of the next day I had got well into the run of them. I had to serve at the meals, which the captain took at regular hours, sitting down with the officer who was off duty; all the day through I would be running with a dram to one or other of my three masters; and at night I slept on a blanket thrown on the deck boards at the aftermost end of the round-house, and right in the draught of the two doors. It was a hard and a cold bed; nor was I suffered to sleep without interruption; for some one would be always coming in from deck to get a dram, and when a fresh watch was to be set, two and sometimes all three would sit down and brew a bowl together. How they kept their health, I know not, any more than how I kept my own.

And yet in other ways it was an easy service. There was no cloth to lay; the meals were either of oatmeal porridge or salt junk, except twice a week, when there was duff: and though I was clumsy enough and (not being firm on my sea-legs) sometimes fell with what I was bringing them,

both Mr. Riach and the captain were singularly patient. I could not but fancy they were making up lee-way, with their consciences, and that they would scarce have been so good with me, if they had not been worse with Ransome.

As for Mr. Shuan, the drink, or his crime, or the two together, had certainly troubled his mind. I cannot say I ever saw him in his proper wits. He never grew used to my being there, stared at me continually (sometimes, I could have thought, with terror) and more than once drew back from my hand when I was serving him. I was pretty sure from the first that he had no clear mind of what he had done, and on my second day in the round-house I had the proof of it. We were alone, and he had been staring at me a long time, when, all at once, up he got, as pale as death, and came close up to me, to my great terror. But I had no cause to be afraid of him.

"You were not here before?" he asked.

"No, sir," said I.

"There was another boy?" he asked again; and when I had answered him, "Ah!" says he, "I thought that," and went and sat down, without another word, except to call for brandy.

You may think it strange, but for all the horror I had, I was still sorry for him. He was a married man, with a wife in Leith; but whether or no he had a family, I have now forgotten; I hope not.

Altogether it was no very hard life for the time it lasted, which (as you are to hear) was not long. I was as well fed as the best of them; even their pickles, which were the great dainty, I was allowed my share of; and had I liked, I might have been drunk from morning to night, like Mr. Shuan. I had company, too, and good company of its sort. Mr. Riach, who had been to the college, spoke to me like a friend when he was not sulking, and told me many curious things, and some that were informing; and even the captain, though he kept me at the stick's end the most part of the time, would sometimes unbuckle a bit, and tell me of the fine countries he had visited.

The shadow of poor Ransome, to be sure, lay on all four of us, and on me and Mr. Shuan, in particular, most heavily. And then I had another trouble of my own. Here I was, doing dirty work for three men that I looked down upon, and one of whom, at least, should have hung upon a gallows; that was for the present; and as for the future, I could only see myself slaving alongside of negroes in the tobacco fields. Mr. Riach, perhaps from caution, would never suffer me to say another word about my story; the captain, whom I tried to approach, rebuffed me like a dog and would not hear a word; and as the days came and went, my heart sank lower, and lower, till I was even glad of the work, which kept me from thinking.

CHAPTER IX.

THE MAN WITH THE BELT OF GOLD.

More than a week went by, in which the ill-luck that had hitherto pursued the *Covenant* upon this voyage grew yet more strongly marked. Some days she made a little way; others, she was driven actually back. At last we were beaten so far to the south that we tossed and tacked to and fro the whole of the ninth day, within sight of Cape Wrath and the wild, rocky coast on either hand of it. There followed on that a council of the officers, and some decision which I did not rightly understand, seeing only the result: that we had made a fair wind of a foul one and were running south.

The tenth afternoon, there was a falling swell and a thick, wet, white fog that hid one end of the brig from the other. All afternoon, when I went on deck, I saw men and officers listening hard over the bulwarks—"for breakers," they said; and though I did not so much as understand the word, I felt danger in the air and was excited.

Maybe about ten at night, I was serving Mr. Riach and the captain at their supper, when the ship struck something with a great sound, and we heard voices singing out. My two masters leaped to their feet.

"She's struck," said Mr. Riach.

"No, sir," said the captain. "We've only run a boat down."

And they hurried out.

The captain was in the right of it. We had run down a boat in the fog, and she had parted in the midst and gone to the bottom with all her crew, but one. This man (as I heard afterward) had been sitting in the stern as a passenger, while the rest were on the benches rowing. At the moment of the blow, the stern had been thrown into the air, and the man (having his hands free, and for all he was encumbered with a frieze overcoat that came below his knees) had leaped up and caught hold of the brig's bowsprit. It showed he had luck and much agility and unusual strength, that he should have thus saved himself from such a pass. And yet, when the captain brought him into the round-house, and I set eyes on him for the first time, he looked as cool as I did.

He was smallish in stature, but well set and as nimble as a goat; his face was of a good open expression, but sunburnt very dark, and heavily freckled and pitted with the smallpox; his eyes were unusually light and had a kind of dancing madness in them, that was both engaging and alarming; and when he took off his great-coat, he laid a pair of fine silver-mounted pistols on the table, and I saw that he was belted with a great sword. His manners, besides, were elegant, and he pledged the captain handsomely. Altogether I thought of him, at the first sight, that here was a man I would rather call my friend than my enemy.

The captain, too, was taking his observations, but rather of the man's clothes than his person. And to be sure, as soon as he had taken off the great-coat, he showed forth mighty fine for the round-house of a merchant brig: having a hat with feathers, a red waistcoat, breeches of black plush, and a blue coat with silver buttons and handsome silver lace: costly clothes, though somewhat spoiled with the fog and being slept in.

"I'm vexed, sir, about the boat," says the captain.

"There are some pretty men gone to the bottom,"

said the stranger, "that I would rather see on the dry land again than half a score of boats."

"Friends of yours?" said Hoseason.

"You have none such friends in your country," was the reply. "They would have died for me like dogs."

"Well, sir," said the captain, still watching him, "there are more men in the world than boats to put them in."

"And that's true, too," cried the other; "and ye seem to be a gentleman of great penetration."

"I have been in France, sir," says the captain; so that it was plain he meant more by the words than showed upon the face of them.

"Well, sir," says the other; "and so has many a pretty man, for the matter of that."

"No doubt, sir," said the captain; "and fine coats."

"Oho!" says the stranger, "is that how the wind sets?" And he laid his hand quickly on his pistols.

"Don't be hasty," said the captain. "Don't do a mischief, before ye see the need for it. Ye've a French soldier's coat upon your back and a Scotch tongue in your head, to be sure; but so has many an honest fellow in these days, and I daresay none the worse of it."

"So?" said the gentleman in the fine coat: "are ye of the honest party?" (meaning, Was he a Jacobite? for each side, in those sort of civil broils, takes the name of honesty for its own).

"Why, sir," replied the captain, "I am a true-blue Protestant, and I thank God for it." (It was the first word of any religion I had ever heard from him, but I learnt afterward he was a great church-goer while on shore.) "But, for all that," says he, "I can be sorry to see another man with his back to the wall."

"Can ye so, indeed?" asks the Jacobite. "Well, sir, to be quite plain with ye, I am one of those honest gentlemen that were in trouble about the years forty-five and six; and (to be still quite plain with ye) if I get into the hands of any of the red-coated gentry, it's like it would go hard with me. Now, sir, I was for France; and there was a French ship cruising here to pick me up; but she gave us the go-by in the fog—as I wish from the heart that ye had done yoursel'! And the best that I can say is this: If ye can set me ashore where I was going, I have that upon me will reward you highly for your trouble."

"In France?" says the captain. "No, sir; that I cannot do. But where ye come from—we might talk of that."

And then, unhappily, he observed me standing in my corner, and packed me off to the galley to get supper for the gentleman. I lost no time, I promise you; and when I came back into the round-house, I found the gentleman had taken a money-belt from about his waist, and poured out a guinea or two upon the table. The captain was looking at the guineas, and then at the belt, and then at the gentleman's face; and I thought he seemed excited.

"Half of it," he cried, "and I'm your man!"

The other swept back the guineas into the belt, and put it on again under his waistcoat. "I have told ye, sir," said he, "that not one doit of it belongs to me. It belongs to my chieftain"—and here he touched his hat—"and while I would be but a silly messenger to grudge some of it that the rest might come safe, I should show myself a hound indeed if I bought my own carcass any too dear. Thirty guineas on the seaside, or sixty if ye set me on the Linnhe Loch. Take it, if ye will; if not, ye can do your worst."

"Ay," said Hoseason. "And if I give ye over to the soldiers?"

"Ye would make a fool's bargain," said the other. "My chief, let me tell you, sir, is forfeited, like every honest man in Scotland. His estate is in the hands of the man they call King George; and it is his officers that collect the rents, or try to collect them. But for the honor of Scotland, the poor tenant bodies take a thought upon their chief lying in exile; and this money is a part of that very rent for which King George is looking. Now, sir, ye seem to me to be a man that understands things: bring this money within the reach of Government, and how much of it'll come to you?"

"Little enough, to be sure," said Hoseason; and then, "If they knew," he added dryly. "But I think, if I was to try, that I could hold my tongue about it."

"Ah, but I'll befool ye there!" cried the gentleman. "Play me false, and I'll play you cunning. If a hand's laid upon me, they shall ken what money it is."

"Well," returned the captain, "what must be must. Sixty guineas, and done. Here's my hand upon it."

"And here's mine," said the other.

And thereupon the captain went out (rather hurriedly, I thought), and left me alone in the round-house with the stranger.

At that period (so soon after the forty-five) there were many exiled gentlemen coming back at the peril of their lives, either to see their friends or to collect a little money; and as for the Highland chiefs that had been forfeited, it was a common matter of talk how their tenants would stint themselves to send them money, and their clansmen outface the soldiery to get it in, and run the gantlet of our great navy to carry it across. All this I had, of course, heard tell of; and now I had a man under my eyes whose life was forfeit on all these counts and upon one more; for he was not only a rebel and a smuggler of rents, but had taken service with King Louis of France. And as if all this were not enough, he had a belt full of golden guineas round his loins. Whatever my opinions, I could not look on such a man without a lively interest.

"And so you're a Jacobite?" said I, as I set meat before him.

"Ay," said he, beginning to eat. "And you, by your long face, should be a Whig?"

"Betwixt and between," said I, not to annoy him; for indeed I was as good a Whig as Mr. Campbell could make me.

"And that's naething," said he. "But I'm saying, Mr. Betwixt-and-Between," he added, "this bottle of yours is dry; and it's hard if I'm to pay sixty guineas and be grudged a dram upon the back of it."

"I'll go and ask for the key," said I, and stepped on deck.

The fog was as close as ever, but the swell almost down. They had laid the brig to, not knowing precisely where they were, and the wind (what little there was of it) not serving well for their true course. Some of the hands were still hearkening for breakers; but the captain and the two officers were in the waist with their heads together. It struck me, I don't know why, that they were after no good; and the first word I heard, as I drew softly near, more than confirmed me.

It was Mr. Riach, crying out as if upon a sudden thought: "Couldn't we wile him out of the round-house?"

"He's better where he is," returned Hoseason; "he hasn't room to use his sword."

"Well, that's true," said Riach; "but he's hard to come at."

"Hut!" said Hoseason. "We can get the man in talk, one upon each side, and pin him by the two arms; or if that'll not hold, sir, we can make a run by both the doors and get him under hand before he has the time to draw."

At this hearing, I was seized with both fear and anger at these treacherous, greedy, bloody men that I sailed with. My first mind was to run away; my second was bolder.

"Captain," said I, "the gentleman is seeking a dram, and the bottle's out. Will you give me the key?"

They all started and turned about.

"Why, here's our chance to get the firearms!" Riach cried; and then to me: "Hark ye, David," he said, "do ye ken where the pistols are?"

"Ay, ay," put in Hoseason. "David kens; David's a good lad. Ye see, David my man, yon wild Hielandman is a danger to the ship, besides being a rank foe to King George, God bless him!"

I had never been so be-Davied since I came on board; but I said yes, as if all I heard were quite natural.

"The trouble is," resumed the captain, "that all our fire-locks, great and little, are in the round-house under this man's nose; likewise the powder. Now, if I, or one of the officers, was to go in and take them, he would fall to thinking. But a lad like you, David, might snap up a horn and a pistol or two without remark. And if ye can do it cleverly, I'll bear it in mind when it'll be good for you to have friends; and that's when we come to Carolina."

Here Mr. Riach whispered him a little.

"Very right, sir," said the captain; and then to myself:

"And see here, David, yon man has a beltful of gold, and I give you my word that you shall have your fingers in it."

I told him I would do as he wished, though indeed I had scarce breath to speak with; and upon that he gave me the key of the spirit locker, and I began to go slowly back to the round-house. What was I to do? They were dogs and thieves; they had stolen me from my own country; they had killed poor Ransome; and was I to hold the candle to another murder? But then, upon the other hand, there was the fear of death very plain before me; for what could a boy and a man, if they were as brave as lions, against a whole ship's company?

I was still arguing it back and forth, and getting no great clearness, when I came into the round-house and saw the Jacobite eating his supper under the lamp; and at that my mind was made up all in a moment. I have no credit by it; it was by no choice of mine, but as if by compulsion, that I walked right up to the table and put my hand on his shoulder.

"Do ye want to be killed?" said I.

He sprang to his feet, and looked a question at me as clear as if he had spoken.

"O!" cried I, "they're all murderers here; it's a ship full of them! They've murdered a boy already. Now it's you."

"Ay, ay," said he; "but they haven't got me yet."

And then looking at me curiously, "Will ye stand with me?"

"That will I!" said I. "I am no thief, nor yet murderer. I'll stand by you."

"Why, then," said he, "what's your name?"

"David Balfour," said I; and then thinking that a man with so fine a coat must like fine people, I added for the first time "of Shaws."

It never occurred to him to doubt me, for a Highlander is used to see great gentlefolk in great poverty; but as he had no estate of his own, my words nettled a very childish vanity he had.

"My name is Stewart," he said, drawing himself up. "Alan Breck, they call me. A king's name is good enough for me, though I bear it plain and have the name of no farm-midden to clap to the hind-end of it."

And having administered this rebuke, as though it were something of a chief importance, he turned to examine our defenses.

The round-house was built very strong, to support the breachings of the seas. Of its five apertures, only the skylight and the two doors were large enough for the passage of a man. The doors, besides, could be drawn close; they were of stout oak, and ran in grooves, and were fitted with hooks to keep them either shut or open, as the need arose. The one that was already shut, I secured in this fashion; but when I was proceeding to slide to the other, Alan stopped me.

"David," said he—"for I cannae bring to mind the name of your landed estate, and so will make so bold as call you David—that door, being open, is the best part of my defenses."

"It would be yet better shut," says I.

"Not so, David," says he. "Ye see, I have but one face; but so long as that door is open and my face to it, the best part of my enemies will be in front of me, where I would aye wish to find them."

Then he gave me from the rack a cutlass (of which there were a few besides the firearms), choosing it with great care, shaking his head and saying he had never in all his life seen poorer weapons; and next he set me down to the table with a powder-horn, a bag of bullets, and all the pistols, which he bade me charge.

"And that will be better work, let me tell you," said he, "for a gentleman of decent birth, than scraping plates and reaching drams to a wheen tarry sailors."

Thereupon he stood up in the midst with his face to the door, and drawing his great sword, made trial of the room he had to wield it in.

"I must strick to the point," he said, shaking his head; "and that's a pity, too. It doesn't set my genius, which is all for the upper guard. And now," said he, "do you keep on charging the pistols, and give heed to me."

I told him I would listen closely. My chest was tight, my mouth dry, the light dark to my eyes; the thought of the numbers that were soon to leap in upon us kept my heart in a flutter; and the sea, which I heard washing round the brig, and where I thought my dead body would be cast ere morning, ran in my mind strangely.

"First of all," said he, "how many are against us?"

I reckoned them up; and such was the hurry of my mind, I had to cast the numbers twice. "Fifteen," said I.

Alan whistled. "Well," said he, "that can't be cured. And now follow me. It is my part to keep this door, where I look for the main battle. In that, ye have no hand. And mind and dinnae fire to this side unless they get me down; for I would rathei have ten foes in front of me than one friend like you cracking pistols at my back."

I told him indeed I was no great shot.

"And that's very bravely said," he cried, in a great admiration of my candor. "There's many a pretty gentleman that wouldnae dare to say it."

"But then, sir," said I, "there is the door behind you, which they may perhaps break in."

"Ay," said he, "and that is a part of your work. No sooner the pistols charged, then ye must climb up into yon bed where ye're handy at the window; and if they lift hand against the door, ye're to shoot. But that's not all. Let's make a bit of a soldier of ye, David. What else have ye to guard?"

"There's the skylight," said I. "But indeed, Mr. Stewart, I would need to have eyes upon both sides to keep the two of them; for when my face is at the one, my back is to the other."

"And that's very true," said Alan. "But have ye no ears to your head?"

"To be sure!" cried I. "I must hear the bursting of the glass!"

"Ye have some rudiments of sense," said Alan grimly.

CHAPTER X.

THE SIEGE OF THE ROUND-HOUSE.

But now our time of truce was come to an end. Those on deck had waited for my coming till they grew impatient; and scarce had Alan spoken, when the captain showed face in the open door.

"Stand!" cried Alan, and pointed his sword at him.

The captain stood, indeed; but he neither winced nor drew back a foot.

"A naked sword?" says he. "This is a strange return for hospitality."

"Do you see me?" said Alan. "I am come of kings; I bear a king's name. My badge is the oak. Do ye see my sword? It has slashed the heads off mair Whigamores than you have toes upon your feet. Call up your vermin to your back, sir, and fall on! The sooner the clash begins, the sooner ye'll taste this steel throughout your vitals."

The captain said nothing to Alan, but he looked over at me with an ugly look. "David," said he, "I'll mind this;" and the sound of his voice went through me with a jar.

Next moment he was gone.

"And now," said Alan, "let your hand keep your head, for the grip is coming."

Alan drew a dirk, which he held in his left hand in case they should run in under his sword. I, on my part, clambered up into the berth with an armful of pistols and something of a heavy heart, and set open the window where I was to watch. It was a small part of the deck that I could overlook, but enough for our purpose. The sea had gone down, and the wind was steady and kept the sails quiet; so that there was a great stillness in the ship, in which I made sure I heard the sound of muttering voices. A little after, and there came a clash of steel upon the deck, by which I knew they were dealing out the cutlasses and one had been let fall; and after that silence again.

I do not know if I was what you call afraid; but my heart beat like a bird's, both quick and little; and there was a dimness came before my eyes which I continually rubbed away, and which continually returned. As for hope, I had none; but only a darkness of despair and a sort of anger against all the world that made me long to sell my life as dear as I was able. I tried to pray, I remember, but that same hurry of my mind, like a man running, would not suffer me to think upon the words; and my chief wish was to have the thing begin and be done with it.

It came all of a sudden when it did, with a rush of feet and a roar, and then a shout from Alan, and a sound of blows and some one crying out as if hurt. I looked back over my shoulder, and saw Mr. Shuan in the doorway, crossing blades with Alan.

"That's him that killed the boy!" I cried.

"Look to your window!" said Alan; and as I turned back to my place, I saw him pass his sword through the mate's body.

It was none too soon for me to look to my own part; for my head was scarce back at the window before five men, carrying a spare yard for a battering-ram, ran past me and took post to drive the door in. I had never fired with a pistol in my life, and not often with a gun; far less against a fellow-creature. But it was now or never; and just as they swung the yard, I cried out, "Take that!" and shot into their midst.

I must have hit one of them, for he sang out and gave back a step, and the rest stopped as if a little disconcerted. Before they had time to recover, I sent another ball over their heads; and at my third shot (which went as wide as the second) the whole party threw down the yard and ran for it.

Then I looked round again into the deck-house. The whole place was full of the smoke of my own firing, just as my ears seemed to be burst with the noise of the shots. But there was Alan, standing as before; only now his sword was running blood to the hilt, and himself so swelled with triumph and fallen into so fine an attitude, that he looked to be invincible. Right before him on the floor was Mr. Shuan, on his hands and knees; the blood was pouring from his mouth, and he was sinking slowly lower, with a terrible, white face; and just as I looked, some of those from behind caught hold of him by the heels and dragged him bodily out of the round-house. I believe he died as they were doing it.

"There's one of your Whigs for ye!" cried Alan; and then turning to me, he asked if I had done much execution.

I told him I had winged one, and thought it was the captain.

"And I've settled two," says he. "No, there's not enough blood let; they'll be back again. To your watch, David. This was but a dram before meat."

I settled back to my place, recharging the three pistols I had fired, and keeping watch with both eye and ear.

Our enemies were disputing not far off upon the deck, and that so loudly that I could hear a word or two above the washing of the seas.

"It was Shuan bungled it," I heard one say.

And another answered him with a "Wheesht, man! He's paid the piper."

After that the voices fell again into the same muttering as before. Only now, one person spoke most of the time, as though laying down a plan, and first one and then another answered him briefly, like men taking orders. By this, I made sure they were coming on again, and told Alan.

"It's what we have to pray for," said he. "Unless we can give them a good distaste of us, and done with it, there'll be nae sleep for either you or me. But this time, mind, they'll be in earnest."

By this my pistols were ready, and there was nothing to do but listen and wait. While the brush lasted, I had not the time to think if I was frighted; but now, when all was still again, my mind ran upon nothing else. The thought of the sharp swords and the cool steel was strong in me; and presently, when I began to hear stealthy steps and a brushing of men's clothes against the round-house wall, and knew they were taking their places in the dark, I could have found it in my mind to cry out aloud.

All this was upon Alan's side; and I had begun to think my share of the fight was at an end, when I heard some one drop softly on the roof above me.

Then there came a single call on the sea-pipe, and that was the signal. A knot of them made one rush of it, cutlass in hand, against the door; and at the same moment, the glass of the skylight was dashed in a thousand pieces, and a man leaped through and landed on the floor. Before he got to his feet, I had clapped a pistol to his back, and might have shot him, too; only at the touch of him (and him alive) my whole flesh misgave me, and I could no more pull the trigger than I could have flown.

He had dropped his cutlass as he jumped, and when he felt the pistol, whipped straight round and laid hold of me, roaring out an oath; and at that my courage came back again, or I grew so much afraid as came to the same thing; for I gave a shriek and shot him in the midst of the body. He gave the most horrible, ugly groan and fell to the floor. The foot of a second fellow, whose legs were dangling through the skylight, struck me at the same time upon the head; and at that I snatched another pistol and shot this one through the thigh, so that he slipped through and tumbled in a lump on his companion's body. There was no talk of missing, any more than there was time to aim; I clapped the muzzle to the very place and fired.

I might have stood and stared at them for long, but I heard Alan shout as if for help, and that brought me to my senses.

He had kept the door so long; but one of the seamen, while he was engaged with others, had run in under his guard and caught him about the body. Alan was dirking him with his left hand, but the fellow clung like a leech. Another had broken in and had his cutlass raised. The door was thronged with their faces. I thought we were lost, and catching up my cutlass, fell on them in flank.

But I had not time to be of help. The wrestler dropped at last; and Alan, leaping back to get his distance, ran upon the others like a bull, roaring as he went. They broke before him like water, turning, and running, and falling one against another in their haste. The sword in his hands flashed like quicksilver into the huddle of our fleeing enemies; and at every flash there came the scream of a man hurt. I was still thinking we were lost, when lo! they were all gone, and Alan was driving them along the deck as a sheepdog chases sheep.

Yet he was no sooner out than he was back again, being as cautious as he was brave; and meanwhile the seamen continued running and crying out as if he was still behind them; and we heard them tumble one upon another into the forecastle, and clap-to the hatch upon the top.

The round-house was like a shambles; three were dead inside, another lay in his death agony across the threshold; and there were Alan and I victorious and unhurt.

He came up to me with open arms. "Come to my arms!" he cried, and embraced and kissed me hard upon both cheeks. "David," said he, "I love you like a brother. And O, man," he cried in a kind of ecstasy, "am I no a bonny fighter?"

Thereupon he turned to the four enemies, passed his sword clean through each of them, and tumbled them out of doors. As he did so, he kept humming and singing and whistling to himself, like a man trying to recall an air; only what he was trying, was to make one. All the while, the flush was in his face, and his eyes were as bright as a five-year-old child's with a new toy. And presently he sat down upon the table, sword in hand; the air that he was making all the time began to run a little clearer, and then clearer still; and then out he burst with a great voice into a Gaelic song.

I have translated it here, not in verse (of which I have no skill) but at least in the king's English. He sang it often afterward, and the thing became popular; so that I have heard it, and had it explained to me, many's the time:

> This is the song of the sword of Alan:
> The smith made it,
> The fire set it;
> Now it shines in the hand of Alan Breck.

Their eyes were many and bright,
Swift were they to behold,
Many the hands they guided:
The sword was alone.

The dun deer troop over the hill,
They are many, the hill is one;
The dun deer vanish,
The hill remains.

Come to me from the hills of heather,
Come from the isles of the sea.
O far-beholding eagles,
Here is your meat.

Now this song which he made (both words and music) in the hour of our victory, is something less than just to me, who stood beside him in the tussle. Mr. Shuan and five more were either killed outright or thoroughly disabled; but of these, two fell by my hand, the two that came by the skylight. Four more were hurt, and of that number, one (and he not the least important) got his hurt from me. So that, altogether, I did my fair share both of the killing and the wounding, and might have claimed a place in Alan's verses. But poets (as a very wise man once told me) have to think upon their rhymes; and in good prose talk, Alan always did me more than justice.

In the meanwhile, I was innocent of any wrong being done me. For not only I knew no word of the Gaelic; but what with the long suspense of the waiting, and the scurry and strain of our two spirits of fighting, and more than all, the horror I had of some of my own share in it, the thing was no sooner over than I was glad to stagger to a seat. There was that tightness on my chest that I could hardly breathe; the thought of the two men I had shot sat upon me like a nightmare; and all upon a sudden, and before I had a guess of what was coming, I began to sob and cry like any child.

Alan clapped my shoulder, and said I was a brave lad and wanted nothing but a sleep.

"I'll take the first watch," said he. "Ye've done well by me, David, first and last; and I wouldn't lose you for all Appin—no, nor for Breadalbane."

So he made up my bed on the floor, and took the first spell, pistol in hand and sword on knee; three hours by the captain's watch upon the wall. Then he roused me up, and I took my turn of three hours; before the end of which it was broad day, and a very quiet morning, with a smooth, rolling sea that tossed the ship and made the blood run to and fro on the round-house floor, and a heavy rain that drummed upon the roof. All my watch there was nothing stirring; and by the banging of the helm, I knew they had even no one at the tiller. Indeed (as I learned afterward) they were so many of them hurt or dead, and the rest in so ill a temper that Mr. Riach and the captain had to take turn and turn (like Alan and me), or the brig might have gone ashore and nobody the wiser. It was a mercy the night had fallen so still, for the wind had gone down as soon as the rain began. Even as it was, I judged by the wailing of a great number of gulls that went crying and fishing round the ship, that she must have drifted pretty near the coast or one of the islands of the Hebrides; and at last, looking out of the door of the round-house, I saw the great stone hills of Skye on the right hand, and, a little more astern, the strange Isle of Rum.

CHAPTER XI.

THE CAPTAIN KNUCKLES UNDER.

Alan and I sat down to breakfast about six of the clock. The floor was covered with broken glass and in a horrid mess of blood, which took away my hunger. In all other ways we were in a situation not only agreeable but merry; having ousted the officers from their own cabin, and having at command all the drink in the ship—both wine and spirits—and all the dainty part of what was eatable, such as the pickles and the fine sort of biscuit. This, of itself, was enough to set us in good humor; but the richest part of it was this, that the two thirstiest men that ever came out of Scotland (Mr. Shuan being dead) were now shut in the fore part of the ship and condemned to what they hated most—cold water.

"And depend upon it," Alan said, "we shall hear more of them ere long. Ye may keep a man from the fighting, but never from his bottle."

We made good company for each other. Alan, indeed, expressed himself most lovingly; and taking a knife from the table, cut me off one of the silver buttons from his coat.

"I had them," says he, "from my father, Duncan Stewart; and now give ye one of them to be a keepsake for last night's work. And wherever ye go and show that button, the friends of Alan Breck will come around you."

He said this as if he had been Charlemagne and commanded armies; and indeed, much as I admired his courage, I was always in danger of smiling at his vanity: in danger, I say, for had I not kept my countenance, I would be afraid to think what a quarrel might have followed.

As soon as we were through with our meal, he rummaged in the captain's locker till he found a clothes brush; and then taking off his coat, began to visit his suit and brush away the stains, with such care and labor as I supposed to have been only usual with women. To be sure, he had no other; and besides (as he said) it belonged to a king and so behooved to be royally looked after.

For all that, when I saw what care he took to pluck out the threads where the button had been cut away, I put a higher value on his gift.

He was still so engaged, when we were hailed by Mr. Riach from the deck, asking for a parley; and I, climbing through the skylight and sitting on the edge of it, pistol in hand and with a bold front, though inwardly in fear of broken glass, hailed him back again and bade him speak out. He came to the edge of the round-house, and stood on a coil of rope, so that his chin was on a level with the roof; and we looked at each other awhile in silence. Mr. Riach, as I do not think he had been very forward in the battle, so he had got off with nothing worse than a blow upon the cheek; but he looked out of heart and very weary, having been all night afoot, either standing watch or doctoring the wounded.

"This is a bad job," said he at last, shaking his head.

"It was none of our choosing," said I.

"The captain," says he, "would like to speak with your friend. They might speak at the window."

"And how do we know what treachery he means?" cried I.

"He means none, David," returned Mr. Riach; "and if he did, I'll tell ye the honest truth, we couldnae get the men to follow."

"Is that so?" said I.

"I'll tell ye more than that," said he. "It's not only the men; it's me. I'm frich'ened, Davie." And he smiled across at me. "No," he continued, "what we want is to be shut of him."

Thereupon I consulted with Alan, and the parley was agreed to and parole given upon either side; but this was not the whole of Mr. Riach's business, and he now begged me for a dram with such instancy and such reminders of his former kindness, that at last I handed him a pannikin with about a gill of brandy. He drank a part, and then carried the rest down upon the deck, to share it (I suppose) with his superior.

A little after, the captain came (as was agreed) to one of the windows, and stood there in the rain, with his arm in a sling, and looking stern and pale, and so old that my heart smote me for having fired upon him.

Alan at once held a pistol in his face.

"Put that thing up!" said the captain. "Have I not passed my word, sir? or do you seek to affront me?"

"Captain," said Alan, "I doubt your word is a breakable. Last night ye haggled and argle-bargled like an apple-wife; and then passed me your word, and gave me your hand to back it; and ye ken very well what was the upshot. Be damned to your word!" says he.

"Well, well, sir," said the captain, "ye'll get little good by swearing." (And truly that was a fault of which the captain was quite free.) "But we have other things to speak," he continued, bitterly. "Ye've made a sore hash of my brig; I haven't hands enough left to work her;

and my first officer (whom I could ill spare) has got your
sword throughout his vitals, and passed without speech.
There is nothing left me, sir, but to put back into the
port of Glasgow after hands; and there (by your leave)
ye will find them that are better able to talk to you."

"Ay?" said Alan; "and faith, I'll have a talk with them
mysel'! Unless there's naebody speaks English in that
town, I have a bonny tale for them. Fifteen tarry sailors
upon the one side, and a man and a halfing boy upon the
other! O, man, it's peetiful!"

Hoseason flushed red.

"No," continued Alan, "that'll no do. Ye'll just have to
set me ashore as we agreed."

"Ay," said Hoseason, "but my first officer is dead—ye
ken best how. There's none of the rest of us acquaint
with this coast, sir; and it's one very dangerous to ships."

"I give ye your choice," says Alan. "Set me on dry
ground in Appin, or Ardgour, or in Morven, or Arisaig,
or Morar; or, in brief, where ye please, within thirty miles
of my own country; except in a country of the Campbells'.
That's a broad target. If ye miss that, ye must be as
feckless at the sailoring as I have found ye at the fighting.
Why, my poor country people in their lit cobles pass from
island to island in all weathers, ay, and by night too, for
the matter of that."

"A coble's not a ship, sir," said the captain. "It has nae
draught of water."

"Well, then, to Glasgow if ye list!" says Alan. "We'll
have the laugh of ye at the least."

"My mind runs little upon laughing," said the captain.
"But all this will cost money, sir."

"Well, sir," says Alan, "I am nae weathercock. Thirty
guineas, if ye land me on the seaside; and sixty, if ye
put me in the Linnhe Loch."

"But see, sir, where we lie, we are but a few hours' sail
from Ardnamurchan," said Hoseason. "Give me sixty, and
I'll set ye there."

"And I'm to wear my brogues and run jeopardy of the
red-coats to please you?" cried Alan. "No, sir, if ye want
sixty guineas, earn them, and set me in my own country."

"It's to risk the brig, sir," said the captain, "and your own lives along with her."

"Take it or want it," says Alan.

"Could ye pilot us at all?" asked the captain, who was frowning to himself.

"Well, it's doubtful," said Alan. "I'm more of a fighting man (as ye have seen for yoursel') than a sailorman. But I have been often enough picked up and set down upon this coast, and should ken something of the lie of it."

The captain shook his head, still frowning.

"If I had lost less money on this unchancy cruise," says he, "I would see you in a rope's-end before I risked my brig, sir. But be it as ye will. As soon as I get a slant of wind (and there's some coming, or I'm the more mistaken) I'll put it in hand. But there's one thing more. We may meet in with a king's ship and she may lay us aboard, sir, with no blame of mine; they keep the cruisers thick upon this coast, ye ken who for. Now, sir, if that was to befall, ye might leave the money."

"Captain," says Alan, "if ye see a pennant, it shall be your part to run away. And now, as I hear you're a little short of brandy in the fore part, I'll offer ye a change; a bottle of brandy against two buckets of water."

That was the last clause of the treaty, and was duly executed on both sides; so that Alan and I could at last wash out the round-house and be quit of the memorials of those whom we had slain, and the captain and Mr. Riach could be happy again in their own way, the name of which was drink.

CHAPTER XII.

I HEAR OF THE RED FOX.

Before we had done cleaning out the round-house, a breeze sprang up from a little to the east of north. This blew off the rain and brought out the sun.

And here I must explain; and the reader would do well to look at a map. On the day when the fog fell and we

ran down Alan's boat, we had been running through the
Little Minch. At dawn after the battle, we lay becalmed
to the east of the Isle of Canna or between that and Isle
Eriska in the chain of the Long Island. Now to get from
there to the Linnhe Loch, the straight course was through
the narrows of the Sound of Mull. But the captain had no
chart; he was afraid to trust his brig so deep among the
islands; and the wind serving well, he preferred to go by
west of Tiree and come up under the southern coast of
the great Isle of Mull.

All day the breeze held in the same point, and rather
freshened than died down; and toward afternoon, a swell
began to set in from round the outer Hebrides. Our
course, to go round about the inner isles, was to the west
of south, so that at first we had this swell upon our beam,
and were much rolled about. But after nightfall, when
we had turned the end of Tiree and began to head more
to the east, the sea came right astern.

Meanwhile, the early part of the day, before the swell
came up, was very pleasant, sailing, as we were, in a
bright sunshine and with many mountainous islands upon
different sides. Alan and I sat in the round-house with
the doors open on each side (the wind being straight
astern) and smoked a pipe or two of the captain's fine
tobacco. It was at this time we heard each other's stories,
which were the more important to me, as I gained some
knowledge of that wild Highland country, on which I
was so soon to land. In those days, so close on the
back of the great rebellion, it was needful a man should
know what he was doing when he went upon the
heather.

It was I that showed the example, telling him all my
misfortune; which he heard with great good nature. Only,
when I came to mention that good friend of mine, Mr.
Campbell the minister, Alan fired up and cried out that
he hated all that were of that name.

"Why," said I, "he is a man you should be proud to
give your hand to."

"I know nothing I would help a Campbell to," says he,
"unless it was a leaden bullet. I would hunt all of that

name like blackcocks. If I lay dying, I would crawl upon my knees to my chamber window for a shot at one."

"Why, Alan," I cried, "what ails ye at the Campbells?"

"Well," says he, "ye ken very well that I am an Appin Stewart, and the Campbells have long harried and wasted those of my name; ay, and got lands of us by treachery—but never with the sword," he cried loudly, and with the word brought down his fist upon the table. But I paid the less attention to this, for I knew it was usually said by those who have the under hand. "There's more than that," he continued, "and all in the same story: lying words, lying papers, tricks fit for a peddler, and the show of what's legal over all, to make a man the more angry."

"You that are so wasteful of your buttons," said I, "I can hardly think you would be a good judge of business."

"My father left me my breeks to cover me, and little besides. And that was how I came to enlist, which was a black spot upon my character at the best of times, and would still be a sore job for me if I fell among the redcoats."

"What?" cried I, "were you in the English army?"

"That was I," said Alan. "But I deserted to the right side at Preston Pans—and that's some comfort."

I could scarcely share this view: holding desertion under arms for an unpardonable fault in honor. But for all I was so young, I was wiser than say my thought. "Dear, dear," says I, "the punishment is death."

"Ay," said hě, "if they got hands on me, it would be a short shrift and a lang tow for Alan! But I have the king of France's commission in my pocket, which would aye be some protection."

"I misdoubt it much," said I.

"I have doubts mysel'," said Alan, dryly.

"And, good Heaven, man," cried I, "you that are a condemned rebel, and a deserter, and a man of the French king's—what tempts ye back into this country? It's a braving of Providence."

"Tut," says Alan, "I have been back every year since forty-six!"

"And what brings ye, man?" cried I.

"Well, ye see, I weary for my friends and country," said he. "France is a braw place, nae doubt; but I weary for the heather and the deer. And then I have bit things that I attend to. Whiles I pick up a few lads to serve the king of France: recruits, ye see; and that's aye a little money. But the heart of the matter is the business of my chief, Ardshiel."

"I thought they called your chief Appin," said I.

"Ay, but Ardshiel is the captain of the clan," said he, which scarcely cleared my mind. "Ye see, David, he that was all his life so great a man, and come of the blood and bearing the name of kings, is now brought down to live in French town like a poor and private person. He that had four hundred swords at his whistle I have seen, with these eyes of mine, buying butter in the market-place, and taking it home in a kale-leaf. This is not only a pain but a disgrace to us of his family and clan. There are the bairns forby, the children and the hope of Appin, that must be learned their letters and how to hold a sword, in that far country. Now, the tenants of Appin have to pay a rent to King George; but their hearts are stanch, they are true to their chief; and what with love and a bit of pressure, and maybe a threat or two, the poor folk scrape up a second rent for Ardshiel. Well, David, I'm the hand that carries it." And he struck the belt about his body, so that the guineas rang.

"Do they pay both?" cried I.

"Ay, David, both," says he.

"What? two rents?" I repeated.

"Ay, David," said he. "I told a different tale to yon captain man; but this is the truth of it. And it's wonderful to me how little pressure is needed. But that's the handi-work of my good kinsman and my father's friend, James of the Glens; James Stewart, that is: Ardshiel's half-brother. He it is that gets the money in, and does the management."

This was the first time I heard the name of that James Stewart, who was afterward so famous at the time of his hanging. But I took little heed at the moment, for all my mind was occupied with the generosity of these poor Highlanders.

"I call it noble," I cried. "I'm a Whig, or little better; but I call it noble."

"Ay," said he, "ye're a Whig, but ye're a gentleman; and that's what does it. Now, if ye were one of the cursed race of Campbell, ye would gnash your teeth to hear tell of it. If ye were the Red Fox." . . . And at that name his teeth shut together, and he ceased speaking. I have seen many a grim face, but never a grimmer than Alan's when he had named the Red Fox.

"And who is the Red Fox?" I asked, daunted, but still curious.

"Who is he?" cried Alan. "Well, and I'll tell you that. When the men of the clans were broken at Culloden, and the good cause went down, and the horses rode over the fetlocks in the best blood of the north, Ardshiel had to flee like a poor deer upon the mountains—he and his lady and his bairns. A sair job we had of it before we got him shipped; and while he still lay in the heather, the English rogues, that couldnae come at his life, were striking at his rights. They stripped him of his powers; they stripped him of his lands; they plucked the weapons from the hands of his clansmen, that had borne arms for thirty centuries; ay, and the very clothes off their backs—so that it's now a sin to wear a tartan plaid, and a man may be cast into jail if he has but a kilt about his legs. One thing they couldnae kill. That was the love the clansmen bore their chief. These guineas are the proof of it. And now, in there steps a man, a Campbell, red-headed Colin of Glenure——"

"Is that him you call the Red Fox?" said I.

"Will ye bring me his brush?" cries Alan, fiercely. "Ah, that's the man. In he steps, and gets papers from King George, to be so-called king's factor on the lands of Appin. And at first he sings small, and is hail-fellow-well-met with Sheamus—that's James of the Glens, my chieftain's agent. But by and by, that came to his ears that I have just told you; how the poor commons of Appin, the farmers and the crofters and the boumen, were wringing their very plaids to get a second rent, and send it over-seas for Ardshiel and his poor bairns. What was it ye called it, when I told ye?"

"I called it noble, Alan," said I.

"And you little better than a common Whig!" cries Alan. "But when it came to Colin Roy, the black Campbell blood in him ran wild. He sat gnashing his teeth at the wine table. What! should a Stewart get a bite of bread, and him not be able to prevent it! Ah! Red Fox, if ever I hold you at a gun's end, the Lord have pity upon ye!" (Alan stopped to swallow down his anger.) "Well, David, what does he do? He declares all the farms to let. And thinks he, in his black heart, I'll soon get other tenants that'll overbid these Stewarts, and Maccolls, and Macrobs (for these are all names in my clan, David), 'and then,' thinks he, 'Ardshiel will have to hold his bonnet on a French roadside.'"

"Well," said I, "what followed?"

Alan laid down his pipe, which he had long since suffered to go out, and set his two hands upon his knees.

"Ay," said he, "ye'll never guess that! For these same Stewarts, and Maccolls, and Macrobs (that had two rents to pay, one to King George by stark force, and one to Ardshiel by natural kindness), offered him a better price than any Campbell in all broad Scotland; and far he sent seeking them—as far as to the sides of Clyde and the cross of Edinburgh—seeking, and fleeching, and begging them to come, where there was a Stewart to be starved and a red-headed hound of a Campbell to be pleasured!"

"Well, Alan," said I, "that is a strange story, and a fine one too. And Whig as I may be, I am glad the man was beaten."

"Him beaten?" echoed Alan. "It's little ye ken of Campbells and less of the Red Fox. Him beaten? No: nor will be, till his blood's on the hillside! But if the day comes, David man, that I can find time and leisure for a bit of hunting, there grows not enough heather in all Scotland to hide him from my vengeance!"

"Man Alan," said I, "ye are neither very wise nor very Christian to blow off so many words of anger. They will do the man ye call the Fox no harm, and yourself no good. Tell me your tale plainly out. What did he next?"

"And that's a good observe, David," said Alan. "Troth and indeed, they will do him no harm; the more's the pity! And barring that about Christianity (of which my opinion is quite otherwise, or I would be nae Christian) I am much of your mind."

"Opinion here or opinion there," said I, "it's a kent thing that Christianity forbids revenge."

"Ah," said he, "it's well seen it was a Campbell taught ye! It would be a convenient world for them and their sort, if there was no such a thing as a lad and a gun behind a heather bush! But that's nothing to the point. That is what he did."

"Ay," said I, "come to that."

"Well, David," said he, "since he couldnae be rid of the royal commons by fair means, he swore he would be rid of them by foul. Ardshiel was to starve: that was the thing he aimed at. And since them that fed him in his exile wouldnae be bought out right or wrong, he would drive them out. Therefore he sent for lawyers, and papers, and red-coats to stand at his back. And the kindly folk of that country must all pack and tramp, every father's son out of his father's house, and out of the place where he was bred and fed, and played when he was a callant. And who are to succeed them? Bareleggit beggars! King George is to whistle for his rents; he maun dow with less; he can spread his butter thinner: what cares Red Colin? If he can hurt Ardshiel, he has his wish; if he can pluck the meat from my chieftain's table, and the bit toys out of his children's hands, he will gang hame singing to Glenure!"

"Let me have a word," said I. "Be sure, if they take less rents, be sure Government has a finger in the pie. It's not this Campbell's fault, man—it's his orders. And if ye killed this Colin to-morrow, what better would ye be? There would be another factor in his shoes, as fast as spur can drive."

"Ye're a good lad in a fight," said Alan; "but man! ye have Whig blood in ye!"

He spoke kindly enough, but there was so much anger
under his contempt that I thought it was wise to change
the conversation. I expressed my wonder how, with the
Highlands covered with troops and guarded like a city
in a siege, a man in his situation could come and go without arrest.

"It's easier than ye would think," said Alan. "A bare
hillside (ye see) is like all one road; if there's a sentry
at one place ye just go by another. And then heather's
a great help. And everywhere there are friends' houses
and friends' byres and haystacks. And besides, when folk
talk of a country covered with troops, it's but a kind of a
by-word at the best. A soldier covers nae mair of it than
his boot-soles. I have fished a water with a sentry on
the other side of the brae, and killed a fine trout; and I
have sat in a heather bush within six feet of another, and
learned a real bonny tune from his whistling. This was
it," said he, and whistled me the air.

"And then, besides," he continued, "it's no sae bad now
as it was in forty-six. The Hielands are what they call
pacified. Small wonder, with never a gun or a sword left
from Cantyre to Cape Wrath, but what tenty folk have
hidden in their thatch! But what I would like to ken,
David, is just how long? Not long, ye would think, with
men like Ardshiel in exile and men like the Red Fox
sitting birling the wine and oppressing the poor at home.
But it's a kittle thing to decide what folk'll bear, and what
they will not. Or why would Red Colin be riding his
horse all over my poor country of Appin, and never a
pretty lad to put a bullet in him?"

And with this Alan fell into a muse, and for a long time
sat very sad and silent.

I will add the rest of what I have to say about my
friend, that he was skilled in all kinds of music, but
principally pipe music; was a well-considered poet in his
own tongue; had read several books both in French and
English; was a dead shot, a good angler, and an excellent
fencer with the small sword as well as with his own particular weapon. For his faults, they were on his face, and
I now knew them all. But the worst of them, his childish

propensity to take offense and to pick quarrels, he greatly laid aside in my case, out of regard for the battle of the round-house. But whether it was because I had done well myself, or because I had been a witness of his own much greater prowess, is more than I can tell. For though he had a great taste for courage in other men, yet he admired it most in Alan Breck.

CHAPTER XIII.

THE LOSS OF THE BRIG.

It was already late at night, and as dark as it ever would be at that season of the year (and that is to say, it was still pretty bright), when Hoseason clapped his head into the round-house door.

"Here," said he, "come out and see if ye can pilot."

"Is this one of your tricks?" asked Alan.

"Do I look like tricks?" cries the captain. "I have other things to think of—my brig's in danger!"

By the concerned look of his face, and, above all, by the sharp tones in which he spoke of his brig, it was plain to both of us he was in deadly earnest; and so Alan and I, with no great fear of treachery, stepped on deck.

The sky was clear; it blew hard, and was bitter cold; a great deal of daylight lingered; and the moon, which was nearly full, shone brightly. The brig was close hauled, so as to round the southwest corner of the Island of Mull; the hills of which (and Ben More above them all, with a wisp of mist upon the top of it) lay full upon the larboard bow. Though it was no good point of sailing for the *Covenant,* she tore through the seas at a great rate, pitching and straining, and pursued by the westerly swell.

Altogether it was no such ill night to keep the seas in; and I had begun to wonder what it was that sat so heavily upon the captain, when the brig rising suddenly on the top of a high swell he pointed and cried to us to look. Away on the lee bow, a thing like a fountain rose out of the moonlit sea, and immediately after we heard a low sound of roaring.

"What do ye call that?" asked the captain gloomily.

"The sea breaking on a reef," said Alan. "And now ye ken where it is; and what better would ye have?"

"Ay," said Hoseason, "if it was the only one."

And sure enough just as he spoke there came a second fountain further to the south.

"There!" said Hoseason. "Ye see for yourself. If I had kent of these reefs, if I had had a chart, or if Shuan had been spared, it's not sixty guineas, no, nor six hundred, would have made me risk my brig in sic a stone-yard! But you, sir, that was to pilot us, have ye never a word?"

"I'm thinking," said Alan, "these'll be what they call the Torran Rocks."

"Are there many of them?" says the captain.

"Truly, sir, I am nae pilot," said Alan; "but it sticks in my mind there are ten miles of them."

Mr. Riach and the captain looked at each other.

"There's a way through them, I suppose?" said the captain.

"Doubtless," said Alan; "but where? But it somehow runs in my mind once more, that it is clearer under the land."

"So?" said Hoseason. "We'll have to haul our wind then, Riach; we'll have to come as near in about the end of Mull as we can take her, sir; and even then we'll have the land to keep the wind off us, and that stoneyard on our lee. Well, we're in for it now, and may as well crack on."

With that he gave an order to the steersman, and sent Riach to the foretop. There were only five men on deck, counting the officers; these were all that were fit (or, at least, both fit and willing) for their work; and two of these were hurt. So, as I say, it fell to Mr. Riach to go aloft, and he sat there looking out and hailing the deck with news of all he saw.

"The sea to the south is thick," he cried; and then, after awhile, "It does seem clearer in by the land."

"Well, sir," said Hoseason to Alan, "we'll try your way

of it. But I think I might as well trust to a blind fiddler. Pray God you're right."

"Pray God I am!" says Alan to me. "But where did I hear it? Well, well, it will be as it must."

As we got nearer to the turn of the land the reefs began to be sown here and there on our very path; and Mr. Riach sometimes cried down to us to change the course. Sometimes, indeed, none too soon; for one reef was so close on the brig's weather board that when a sea burst upon it the lighter sprays fell upon her deck and wetted us like rain.

The brightness of the night showed us these perils as clearly as by day, which was, perhaps, the more alarming. It showed me, too, the face of the captain as he stood by the steersman, now on one foot, now on the other, and sometimes blowing in his hands, but still listening and looking and as steady as steel. Neither he nor Mr. Riach had shown well in the fighting; but I saw they were brave in their own trade, and admired them all the more because I found Alan very white.

"Ochone, David," said he, "this is no the kind of death I fancy."

"What, Alan!" I cried, "you're not afraid?"

"No," said he, wetting his lips, "but you'll allow yourself, it's a cold ending."

By this time, now and then sheering to one side or the other to avoid a reef, but still hugging the wind and the land, we had got round Iona and begun to come alongside Mull. The tide of the tail of the land ran very strong, and threw the brig about. Two hands were put to the helm, and Hoseason himself would sometimes lend a help; and it was strange to see three strong men throw their weight upon the tiller, and it (like a living thing) struggle against and drive them back. This would have been the greater danger, had not the sea been for some while free of obstacles. Mr. Riach, besides, announced from the top that he saw clear water ahead.

"Ye were right," said Hoseason to Alan. "Ye have saved the brig, sir; I'll mind that when we come to clear accounts." And I believe he not only meant what he said, but would have done it; so high a place did the *Covenant* hold in his affections.

But this is matter only for conjecture, things having gone otherwise than he forecast.

"Keep her away a point," sings out Mr. Riach. "Reef to windward!"

And just at the same time the tide caught the brig, and threw the wind out of her sails. She came round into the wind like a top, and the next moment struck the reef with such a dunch as threw us all flat upon the deck, and came near to shake Mr. Riach from his place upon the mast.

I was on my feet in a minute. The reef on which we had struck was close in under the southwest end of Mull, off a little isle they call Earraid, which lay low and black upon the larboard. Sometimes the swell broke clean over us; sometimes it only ground the poor brig upon the reef, so that we could hear her beat herself to pieces; and what with the great noise of the sails, and the singing of the wind, and the flying of the spray in the moonlight, and the sense of danger, I think my head was partly turned, for I could scarcely understand the things I saw.

Presently, I observed Mr. Riach and the seamen busy round the skiff; and still in the same blank, ran over to assist them; and as soon as I set my hand to work, my mind came clear again. It was no very easy task, for the skiff lay amidships and was full of hamper, and the breaking of the heavier seas continually forced us to give over and hold on; but we all wrought like horses while we could.

Meanwhile such of the wounded as could move came clambering out of the forescuttle and began to help; while the rest that lay helpless in their bunks harrowed me with screaming and begging to be saved.

The captain took no part. It seemed he was struck stupid. He stood holding by the shrouds, talking to himself and groaning out aloud whenever the ship hammered on the rock. His brig was like wife and child to him; he had looked on, day by day, at the mishandling of poor Ransome;

but when it came to the brig, he seemed to suffer along with her.

All the time of our working at the boat, I remember only one other thing: that I asked Alan, looking across at the shore, what country it was; and he answered, it was the worst possible for him, for it was a land of the Campbells.

We had one of the wounded men told off to keep a watch upon the seas and cry us warning. Well, we had the boat about ready to be launched, when this man sang out pretty shrill: "For God's sake, hold on!" We knew by his tone that it was something more than ordinary; and sure enough, there followed a sea so huge that it lifted the brig right up and canted her over on her beam. Whether the cry came too late or my hold was too weak, I know not; but at the sudden tilting of the ship, I was cast clean over the bulwarks into the sea.

I went down, and drank my fill; and then came up, and got a blink of the moon; and then down again. They say a man sinks the third time for good. I cannot be made like other folk, then, for I would not like to write how often I went down or how often I came up again. All the while, I was being hurled along, and beaten upon and choked, and then swallowed whole; and the thing was so distracting to my wits, that I was neither sorry nor afraid.

Presently, I found I was holding to a spar, which helped me somewhat. And then all of a sudden I was in quiet water, and began to come to myself.

It was the spare yard I had got hold of, and I was amazed to see how far I had traveled from the brig. I hailed her, indeed; but it was plain she was already out of cry. She was still holding together; but whether or not they had yet launched the boat, I was too far off and too low down to see.

While I was hailing the brig, I spied a tract of water lying between us, where no great waves came, but which yet boiled white all over and bristled in the moon with rings and bubbles. Sometimes the whole tract swung to one side, like the tail of a live serpent; sometimes, for a glimpse, it all would disappear and then boil up again.

What it was I had no guess, which for the time increased
my fear of it; but I now know it must have been the
roost or tide-race, which had carried me away so fast
and tumbled me about so cruelly, and at last, as if tired
of that play, had flung out me and the spare yard upon
its landward margin.

I now lay quite becalmed, and began to feel that a
man can die of cold as well as of drowning. The shores
of Earraid were close in; I could see in the moonlight the
dots of heather and the sparkling of the mica in the rocks.

"Well," thought I to myself, "if I cannot get as far as
that, it's strange."

I had no skill of swimming, Essen water being small in
our neighborhood; but when I laid hold upon the yard
with both arms, and kicked out with both feet, I soon
began to find that I was moving. Hard work it was, and
mortally slow; but in about an hour of kicking and splash-
ing, I had got well in between the points of a sandy bay
surrounded by low hills.

The sea was here quite quiet; there was no sound of
any surf; the moon shone clear; and I thought in my heart
I had never seen a place so desert and desolate. But it
was dry land; and when at last it grew so shallow that I
could leave the yard and wade ashore upon my feet, I
cannot tell if I was more tired or more grateful. Both at
least, I was: tired as I never was before that night; and
grateful to God, as I trust I have been often, though never
with more cause.

CHAPTER XIV.

THE ISLET.

With my stepping ashore, I began the most unhappy
part of my adventures. It was half-past twelve in the
morning, and though the wind was broken by the land,
it was a cold night. I dared not sit down (for I thought I
should have frozen), but took off my shoes and walked

to and fro upon the sand, barefoot and beating my breast, with infinite weariness. There was no sound of man or cattle; not a cock crew, though it was about the hour of their first waking; only the surf broke outside in the distance, which put me in mind of my perils and those of my friend. To walk by the sea at that hour of the morning, and in a place so desert-like and lonesome, struck me with a kind of fear.

As soon as the day began to break, I put on my shoes and climbed a hill—the ruggedest scramble I ever undertook—falling, the whole way, between big blocks of granite or leaping from one to another. When I got to the top the dawn was come. There was no sign of the brig, which must have lifted from the reef and sunk. The boat, too, was nowhere to be seen. There was never a sail upon the ocean; and in what I could see of the land, was neither house nor man.

I was afraid to think what had befallen my shipmates, and afraid to look longer at so empty a scene. What with my wet clothes and weariness, and my belly that now began to ache with hunger, I had enough to trouble me without that. So I set off eastward along the south coast, hoping to find a house where I might warm myself, and perhaps get news of those I had lost. And at the worst, I considered the sun would soon rise and dry my clothes.

After a little, my way was stopped by a creek or inlet of the sea, which seemed to run pretty deep into the land; and as I had no means to get across, I must needs change my direction to go about the end of it. It was still the roughest kind of walking; indeed the whole, not only of Earraid, but of the neighboring part of Mull (which they call the Ross) is nothing but a jumble of granite rocks with heather in among. At first the creek kept narrowing as I had looked to see; but presently to my surprise it began to widen out again. At this I scratched my head, but had still no notion of the truth; until at last I came to a rising ground, and it burst upon me all in a moment that I was cast upon a little, barren isle, and cut off on every side by the salt seas.

Instead of the sun rising to dry me, it came on to rain, with a thick mist; so that my case was lamentable.

The time I spent upon the island is still so horrible a thought to me, that I must pass it lightly over. In all the books I have read of people cast away, they had either their pockets full of tools, or a chest of things would be thrown upon the beach along with them, as if on purpose. My case was very different. I had nothing in my pockets but money and Alan's silver button; and being inland bred, I was as much short of knowledge as of means.

I knew indeed that shell-fish were counted good to eat; and among the rocks of the isle I found a great plenty of limpets, which at first I could scarcely strike from their places, not knowing quickness to be needful. There were, besides, some of the little shells that we call buckies; I think periwinkle is the English name. Of these two I made my whole diet, devouring them cold and raw as I found them; and so hungry was I, that at first they seemed to me delicious.

Perhaps they were out of season, or perhaps there was something wrong in the sea about my island. But at least I had no sooner eaten my first meal than I was seized with giddiness and retching, and lay for a long time no better than dead. A second trial of the same food (indeed I had no other) did better with me and revived my strength. But as long as I was on the island, I never knew what to expect when I had eaten; sometimes all was well, and sometimes I was thrown into a miserable sickness; nor could I ever distinguish what particular fish it was that hurt me.

All day it streamed rain; the island ran like a sop; there was no dry spot to be found; and when I lay down that night, between two boulders that made a kind of roof, my feet were in a bog.

The second day, I crossed the island to all sides. There was no one part of it better than another; it was all desolate and rocky; nothing living on it but game birds which I lacked the means to kill, and the gulls which haunted the outlying rocks in a prodigious number. But the creek, or straits, that cut off the isle from the main land of the

Ross, opened out on the north into a bay, and the bay again opened into the Sound of Iona; and it was the neighborhood of this place that I chose to be my home; though if I had thought upon the very name of home in such a spot, I must have burst out crying.

I had good reasons for my choice. There was in this part of the isle a little hut of a house like a pig's hut, where fishers used to sleep when they came there upon their business; but the turf roof of it had fallen entirely in; so that the hut was of no use to me, and gave me less shelter than my rocks. What was more important, the shell-fish on which I lived grew there in great plenty; when the tide was out I could gather a peck at a time: and this was doubtless a convenience. But the other reason went deeper. I had become in no way used to the horrid solitude of the isle, but still looked round me on all sides (like a man that was hunted) between fear and hope that I might see some human creature coming. Now, from a little up the hillside over the bay, I could catch a sight of the great, ancient church and the roofs of the people's houses in Iona. And on the other hand, over the low country of the Ross, I saw smoke go up, morning and evening, as if from a homestead in a hollow of the land.

I used to watch this smoke, when I was wet and cold, and had my head half turned with loneliness; and think of the fireside and the company, till my heart burned. It was the same with the roofs of Iona. Altogether, this sight I had of men's homes and comfortable lives, although it put a point on my own sufferings, yet it kept hope alive, and helped me to eat my raw shell-fish (which had soon grown to be a disgust) and saved me from the sense of horror I had whenever I was quite alone with dead rocks, and fowls, and the rain, and the cold sea.

As I was jumping about after my limpets, I was started by a guinea piece, which fell upon a rock in front of me and glanced off into the sea. When the sailors gave me my money again, they kept back not only about a third of the whole sum, but my father's leather purse; so that from that day out, I carried my gold loose in a pocket with a button. I now saw there must be a hole, and clapped my hand to the place in a great hurry. But this was to lock the stable door after the steed was stolen. I had left the shore at Queensferry with near on fifty pounds; now I found no more than two guinea pieces and a silver shilling.

It is true I picked up a third guinea a little after, where it lay shining on a piece of turf. That made a fortune of three pounds and four shillings, English money, for a lad, the rightful heir of an estate, and now starving on an isle at the extreme end of the wild Highlands.

This state of my affairs dashed me still further; and indeed my plight on that third morning was truly pitiful. My clothes were beginning to rot; my stockings in particular were quite worn through, so that my shanks went naked; my hands had grown quite soft with the continual soaking; my throat was very sore, my strength had much abated, and my heart so turned against the horrid stuff I was condemned to eat, that the very sight of it came near to sicken me.

And yet the worst was not yet come.

There is a pretty high rock on the northwest of Earraid, which (because it had a flat top and overlooked the sound) I was much in the habit of frequenting; not that ever I stayed in one place, save when asleep, my misery giving me no rest. Indeed, I wore myself down with continual and aimless goings and comings in the rain.

As soon, however, as the sun came out, I lay down on the top of that rock to dry myself. The comfort of the sunshine is a thing I cannot tell. It set me thinking hopefully of my deliverance, of which I had begun to despair; and I scanned the sea and the Ross with a fresh interest. On the south of my rock, a part of the island jutted out and hid the open ocean, so that a boat could thus come quite near me upon that side, and I be none the wiser.

Well, all of a sudden, a coble with a brown sail and a pair of fishers aboard of it, came flying round that corner of the isle, bound for Iona. I shouted out, and then fell on my knees on the rock and reached up my hands and prayed to them. They were near enough to hear—I could even see the color of their hair; and there was no doubt but they observed me, for they cried out in the Gaelic tongue and laughed. But the boat never turned aside, and flew on, right before my eyes, for Iona.

I could not believe such wickedness, and ran along the shore from rock to rock, crying on them piteously; even after they were out of reach of my voice, I still cried and waved to them; and when they were quite gone, I thought my heart would have burst. I wept and roared like a wicked child, tearing up the turf with my nails and grinding my face in the earth. If a wish would kill men, those two fishers would never have seen morning; and I should likely have died upon my island.

The next day (which was the fourth of this horrible life of mine) I found my bodily strength run very low. But the sun shone, the air was sweet, and what I managed to eat of the shell-fish agreed well with me and revived my courage.

I was scarce back on my rock (where I went always the first thing after I had eaten) before I observed a boat coming down the sound and with her head, as I thought, in my direction.

I began at once to hope and fear exceedingly; for I thought these men might have thought better of their cruelty and be coming back to my assistance. But another disappointment, such as yesterday's was more than I could bear. I turned my back, accordingly, upon the sea, and did not look again till I had counted many hundreds. The boat was still heading for the island. The next time I counted the full thousand, as slowly as I could, my heart beating so as to hurt me. And then it was out of all question. She was coming straight to Earraid!

I could no longer hold myself back, but ran to the seaside and out, from one rock to another, as far as I could go. It is a marvel I was not drowned; for when I was brought to a stand at last, my legs shook under me, and my mouth was so dry, I must wet it with the sea-water before I was able to shout.

All this time the boat was coming on; and now I was able to perceive it was the same boat and the same two men as yesterday. This I knew by their hair, which the one had of a bright yellow and the other black. But now there was a third man along with them, who looked to be of a better class.

As soon as they were come within easy speech, they let down their sail and lay quiet. In spite of my supplications, they drew no nearer in, and what frightened me most of all, the new man tee-hee'd with laughter as he talked and looked at me.

Then he stood up in the boat and addressed me a long while, speaking fast and with many wavings of his hand. I told him I had no Gaelic; and at this be became very angry, and I began to suspect he thought he was talking English. Listening very close, I caught the word "what-effer," several times; but all the rest was Gaelic, and might have been Greek and Hebrew for me.

"Whatever," said I, to show him I had caught a word.

"Yes, yes—yes, yes," says he, and then he looked at the other men, as much as to say, "I told you I spoke English," and began again as hard as ever in the Gaelic. This time I picked out another word, "tide." Then I had a flash of hope. I remembered he was always waving his hand toward the mainland of the Ross.

"Do you mean when the tide is out——?" I cried, and could not finish.

"Yes, yes," said he. "Tide."

At that I turned tail upon their boat (where my adviser had once more begun to tee-hee with laughter), leaped back the way I had come, from one stone to another, and set off running across the isle as I had never run before. In about half an hour I came out upon the shores of the creek; and, sure enough, it was shrunk into a little trickle of water, through which I dashed, not above my knees, and landed with a shout on the main island.

CHAPTER XV.

THE LAD WITH THE SILVER BUTTON: THROUGH THE ISLE OF MULL.

The Ross of Mull, which I had now got upon, was rugged and trackless, like the isle I had just left; being

all bog, and brier, and big stone. There may be roads
for them that know that country well; but for my part
I had no better guide than my own nose, and no other
landmark than Ben More.

I aimed as well as I could for the smoke I had seen so
often from the island; and with all my great weariness and
the difficulty of the way, came upon the house at the bottom of a little hollow, about five or six at night. It was
low and longish, roofed with turf and built of unmortared
stones; and on a mound in front of it, an old gentleman
sat smoking his pipe in the sun.

With what little English he had, he gave me to understand that my shipmates had got safe ashore, and had
broken bread in that very house on the day after.

"Was there one," I asked, "dressed like a gentleman?"

He said they all wore rough great-coats; but to be sure,
the first of them, the one that came alone, wore breeches
and stockings, while the rest had sailors' trousers.

"Ah," said I, "and he would have a feathered hat?"

He told me, no, that he was bare-headed like myself.

At first I thought Alan might have lost his hat; and
then the rain came in my mind, and I judged it more
likely he had it out of harm's way, under his great-coat.
This set me smiling, partly because my friend was safe,
partly to think of his vanity in dress.

And then the old gentleman clapped his hand to his
brow, and cried out that I must be the lad with the silver
button.

"Why, yes!" said I, in some wonder.

"Well, then," said the old gentleman, "I have a word
for you that you are to follow your friend to his country,
by Torosay."

He then asked me how I had fared, and I told him
my tale. A south-country man would certainly have
laughed; but this old gentleman (I call him so because
of his manners, for his clothes were dropping off his back)
heard me all through with nothing but gravity and pity.
When I had done, he took me by the hand, led me into his
hut (it was no better) and presented me before his wife,
as if she had been the queen and I a duke.

The good woman set oat-bread before me and a cold grouse, patting my shoulder and smiling to me all the time, for she had no English; and the old gentleman (not to be behind) brewed me a strong punch out of their country spirit. All the while I was eating, and after that when I was drinking the punch, I could scarce come to believe in my good fortune; and the house, though it was thick with the peat-smoke and as full of holes as a colander, seemed like a palace.

The punch threw me in a strong sweat and a deep slumber; the good people let me lie; and it was near noon of the next day before I took the road, my throat already easier and my spirits quite restored by good fare and good news. The old gentleman, although I pressed him hard, would take no money, and gave me an old bonnet for my head; though I am free to own I was no sooner out of view of the house than I very zealously washed this gift of his in a wayside fountain.

Thought I to myself: "If these are the wild Highlanders, I could wish my own folk wilder."

I not only started late, but I must have wandered nearly half the time. True, I met plenty of people, grubbing in little miserable fields that would not keep a cat, or herding little kine about the bigness of asses. The Highland dress being forbidden by law since the rebellion, and the people condemned to the lowland habit, which they much disliked, it was strange to see the variety of their array. Some went bare, only for a hanging cloak or greatcoat, and carried their trousers on their backs like a useless burthen; some had made an imitation of the tartan with little parti-colored stripes patched together like an old wife's quilt; others, again, still wore the Highland philabeg, but by putting a few stitches between the legs, transformed it into a pair of trousers like a Dutchman's. All those makeshifts were condemned and punished, for the law was harshly applied, in hopes to break up the clan spirit; but in that out-of-the-way, seabound isle, there were few to make remarks and fewer to tell tales.

At about eight at night, and already very weary, I came to a lone house, where I asked admittance and was refused until I bethought me of the power of money in so poor a country, and held up one of my guineas in my finger and thumb. Thereupon, the man of the house, who had hitherto pretended to have no English' and driven me from his door by signals, suddenly began to speak as clearly as was needful, and agreed for five shillings to give me a night's lodging and guide me the next day to Torosay.

At Torosay, on the Sound of Mull and looking over to the mainland of Morven, there was an inn with an innkeeper, who was a Maclean, it appeared, of a very high family; for to keep an inn is thought even more genteel in the Highlands than it is with us, perhaps as partaking of hospitality, or perhaps because the trade is idle and drunken. He spoke good English, and finding me to be something of a scholar, tried me first in French, where he easily beat me, and then in Latin, in which I don't know which of us did best. This pleasant rivalry put us at once upon friendly terms; and I sat up and drank punch with him (or, to be more correct, sat up and watched him drink it) until he was so tipsy that he wept upon my shoulder.

I tried him, as if by accident, with a sight of Alan's button; but it was plain he had never seen or heard of it. Indeed, he bore some grudge against the family and friends of Ardshiel, and before he was drunk he read me a lampoon, in very good Latin, but with a very ill meaning, which he had made in elegiac verses upon a person of that house.

At last, when my landlord could drink no more, he showed me to a bed, and I lay down in very good spirits; having traveled the greater part of that big and crooked Island of Mull, from Earraid to Torosay, fifty miles as the crow flies, and (with my wanderings) much nearer a hundred, in four days and with little fatigue. Indeed, I was by far in better heart and health of body at the end of that long tramp than I had been at the beginning.

CHAPTER XVI.

THE LAD WITH THE SILVER BUTTON: ACROSS MORVEN.

There is a regular ferry from Torosay to Kinlochaline on the mainland. Both shores of the sound are in the country of the strong clan of the Macleans, and the people that passed the ferry with me were almost all of that clan. The skipper of the boat, on the other hand, was called Neil Roy Macrob; and since Macrob was one of the names of Alan's clansmen, and Alan himself had sent me to that ferry, I was eager to come to private speech of Neil Roy.

In the crowded boat this was of course impossible, and the passage was a very slow affair. There was no wind, and as the boat was wretchedly equipped, we could pull but two oars on one side, and one on the other. The men gave way, however, with a good will, the passengers taking spells to help them, and the whole company giving the time in Gaelic boat-songs. And what with the songs, and the sea air, and the good nature and spirit of all concerned, and the bright weather, the passage was a pretty thing to have seen.

At Kinlochaline I got Neil Roy upon one side on the beach, and said I made sure he was one of Appin's men.

"And what for no?" said he.

"I am seeking somebody," said I; "and it comes in my mind that you will have news of him. Alan Breck Stewart is his name." And very foolishly, instead of showing him the button, I sought to pass a shilling in his hand.

At this he drew back. "I am very much affronted," he said; "and this is not the way that one shentleman should behave to another at all. The man you ask for is in France; but if he was in my sporran," says he, "and your belly full of shillings, I would not hurt a hair upon his body."

I saw I had gone the wrong way to work, and without wasting time upon apologies, showed him the button lying in the hollow of my palm.

"Aweel, aweel," said Neil; "and I think ye might have begun with that end of the stick, whatever! But if ye are the lad with the silver button, all is well, and I have the word to see that ye come safe. But if ye will pardon me to speak plainly," says he, "there is a name that you should never take into your mouth, and that is the name of Alan Breck; and there is a thing that ye would never do, and that is to offer your dirty money to a Hieland shentleman."

It was not very easy to apologize; for I could scarce tell him (what was the truth) that I had never dreamed he would set up to be a gentleman until he told me so. Neil on his part had no wish to prolong his dealings with me, only to fulfill his orders and be done with it; and he made haste to give me my route. This was to lie the night in Kinlochaline in the public inn; to cross Morven the next day to Ardgour, and lie the night in the house of one John of the Claymore, who was warned that I might come; the third day, to be set across one loch at Corran and another at Balachulish, and then ask my way to the house of James of the Glens, at Aucharn in Duror of Appin. There was a good deal of ferrying as you hear; the sea in all this part running deep into the mountains and winding about their roots. It makes the country strong to hold and difficult to travel, but full of prodigious, wild and dreadful prospects.

I had some other advice from Neil; to speak with no one by the way, to avoid Whigs, Campbells, and the "red soldiers;" to leave the road and lie in a bush, if I saw any of the latter coming, "for it was never chancy to meet in with them;" and in brief, to conduct myself like a robber or a Jacobite agent, as perhaps Neil thought me.

The inn at Kinlochaline was the most beggarly, vile place that ever pigs were styed in, full of smoke, vermin, and silent Highlanders. I was not only discontented with my lodgings, but with myself for my mismanagement of Neil, and thought I could hardly be worse off.

Early in my next day's journey, I overtook a little, stout, solemn man, walking very slowly with his toes turned out, sometimes reading in a book and sometimes marking the place with his finger, and dressed decently and plainly in something of a clerical style.

This I found to be a catechist, one of those sent out by the Edinburgh Society for Propagating Christian

Knowledge, to evangelize the more savage places of the Highlands. His name was Henderland; he spoke with the broad
south-country tongue, which I was beginning to weary for
the sound of; and besides common countryship, we soon found
we had a more particular bond of interest. For my good
friend, the minister of Essendean, had translated into the
Gaelic in his by-time a number of hymns and pious books,
which Henderland used in his work and held in great esteem.
Indeed it was one of these he was carrying and reading
when we met.

We fell into company at once, our ways lying together
as far as Kingairloch. As we went, he stopped and spoke
with all the wayfarers and workers that we met or passed;
and though of course I could not tell what they discoursed
about, yet I judged Mr. Henderland must be well liked in
the countryside, for I observed many of them to bring out
their mulls and share a pinch of snuff with him.

I told him as far in my affairs as I judged wise: as far,
that is, as they were none of Alan's; and gave Balachulish
as the place I was traveling to, to meet a friend; for I
thought Aucharn, or even Duror, would be too particular
and might put him on the scent.

On his part, he told me much of his work and the people
he worked among, the hiding priests and Jacobites, the Dis-
arming Act, the dress, and many other curiosities of the time
and place. He seemed moderate: blaming Parliament in several points, and especially because they had framed the Act
more severely against those who wore the dress than against
those who carried weapons.

This moderation put it in my mind to question him of
the Red Fox and the Appin tenants: questions which, I
thought, would seem natural enough in the mouth of one
traveling to that country.

He said it was a bad business. "It's wonderful," said
he, "where the tenants find the money, for their life is mere
starvation. (Ye don't carry such a thing as snuff, do ye,
Mr. Balfour? No. Well, I'm better wanting it.) But
these tenants (as I was saying) are doubtless partly driven
to it. James Stewart in Duror (that's him they call James
of the Glens) is half-brother to Ardshiel, the captain of the

clan; and he is a man much looked up to, and drives very hard. And then there's one they call Alan Breck——"

"Ah!" cried I, "what of him?"

"What of the wind that bloweth where it listeth?" said Henderland. "He's here and awa; here to-day and gone to-morrow; a fair heather-cat. He might be glowering at the two of us out of yon whin-bush, and I wouldnae wonder! Ye'll no carry such a thing as snuff, will ye?"

I told him no, and that he had asked the same thing more than once.

"It's highly possible," said he, sighing. "But it seems strange ye shouldnae carry it. However, as I was saying, this Alan Breck is a bold, desperate customer, and well kent to be James' right hand. His life is forfeit already; he would boggle at naething; and maybe, if a tenant-body was to hang back, he would get a dirk in his wame."

"You make a poor story of it all, Mr. Henderland," said I. "If it is all fear upon both sides, I care to hear no more of it."

"Na," said Mr. Henderland, "but there's love too, and self-denial that should put the like of you and me to shame. There's something fine about it; no perhaps Christian, but humanly fine. Even Alan Breck, by all that I hear, is a chield to be respected. There's many a lying sneck-draw sits close in kirk in our own part of the country, and stands well in the world's eye, and maybe is a far worse man, Mr. Balfour, than yon misguided shedder of man's blood. Ay, ay, we might take a lesson by them. Ye'll perhaps think I've been too long in the Hielands?" he added, smiling to me.

I told him not at all; that I had seen much to admire among the Highlanders; and if he came to that, Mr. Campbell himself was a Highlander.

"Ay," said he, "that's true. It's a fine blood."

"And what is the king's agent about?" I asked.

"Colin Campbell?" says Henderland. "Putting his head in a bees' byke!"

"He is to turn the tenants out by force, I hear?" said I.

"Yes," says he, "but the business has gone back and forth, as folks say. First, James of the Glens rode to Edinburgh and got some lawyer (a Stewart, nae doubt—they all hing together like bats in a steeple) and had the proceedings stayed. And then Colin Campbell cam' in again, and had the upper hand before the Barons of Exchequer. And now they tell me the first of the tenants are to flit to-morrow. It's to begin at Duror under James' very windows, which doesnae seem wise by my humble way of it."

"Do you think they'll fight?" I asked.

"Well," says Henderland, "they're disarmed—or supposed to be—for there's still a good deal of cold iron lying by in quiet places. And then Colin Campbell has the sogers coming. But for all that, if I was his lady wife, I wouldnae be well pleased till I got him home again. They're queer customers, the Appin Stewarts."

I asked if they were worse than their neighbors.

"No they," said he. "And that's the worst part of it. For if Colin Roy can get his business done in Appin, he has it all to begin again in the next country, which they call Mamore, and which is one of the countries of the Camerons. He's king's factor upon both, and from both he has to drive out the tenants; and indeed, Mr. Balfour (to be open with ye) it's my belief that if he escapes the one lot, he'll get his death by the other."

So we continued talking and walking the great part of the day; until at last, Mr. Henderland, after expressing his delight in my company, and satisfaction at meeting with a friend of Mr. Campbell's, proposed that I should make a short stage, and lie the night in his house a little beyond Kingairloch.

We had no sooner come to the door of Mr. Henderland's dwelling, than to my great surprise (for I was now used to the politeness of Highlanders) he burst rudely past me, dashed into the room, caught up a jar and a small horn spoon, and began ladling snuff into his nose in most excessive quantities. Then he had a hearty fit of sneezing, and looked round upon me with a rather silly smile.

"It's a vow I took," says he. "I took a vow upon me that I would nae carry it. Doubtless it's a great privation; but when I think upon the martyrs, not only to the Scottish Covenant but to other points of Christianity, I think shame to mind it."

As soon as we had eaten (and porridge and whey was the best of the good man's diet) he took a grave face and said he had a duty to perform by Mr. Campbell, and that was to inquire into my state of mind toward God. I was inclined to smile at him, since the business of the snuff; but he had not spoken long before he brought the tears into my eyes. There are two things that men should never weary of, goodness and humility; we get none too much of them in this rough world and among cold, proud people; but Mr. Henderland had their very speech upon his tongue. And though I was a good deal puffed up with my adventures and with having come off, as the saying is, with flying colors, yet he soon had me on my knees beside a simple, poor old man, and both proud and glad to be there.

CHAPTER XVII.

THE DEATH OF THE RED FOX.

The next day Mr. Henderland found for me a man who had a boat of his own and was to cross the Linnhe Loch that afternoon into Appin, fishing. Him he prevailed on to take me, for he was one of his flock; and in this way I saved a long day's travel and the price of the two public ferries I must otherwise have passed.

A little after we had started, the sun shone upon a little moving clump of scarlet close in along the waterside to the north. It was much of the same red as soldiers' coats; every now and then, too, there came little sparks and lightnings, as though the sun had struck upon bright steel.

I asked my boatman what it should be; and he answered he supposed it was some of the red soldiers coming in from Fort William into Appin, against the poor tenantry of the country. Well, it was a sad sight to me; and whether it was because of my thoughts of Alan, or from something prophetic in my bosom, although this was but the second time I had seen King George's troops, I had no good will to them.

At last we came so near the point of land at the entering in of Loch Leven that I begged to be set on shore. My boatman (who was an honest fellow and mindful of his promise to the catechist) would fain have carried me on to Balachulish; but as this was to take me farther from my secret destination, I insisted, and was set on shore at last under the wood of Lettermore in Alan's country of Appin.

This was a wood of birches, growing on a steep, craggy side of a mountain that overhung the loch. It had many openings and ferny dells; and a road or bridle track ran north and south through the midst of it, by the edge of which, where was a spring, I sat down to eat some oat-bread of Mr. Henderland's and think upon my situation.

As I was so sitting and thinking, a sound of men and horses came to me through the wood; and presently after, at a turning of the road, I saw four travelers come into view. The way was in this part so rough and narrow that they came single and led their horses by the reins. The first was a great, red-headed gentleman, of an imperious and flushed face, who carried his hat in his hand and fanned himself, for he was in a breathing heat. The second, by his decent black garb and white wig, I correctly took to be a lawyer. The third was a servant, and wore some part of his clothes in tartan, which showed that his master was of a Highland family, and either an outlaw or else in singular good odor with the Government, since the wearing of tartan was against the Act. If I had been better versed in these things, I would have known the tartan to be of the Argyle (or Campbell) colors. This servant had a good-sized portmanteau strapped on his horse, and a net of lemons (to brew punch with) hanging at the saddle-bow; as was often enough the custom with luxurious travelers in that part of the country.

As for the fourth, who brought up the tail, I had seen his like before, and knew him at once to be a sheriff's officer.

I had no sooner seen these people coming than I made up my mind (for no reason that I can tell) to go through with my adventure; and when the first came alongside of me, I rose up from the bracken and asked him the way to Aucharn.

He stopped and looked at me, as I thought, a little oddly; and then, turning to the lawyer, "Mungo," said he, "there's many a man would think this more of a warning than two pyats. Here am I on my road to Duror on the job ye ken; and here is a young lad starts up out of the bracken, and speers if I am on the way to Aucharn."

"Glenure," said the other, "this is an ill subject for jesting."

These two had now drawn close up and were gazing at me, while the two followers had halted about a stone-cast in the rear.

"And what seek ye in Aucharn?" said Colin Roy Campbell of Glenure; him they call the Red Fox; for he it was I had stopped.

"The man that lives there," said I.

"James of the Glens?" says Glenure, musingly: and then to the lawyer: "Is he gathering his people, think ye?"

"Anyway," says the lawyer, "we shall do better to bide where we are, and let the soldiers rally us."

"If you are concerned for me," said I, "I am neither of his people nor yours, but an honest subject of King George, owing no man and fearing no man."

"Why, very well said," replies the factor. "But if I may make so bold as ask, what does this honest man so far from his country? and why does he come seeking the brother of Ardshiel? I have power here, I must tell you. I am king's factor upon several of these estates, and have twelve files of soldiers at my back."

"I have heard a waif word in the country," said I, a little nettled, "that you were a hard man to drive."

He still kept looking at me, as if in doubt.

"Well," said he, at last, "your tongue is bold, but I am no unfriend to plainness. If ye had asked me the way to the door of James Stewart on any other day but this, I would have set ye right and bidden ye God speed. But to-day—eh, Mungo?" And he turned again to look at the lawyer.

But just as he turned there came the shot of a firelock

from higher up the hill; and with the very sound of it Glenure fell upon the road.

"O, I am dead!" he cried, several times over.

The lawyer had caught him up and held him in his arms, the servant standing over and clasping his hands. And now the wounded man looked from one to another with scared eyes, and there was a change in his voice that went to the heart.

"Take care of yourselves," says he. "I am dead."

He tried to open his clothes as if to look for the wound, but his fingers slipped on the buttons. With that he gave a great sigh, his head rolled on his shoulder, and he passed away.

The lawyer said never a word, but his face was as sharp as a pen and as white as the dead man's; the servant broke out into a great noise of crying and weeping, like a child; and I, on my side, stood staring at them in a kind of horror. The sheriff's officer had run back at the first sound of the shot, to hasten the coming of the soldiers.

At last the lawyer laid down the dead man in his blood upon the road, and got to his own feet with a kind of stagger.

I believe it was his movement that brought me to my senses; for he had no sooner done so than I began to scramble up the hill, crying out, "The murderer! the murderer."

So little a time had elapsed, that when I got to the top of the first steepness, and could see some part of the open mountain, the murderer was still moving away at no great distance. He was a big man, in a black coat, with metal buttons, and carried a long fowling-piece.

"Here!" I cried. "I see him!"

At that the murderer gave a little, quick look over his shoulder, and began to run. The next moment he was lost in a fringe of birches; then he came out again on the upper side, where I could see him climbing like a jackanapes, for that part was again very steep; and then he dipped behind a boulder, and I saw him no more.

All this time I had been running on my side, and had got a good way up, when a voice cried upon me to stand.

I was at the edge of the upper wood, and so now, when I

halted and looked back, I saw all the open part of the hill below me. The lawyer and the sheriff's officer were standing just above the road, crying and waving on me to come back; and on their left, the redcoats, musket in hand, were beginning to struggle singly out of the lower wood.

"Why should I come back?" I cried. "Come you on!"

"Ten pounds if ye take that lad!" cried the lawyer. "He's an accomplice. He was posted here to hold us in talk."

At that word (which I could hear quite plainly, though it was to the soldiers and not to me that he was crying it) my heart came in my mouth with quite a new kind of terror. Indeed, it is one thing to stand the danger of your life, and quite another to run the peril of both life and character. The thing, besides, had come so suddenly, like thunder out of a clear sky, that I was all amazed and helpless.

The soldiers began to spread, some of them to run, and others to put up their pieces and cover me; and still I stood.

"Duck in here among the trees," said a voice, close by.

Indeed, I scarce knew what I was doing, but I obeyed; and as I did so, I heard the firelocks bang and the balls whistle in the birches.

Just inside the shelter of the trees I found Alan Breck standing, with a fishing-rod. He gave me no salutation; indeed it was no time for civilities; only "Come!" says he, and set off running along the side of the mountain toward Balachulish; and I, like a sheep, to follow him.

Now we ran among the birches; now stooping behind low humps upon the mountain side; now crawling on all-fours among the heather. The pace was deadly, my heart seemed bursting against my ribs; and I had neither time to think nor breath to speak with. Only I remember seeing with wonder, that Alan every now and then would straighten himself to his full height and look back; and every time he did so, there came a great far-away cheering and crying of the soldiers.

Quarter of an hour later, Alan stopped, clapped down flat in the heather, and turned to me.

"Now," said he, "it's earnest. Do as I do for your life."

And at the same speed, but now with infinitely more precaution, we traced back again across the mountain side by the same way that we had come, only perhaps higher; till at last Alan threw himself down in the upper wood of Lettermore, where I had found him at the first, and lay, with his face in the bracken, panting like a dog.

My own sides so ached, my head so swam, my tongue so hung out of my mouth with heat and dryness, that I lay beside him like one dead.

CHAPTER XVIII.

I TALK WITH ALAN IN THE WOOD OF LETTERMORE.

Alan was the first to come round. He rose, went to the border of the wood, peered out a little, and then returned and sat down.

"Well," said he, "yon was a hot burst, David."

I said nothing, nor so much as lifted my face. I had seen murder done, and a great, ruddy, jovial gentleman struck out of life in a moment; the pity of that sight was still sore within me, and yet that was but a part of my concern. Here was murder done upon the man Alan hated; here was Alan skulking in the trees and running from the troops; and whether his was the hand that fired or only the head that ordered, signified but little. By my way of it, my only friend in that wild country was blood-guilty in the first degree; I held him in horror; I could not look upon his face; I would have rather lain alone in the rain on my cold isle, than in that warm wood beside a murderer.

"Are ye still wearied?" he asked again.

"No," said I, still with my face in the bracken; "no, I am not wearied now, and I can speak. You and me must part," I said. "I liked you very well, Alan; but your ways are not mine, and they're not God's; and the short and the long of it is just that we must part."

"I will hardly part from ye, David, without some kind of reason for the same," said Alan, mighty gravely. "If ye ken anything against my reputation, it's the least thing that ye should do, for old acquaintance sake, to let me hear the name of it; and if ye have only taken a distaste to my society, it will be proper for me to judge if I'm insulted."

"Alan," said I, "what is the sense of this? Ye ken very well yon Campbell-man lies in his blood upon the road."

He was silent for a little; then says he, "Did ever ye hear tell of the story of the Man and the Good People?"— by which he meant the fairies.

"No," said I, "nor do I want to hear it."

"With your permission, Mr. Balfour, I will tell it you, whatever," says Alan. "The man, ye should ken, was cast upon a rock in the sea, where it appears the Good People were in use to come and rest as they went through to Ireland. The name of this rock is called the Skerryvore, and it's not far from where we suffered shipwreck. Well, it seems the man cried so sore, if he could just see his little bairn before he died! that at last the king of the Good People took peety upon him, and sent one flying that brought back the bairn in a bag and laid it down beside the man where he lay sleeping. So when the man woke, there was a poke beside him and something into the inside of it that moved. Well, it seems he was one of these gentry that think aye the worst of things; and for greater security, he stuck his dirk throughout that poke before he opened it, and there was his bairn dead. I am thinking to myself, Mr. Balfour, that you and the man are very much alike."

"Do you mean you had no hand in it?" cried I, sitting up.

"I will tell you first of all, Mr. Balfour of Shaws, as one friend to another," said Alan, "that if I were going to kill a gentleman, it would not be in my own country, to bring trouble on my clan; and I would not go wanting sword and gun, and with a long fishing-rod upon my back."

"Well," said I, "that's true!"

"And now," continued Alan, taking out his dirk and laying his hand upon it in a certain manner, "I swear upon the Holy Iron I had neither art nor part, act nor thought in it."

"I thank God for that," cried I, and offered him my hand. He did not appear to see it.

"And here is a great deal of work about a Campbell!" said he. "They are not so scarce, that I ken!"

"At least," said I, "you cannot justly blame me, for you

know very well what you told me in the brig. But the temptation and the act are different, I thank God again for that. We may all be tempted; but to take a life in cold blood, Alan!" And I could say no more for the moment. "And do you know who did it?" I added. "Do you know that man in the black coat?"

"I have nae clear mind about his coat," said Alan, cunningly; "but it sticks in my head that it was blue."

"Blue or black, did ye know him?" said I.

"I couldnae just conscientiously swear to him," says Alan. "He gaed very close by me, to be sure, but it's a strange thing that I should just have been tying my brogues."

"Can you swear that you don't know him, Alan?" I cried, half angered, half in a mind to laugh at his evasions.

"Not yet," says he; "but I've a grand memory for forgetting, David."

"And yet there was one thing I saw clearly," said I; "and that was, that you exposed yourself and me to draw the soldiers."

"It's very likely," said Alan; "and so would any gentleman. You and me were innocent of that transaction."

"The better reason, since we were falsely suspected, that we should get clear," I cried. "The innocent should surely come before the guilty."

"Why, David," said he, "the innocent have aye a chance to get assoiled in court; but for the lad that shot the bullet, I think the best place for him will be the heather. Them that havenae dipped their hands in any little difficulty, should be very mindful of the case of them that have. And that is the good Christianity. For it was the other way round about, and the lad whom I couldnae just clearly see had been in our shoes, and we in his (as might very well have been), I think we would be a good deal obliged to him oursel's if he would draw the soldiers."

When it came to this, I gave Alan up. But he looked so innocent all the time, and was in such clear good faith in what he said, and so ready to sacrifice himself for what he deemed his duty, that my mouth was closed. Mr. Henderland's words came back to me: that we ourselves might take a lesson by these wild Highlanders. Well, here I had taken

mine. Alan's morals were all tail-first; but he was ready
to give his life for them, such as they were.

"Alan," said I, "I'll not say it's the good Christianity
as I understand it, but it's good enough. And here I offer
ye my hand for the second time."

Whereupon he gave me both of his, saying surely I had
cast a spell upon him, for he could forgive me anything.
Then he grew very grave, and said we had not much time
to throw away, but must both flee that country: he, because
he was a deserter, and the whole of Appin would now be
searched like a chamber, and every one obliged to give a
good account of himself; and I, because I was certainly
involved in the murder.

"O!" says I, willing to give him a little lesson, "I have
no fear of the justice of my country."

"As if this was your country!" said he. "Or as if ye
would be tried here, in a country of Stewarts!"

"It's all Scotland," said I.

"Man, I whiles wonder at ye," said Alan. "This is a
Campbell that's been killed. Well, it'll be tried in Inverara,
the Campbells' head place; with fifteen Campbells in the
jury-box, and the biggest Campbell of all (and that's the
duke) sitting cocking on the bench. Justice, David? The
same justice, by all the world, as Glenure found a while ago
at the roadside."

This frighted me a little, I confess, and would have
frighted me more if I had known how nearly exact were
Alan's predictions; indeed it was but in one point that he
exaggerated, there being but eleven Campbells on the jury;
though as the other four were equally in the duke's dependence, it mattered less than might appear. Still, I cried
out that he was unjust to the Duke of Argyle, who (for all
he was a Whig) was yet a wise and honest nobleman.

"Hoot!" said Alan, "the man's a Whig, nae doubt; but
I would never deny he was a good chieftain to his clan.
And what would the clan think if there was a Campbell
shot, and naebody hanged, and their own chief the justice
general? But I have often observed," says Alan, "that you
Low country bodies have no clear idea of what's right and
wrong."

At this I did at last laugh out aloud; when to my surprise, Alan joined in and laughed as merrily as myself.

"Na, na," said he, "we're in the Hielands, David; and when I tell ye to run, take my word and run. Nae doubt it's a hard thing to skulk and starve in the heather, but it's harder yet to lie shackled in a redcoat prison."

I asked him whither we should flee; and as he told me "to the Lowlands," I was a little better inclined to go with him; for indeed I was growing impatient to get back and have the upper hand of my uncle. Besides Alan made so sure there would be no question of justice in the matter, that I began to be afraid he might be right. Of all deaths, I would truly like least to die by the gallows; and the picture of that uncanny instrument came into my head with extraordinary clearness (as I had once seen it engraved at the top of a peddler's ballad) and took away my appetite for courts of justice.

"I'll chance it, Alan," said I. "I'll go with you."

"But mind you," said Alan, "it's no small thing. Ye maun lie bare and hard, and brook many an empty belly. Your bed shall be the moorcock's, and your life shall be like the hunted deer's, and ye shall sleep with your hand upon your weapon. Ay, man, ye shall taigle many a weary foot, or we get clear! I tell ye this at the start, for it's a life that I ken well. But if ye ask what other chance ye have, I answer: Nane. Either take to the heather with me, or else hang."

"And that's a choice very easily made," said I; and we shook hands upon it.

"And now let's take another keek at the redcoats," says Alan, and he led me to the northeastern fringe of the wood.

Looking out between the trees, we could see a great side of mountain, running down exceedingly steep into the waters of the loch. It was a rough part, all hanging stone, and heather, and bit scrags of birchwood; and away at the far end toward Balachulish, little wee red soldiers were dipping up and down over hill and howe, and growing smaller every minute. There was no cheering now, for I think they had other uses for what breath was left them; but they still stuck to the trail, and doubtless thought that we were close in front of them.

Alan watched them, smiling to himself.

"Ay," said he, "they'll be gey weary before they've got to the end of that employ! And so you and me, David, can sit down and eat a bite, and breathe a bit longer, and take a dram from my bottle. Then we'll strike for Aucharn, the house of my kinsman, James of the Glens, where I must get my clothes, and my arms, and money to carry us along; and then, David, we'll cry 'Forth, Fortune!' and take a cast among the heather."

So we sat again and ate and drank, in a place whence we could see the sun going down into a field of great, wild and houseless mountains, such as I was now condemned to wander in with my companion. Partly as we so sat, and partly afterward on the way to Aucharn, each of us narrated his adventures; and I shall here set down so much of Alan's as seems either curious or needful.

It appears he ran to the bulwarks as soon as the wave was passed; saw me, and lost me, and saw me again, as I tumbled in the roost; and at last had one glimpse of me clinging on the yard. It was this that put him in some hope I would maybe get to land after all, and made him leave these clues and messages which had brought me (for my sins) to that unlucky country of Appin.

In the meanwhile, those still on the brig had got the skiff launched, and one or two were on board of her already, when there came a second wave greater than the first, and heaved the brig out of her place, and would certainly have sent her to the bottom, had she not struck and caught on some projection of the reef.. When she had struck first, it had been bows-on, so that the stern had hitherto been lowest. But now her stern was thrown in the air, and the bows plunged under the sea; and with that, the water began to pour into the forescuttle like the pouring of a mill-dam.

It took the color out of Alan's face, even to tell what followed. For there were still two men lying impotent in their bunks; and these, seeing the water pour in and thinking the ship had foundered, begun to cry out aloud, and that with such harrowing cries that all who were on deck tumbled

one after another into the skiff and fell to their oars. They
were not two hundred yards away, when there came a third
great sea; and at that the brig lifted clean over the reef;
her canvas filled for a moment, and she seemed to sail in
chase of them, but settling all the while; and presently she
drew down and down, as if a hand was drawing her; and
the sea closed over the *Covenant* of Dysart.

Never a word they spoke as they pulled ashore, being
stunned with the horror of that screaming; but they had
scarce set foot upon the beach when Hoseason woke up, as
if out of a muse, and bade them lay hands upon Alan. They
hung back indeed, having little taste for the employment; but
Hoseason was like a fiend; crying that Alan was alone, that
he had a great sum about him, that he had been the means
of losing the brig and drowning all their comrades, and
that here was both revenge and wealth upon a single cast. It
was seven against one; in that part of the shore there was
no rock that Alan could set his back to; and the sailors
began to spread out and come behind him.

"And then," said Alan, "the little man with the red head
—I havenae mind of the name that he is called."

"Riach," said I.

"Ay," said Alan, "Riach! Well, it was him that took
up the clubs for me, asked the men if they werenae feared
of a judgment, and says he, 'Dod, I'll put my back to the
Hielandman's mysel'.' That's none such an entirely bad
little man, yon little man with the red head," said Alan. "He
has some spunks of decency."

"Well," said I, "he was kind to me in his way."

"And so he was to Alan," said he; "and by my troth, I
found his way a very good one! But ye see, David, the loss
of the ship and the cries of these poor lads sat very ill
upon the man; and I'm thinking that would be the cause
of it."

"Well, I would think so," said I; "for he was as keen as
any of the rest at the beginning. But how did Hoseason
take it?"

"It sticks in my mind that he would take it very ill," says
Alan. "But the little man cried to me to run, and indeed I
thought it was a good observe, and ran. The last that I

saw they were all in a knot upon the beach, like folk that were not agreeing very well together."

"What do you mean by that?" said I.

"Well, the fists were going," said Alan; "and I saw one man go down like a pair of breeks. But I thought it would be better no to wait. Ye see there's a strip of Campbells in that end of Mull, which is no good company for a gentleman like me. If it hadnae been for that I would have waited and looked for ye mysel', let alone giving a hand to the little man." (It was droll how Alan dwelt on Mr. Riach's stature, for, to say the truth, the one was not much smaller than the other.) "So," says he, continuing, "I set my best foot forward, and whenever I met in with any one I cried out there was a wreck ashore. Man, they didnae stop to fash with me! Ye should have seen them linking for the beach! And when they got there they found they had had the pleasure of a run, which is aye good for a Campbell. I'm thinking it was a judgment on the clan that the brig went down in the lump and didnae break. But it was a very unlucky thing for you, that same; for if any wreck had come ashore they would have hunted high and low, and would soon have found ye."

CHAPTER XIX.

THE HOUSE OF FEAR.

Night fell as we were walking, and the clouds, which had broken up in the afternoon, settled in and thickened, so that it fell, for the season of the year, extremely dark. The way we went was over rough mountain sides; and though Alan pushed on with an assured manner, I could by no means see how he directed himself.

At last, about half-past ten of the clock, we came to the top of a brae, and saw lights below us. It seemed a house door stood open and let out a beam of fire and candle light; and all round the house and steading five or six persons were moving hurriedly about, each carrying a lighted brand.

"James must have tint his wits," said Alan. "If this was the soldiers instead of you and me he would be in a bonny mess. But I daresay he'll have a sentry on the road, and he would ken well enough no soldiers would find the way that we came."

Hereupon he whistled three times, in a particular manner. It was strange to see how, at the first sound of it, all the moving torches came to a stand, as if the bearers were affrighted, and how, at the third, the bustle began again as before.

Having thus set folks' minds at rest, we came down the brae, and were met at the yard gate (for this place was like a well-doing farm) by a tall, handsome man of more than fifty, who cried out to Alan in the Gaelic.

"James Stewart," said Alan, "I will ask ye to speak in Scotch, for here is a young gentleman with me that has nane of the other. This is him," he added, putting his arm through mine, "a young gentleman of the Lowlands, and a laird in his country too, but I am thinking it will be the better for his health if we give his name the go-by."

James of the Glens turned to me for a moment, and greeted me courteously enough; the next he had turned to Alan.

"This has been a dreadful accident," he cried. "It will bring trouble on the country." And he wrung his hands.

"Hoots!" said Alan, "ye must take the sour with the sweet, man. Colin Roy is dead, and be thankful for that!"

"Ay," said James, "and by my troth, I wish he was alive again! It's all very fine to blow and boast beforehand; but now it's done, Alan; and who's to bear the blame of it? The accident fell out in Appin—mind ye that, Alan; it's Appin that must pay; and I am a man that has a family."

While this was going on, I looked about me at the servants. Some were on ladders, digging in the thatch of the house or the farm buildings, from which they brought out guns, swords, and different weapons of war; others carried them away; and by the sound of mattock blows from somewhere further down the brae, I suppose they buried them. Though they were all so busy, there prevailed no kind of order in their efforts; men struggled together for the same gun and ran into each other with their burning torches, and James was continually turning about from his talk with Alan, to cry out orders which were apparently never understood. The faces in the torchlight were like those of people overborne with hurry and panic; and, though none spoke above his breath, their speech sounded both anxious and angry.

It was about this time that a lassie came out of the house carrying a pack or bundle; and it has often made me smile to think how Alan's instinct awoke at the mere sight of it.

"What's that the lassie has?" he asked.

"We're just setting the house in order, Alan," said James, in his frightened and somewhat fawning way. "They'll search Appin with candles, and we must have all things straight. We're digging the bit guns and swords into the moss, ye see; and these, I am thinking, will be your ain French clothes."

"Bury my French clothes!" cried Alan. "Troth no!" And he laid hold upon the packet and retired into the barn to shift himself, recommending me in the meanwhile to his kinsman.

This was all wretched for a stranger like myself to hear and see; and I was right glad when Alan returned, looking like himself in his fine French clothes, though (to be sure) they were now grown almost too battered and withered to deserve that name. I was then taken out in my turn by another of the sons, and given that change of clothing (of which I had stood so long in need), and a pair of Highland brogues, made of deer-leather, rather strange at first, but after a little practice very easy to the feet.

By the time I came back, Alan must have told his story; for it seemed understood that I was to fly with him, and they were all busy upon our equipment. They gave us each a sword and pistols, though I professed my inability to use the former; and with these, and some ammunition, a bag of oatmeal, an iron pan, and a bottle of right French brandy, we were ready for the heather. Money, indeed, was lacking. I had about two guineas left; Alan's belt having been dispatched by another hand, that trusty messenger had no more than seventeenpence to his whole fortune; and as for James, it appears he had brought himself so low with journeys to Edinburgh and legal expenses on behalf of the tenants, that he could only scrape together three and fivepence halfpenny; the most of it in coppers.

"This'll no do," said Alan.

"Ye must find a safe bit somewhere near by," said James, "and get word sent to me. Ye see, ye'll have to get this business prettily off, Alan. This is no time to be stayed for a guinea or two. They're sure to get wind of ye, sure to seek ye, and by my way of it, sure to lay on ye the wyte of this day's accident. If it falls on you, it falls on me that am your near kinsman and harbored ye while ye were in the country. And if it comes on me——" he paused, and bit his fingers, with a white face. "It would be a painful thing for our friends if I was to hang," said he.

"It would be an ill day for Appin," says Alan.

"It's a day that sticks in my throat," said James. "O man, man, man—man, Alan! you and me have spoken like two fools!" he cried, striking his hand upon the wall so that the house rang again.

"Well, and that's true, too," said Alan; "and my friend from the Lowlands here" (nodding at me) "gave me a good word upon that head, if I would only have listened to him."

"But see here," said James, returning to his former manner, "if they lay me by the heels, Alan, it's then that you'll be needing the money; for with all that I have said, and that you have said, it will look very black against the two of us; do ye mark that? Well, follow me out, and ye'll see that I'll have to get a paper out against ye mysel'; I'll have to offer a reward for ye; ay, will I! It's a sore thing to do between such near friends; but if I get the blame of this dreadful accident, I'll have to fend for myself, man. Do ye see that?"

He spoke with a pleading earnestness, taking Alan by the breast of the coat.

"Ay," said Alan, "I see that."

"And ye'll have to be clear of the country, Alan—ay, and clear of Scotland—you and your friend from the Lowlands, too. For I'll have to paper your friend from the Lowlands. Ye see that, Alan—say that ye see that!"

I thought Alan flushed a bit. "This is unco hard on me

that brought him here, James," said he, throwing his head back. "It's like making me a traitor!"

"Now, Alan, man!" cried James, "look things in the face! He'll be papered anyway; Mungo Campbell'll be sure to paper him; what matters if I paper him, too? And then, Alan, I am a man that has a family." And then after a little pause on both sides: "And, Alan, it'll be a jury of Campbells," said he.

"There's one thing," said Alan, musingly, "that naebody kens his name."

"Nor yet they shallnae, Alan! There's my hand on that," cried James, for all the world as if he had really known my name and was foregoing some advantage. "But just the habit he was in, and what he looked like, and his age, and the like? I couldnae well do less."

"I wonder at your father's son," cried Alan, sternly. "Would ye sell the lad with a gift? would ye change his clothes and then betray him?"

"No, no, Alan," said James. "No, no: the habit he took off—the habit Mungo saw him in." But I thought he seemed crestfallen; indeed, he was clutching at every straw; and all the time, I daresay, saw the faces of his hereditary foes on the bench and in the jury-box, and the gallows in the background.

"Well, sir," says Alan, turning to me, "what say ye to that? Ye are here under the safeguard of my honor; and it's my part to see nothing done but what shall please you."

"I have but one word to say," said I; "for to all this dispute I am a perfect stranger. But the plain common sense is to set the blame where it belongs, and that is on the man that fired the shot. Paper him, as ye call it, set the hunt on him; and let honest, innocent folk show their faces in safety."

But at this both Alan and James cried out in horror; bidding me hold my tongue, for that was not to be thought of, and asking me "What the Camerons would think?" (which again confirmed me, it must have been a Cameron from Mamore that did the act) and if I did not see that the lad might be caught? "Ye havenae surely thought of that?"

said they, with such innocent earnestness, that my hands dropped at my side, and I despaired of argument.

"Very well, then," said I, "paper me, if you please, paper Alan, paper King George! We're all three innocent, and that seems to be what's wanted! But at least, sir," said I to James, recovering from my little fit of annoyance, "I am Alan's friend, and if I can be helpful to friends of his, I will not stumble at the risk."

I thought it best to put a fair face on my consent, for I saw Alan troubled; and besides (thinks I to myself) as soon as my back is turned, they will paper me, as they call it, whether I consent or not. But in this I saw I was wrong; for I had no sooner said the words, than Mrs. Stewart leaped out of her chair, came running over to us, and wept first upon my neck and then on Alan's, blessing God for our goodness to her family.

"As for you, Alan, it was no more than your bounden duty," she said. "But for this lad that has come here and seen us at our worst, and seen the goodman fleeching like a suitor, him that by rights should give his commands like any king—as for you, my lad," she says, "my heart is wae not to have your name, but I have your face; and as long as my heart beats under my bosom, I will keep it, and think of it, and bless it." And with that she kissed me, and burst once more into such sobbing, that I stood abashed.

"Hoot, hoot," said Alan, looking mighty silly. "The day comes unco soon in this month of July; and to-morrow there'll be a fine to-do in Appin, a fine riding of dragoons, and crying of 'Cruachan!' and running of redcoats; and it behooves you and me to be the sooner gone."

Thereupon we said farewell, and set out again, bending somewhat eastward, in a fine mild dark night, and over much the same broken country as before.

CHAPTER XX.

THE FLIGHT IN THE HEATHER: THE ROCKS.

Sometimes we walked, sometimes ran; and as it drew on to morning, walked ever the less and ran the more.

For all our hurry, day began to come in while we were still far from any shelter. It found us in a prodigious valley, strewn with rocks and where ran a foaming river. Wild mountains stood around it; there grew there neither grass nor trees; and I have sometimes thought since then, that it may have been the valley called Glencoe, where the massacre was in the time of King William. But for the details of our itinerary, I am all to seek; our way lying now by short cuts, now by great detours; our pace being so hurried; our time of journeying usually by night; and the names of such places as I asked and heard being in the Gaelic tongue and the more easily forgotten.

The first peep of morning, then, showed us this horrible place, and I could see Alan knit his brow.

"This is no fit place for you and me," he said. "This is a place they're bound to watch."

And with that he ran harder than ever down to the waterside, in a part where the river was split in two among three rocks. It went through with a horrid thundering that made my belly quake; and there hung over the lynn a little mist of spray. Alan looked neither to the right nor to the left, but jumped clean upon the middle rock and fell there on his hands and knees to check himself, for that rock was small and he might have pitched over on the far side. I had scarce time to measure the distance or to understand the peril before I had followed him, and he had caught and stopped me.

So there we stood, side by side upon a small rock slippery with spray, a far broader leap in front of us, and the river dinning upon all sides. When I saw where I was there came on me a deadly sickness of fear, and I put my hand over my eyes. Alan took me and shook me; I saw he was speaking, but the roaring of the falls and the trouble of my mind prevented me from hearing; only I saw his face was red with anger, and that he stamped upon the rock. The same look showed me the water raging by and the mist hanging in the air; and with that, I covered my eyes again and shuddered.

The next minute Alan had set the brandy bottle to my lips, and forced me to drink about a gill, which sent the blood into my head again. Then, putting his hands to his mouth and his mouth to my ear, he shouted, "Hang or drown!" and turning his back upon me, leaped over the farther branch of the stream, and landed safe.

I was now alone upon the rock, which gave me the more room; the brandy was singing in my ears; I had this good example fresh before me, and just wit enough to see that if I did not leap at once, I should never leap at all. I bent low on my knees and flung myself forth, with that kind of anger of despair that has sometimes stood me in stead of courage. Sure enough, it was but my hands that reached the full length; these slipped, caught again, slipped again; and I was sliddering back into the lynn, when Alan seized me, first by the hair, then by the collar, and with a great strain dragged me into safety.

Never a word he said, but set off running again for his life, and I must stagger to my feet and run after him. I had been weary before, but now I was sick and bruised, and partly drunken with the brandy; I kept stumbling as I ran, I had a stitch that came near to overmaster me; and when at last Alan paused under a great rock that stood there among a number of others, it was none too soon for David Balfour.

A great rock, I have said; but by rights it was two rocks leaning together at the top, both some twenty feet high, and at the first sight inaccessible. Even Alan (though you may say he had as good as four hands) failed twice in an attempt to climb them; and it was only at the third trial, and then by standing on my shoulders and leaping up with such force as I thought must have broken my collar-bone, that he secured a lodgment. Once there, he let down his leathern girdle; and with the aid of that, and a pair of shallow footholds in the rock, I scrambled up beside him.

Then I saw why we had come there; for the two rocks, both being somewhat hollow on the top and sloping one to the other, made a kind of dish or saucer, where as many as three or four men might have lain hidden.

All this while, Alan had not said a word, and had run and climbed with such a savage, silent frenzy of hurry, that I knew he was in mortal fear of some miscarriage. Even now we were on the rock he said nothing, nor so much as relaxed the frowning look upon his face; but clapped flat down, and keeping only one eye above the edge of our place of shelter, scouted all round the compass. The dawn had come quiet clear; we could see the stony sides of the valley, and its bottom, which was bestrewed with rocks, and the river, which went from one side to another, and made white falls; but nowhere the smoke of a house, nor any living creature but some eagles screaming round a cliff.

Then at last Alan smiled.

"Ay," said he, "now we have a chance;" and then looking at me with amusement, "Ye're no very brisk at the jumping," said he.

At this I suppose I colored with mortification, for he added at once, "Hoots! small blame to ye! To be feared of a thing and yet to do it, is what makes the prettiest kind of a man. And then there was water there, and water's a think that dauntons even me. No, no," said Alan, "it's no you that's to blame, it's me."

I asked him why.

"Why," said he, "I have proved myself a gomeral this night. For first of all I take a wrong road, and that in my own country of Appin; so that the day has caught us where we should never have been; and thanks to that, we lie here in some danger and mair discomfort. And next (which is the worst of the two, for a man that has been so much among the heather as myself) I have come wanting a water-bottle, and here we lie for a long summer's day with naething but neat spirit. Ye may think that a small matter; but before it comes night, David, ye'll give me news of it."

I was anxious to redeem my character, and offered, if he would pour out the brandy, to run down and fill the bottle at the river.

"I wouldnae waste the good spirit either," says he. "It's been a good friend to you this night, or in my poor opinion, ye would still be cocking on yon stone. And what's mair," says he, "ye may have observed (you that's a man of so much penetration) that Alan Breck Stewart was perhaps walking quicker than his ordinar'."

"You!" I cried, "you were running fit to burst."

"Was I so?" said he. "Well, then, ye may depend upon it, there was nae time to be lost. And now here is enough said; gang you to your sleep, lad, and I'll watch."

Accordingly, I lay down to sleep; a little peaty earth had rifted in between the top of the two rocks, and some bracken grew there, to be a bed to me; the last thing I heard was still the crying of the eagles.

I daresay it would be nine in the morning when I was roughly awakened, and found Alan's hand pressed upon my mouth.

"Wheest!" he whispered. "Ye were snoring."

"Well," said I, surprised at his anxious and dark face, "and why not."

He peered over the edge of the rock, and signed to me to do the like.

It was now high day, cloudless, and very hot. The valley was as clear as in a picture. About half a mile up the water was a camp of red-coats; a big fire blazed in their midst, at which some were cooking; and near by, on the top of a rock about as high as ours, there stood a sentry, with the sun sparkling on his arms. All the way down along the riverside were posted other sentries; here near together, there widelier scattered; some planted like the first, on places of command, some on the ground level, and marching and counter-marching, so as to meet half way. Higher up the glen, where the ground was more open, the chain of posts was continued by horse-soldiers, whom we could see in the distance riding to and fro. Lower down, the infantry continued; but as the stream was suddenly swelled by the confluence of a considerable burn, they were more widely set, and only watched the fords and stepping-stones.

I took but one look at them and ducked again into my place. It was strange indeed to see this valley, which had lain so solitary in the hour of dawn, bristling with arms and dotted with red-coats and breeches.

"Ye see," said Alan, "this was what I was afraid of, Davie: that they would watch the burnside. They began to come in about two hours ago, and, man! but ye're a grand hand at the sleeping! We're in a narrow place. If they get up the sides of the hill, they could easy spy us with a glass; but if they'll only keep in the foot of the valley, we'll do yet. The posts are thinner down the water; and come night, we'll try our hand at getting by them."

"And what are we to do till night?" I asked.

"Lie here," says he, "and birstle."

That one good Scotch word, birstle, was indeed the most of the story of the day that we had now to pass. You are to remember that we lay on the bare top of a rock, like scones upon a girdle; the sun beat upon us cruelly; the rock grew so heated, a man could scarce endure the touch of it; and the little patch of earth and fern, which kept cooler, was only large enough for one at a time. We took turn about to lie on the naked rock, which was indeed like the position of that saint that was martyred on a gridiron; and it ran in my mind how strange it was that, in the same climate and at only a few days distance, I should have suffered so cruelly, first from cold upon my island, and now from heat upon this rock.

All the while we had no water, only raw brandy for a drink, which was worse than nothing; but we kept the bottle as cool as we could, burying it in the earth, and got some relief by bathing our breasts and temples.

The soldiers kept stirring all day in the bottom of the valley, now changing guard, now in patrolling parties hunting among the rocks. These lay round in so great a number, that to look for men among them was like looking for a needle in a bottle of hay; and being so hopeless a task, it was gone about with the less care. Yet we could see the soldiers pike their bayonets among the heather, which sent a cold thrill into my vitals; and they would sometimes hang about our rock, so that we scarce dared to breathe.

It was in this way that I first heard the right English speech; one fellow as he went by actually clapping his hand upon the sunny face of the rock on which we lay, and pluck-ing it off again with an oath.

The tediousness and pain of these hours upon the rocks grew only the greater as the day went on; the rock getting still the hotter and the sun fiercer. There were giddiness, and sickness, and sharp pangs like rheumatism, to be supported. I minded then, and have often minded since, on the lines in our Scotch Psalm:—

> "The moon by night thee shall not smite,
> Nor yet the sun by day;"

and indeed it was only by God's blessing that we were neither of us sun-smitten.

At last, about two, it was beyond men's bearing, and there was now temptation to resist, as well as pain to thole. For the sun being now got a little into the west, there came a patch of shade on the east side of our rock, which was the side sheltered from the soldiers.

"As well one death as another," said Alan, and slipped over the edge and dropped on the ground on the shadowy side.

I followed him at once, and instantly fell all my length, so weak was I and so giddy with that long exposure. Here, then, we lay for an hour or two, aching from head to foot, as weak as water, and lying quite naked to the eye of any soldier who should have strolled that way. None came, however, all passing by on the other side; so that our rock continued to be our shield even in this new position.

Presently we began again to get a little strength; and as the soldiers were now lying closer along the riverside, Alan proposed that we should try a start. I was by this time afraid of but one thing in the world; and that was to be set back upon the rock; anything else was welcome to me; so we got ourselves at once in marching order, and began to slip from rock to rock one after the other, now crawling flat on our bellies in the shade, now making a run for it, heart in mouth.

By sundown, we had made some distance, even by our slow rate of progress, though to be sure the sentry on the rock was still plainly in our view. But now we came on something that put all fears out of season; and that was a deep, rushing burn that tore down, in that part, to join the glen-river. At the sight of this, we cast ourselves on the ground and plunged head and shoulders in the water; and I cannot tell which was the more pleasant, the great shock as the cool stream went over us, or the greed with which we drank of it.

We lay there (for the banks hid us), drank again and again, bathed our chests, let our wrists trail in the running water till they ached with the chill; and at last, being wonderfully renewed, we got out the meal-bag and made drammach in the iron pan. This, though it is but cold water mingled with oatmeal, yet makes a good enough dish for a hungry man; and where there are no means of making fire, or (as in our case) good reason for not making one, it is the chief stand-by of those who have taken to the heather.

As soon as the shadow of the night had fallen, we set forth again, at first with the same caution, but presently with more boldness, standing our full height and stepping out at a good pace of walking. The way was very intricate, lying up the steep sides of mountains and along the brows of cliffs; clouds had come in with the sunset, and the night was dark and cool; so that I walked without much fatigue, but in continual fear of falling and rolling down the mountains, and with no guess at our direction.

CHAPTER XXI.

THE FLIGHT IN THE HEATHER: THE HEUGH OF CORRYNAKIEGH.

Early as day comes in the beginning of July, it was still dark when we reached our destination, a cleft in the head of a great mountain, with a water running through the midst, and upon the one hand a shallow cave in a rock. Birches grew there in a thin, pretty wood, which a little further on was changed into a wood of pines. The burn was full of trout; the wood of cushat-doves; on the opening side of the mountain beyond, whaups would be always whistling and cuckoos were plentiful. From the mouth of the cleft we looked down upon a part of Mamore, and on the sea-loch that divides that country from Appin; and this from so great a height, as made it my continual wonder and pleasure to sit and behold them.

The name of the cleft was the Heugh of Corrynakiegh; and although from its height and being so near upon the sea it was often beset with clouds, yet it was on the whole a pleasant place, and the five days we lived in it went happily.

In the meanwhile, you are not to suppose that we neglected our chief business, which was to get away.

"It will be many a long day," Alan said to me on our first morning, "before the red-coats think upon seeking Corrynakiegh; so now we must get word sent to James, and he must find the siller for us."

"And how shall we send that word?" says I. "We are here in a desert place, which yet we dare not leave; and unless ye get the fowls of the air to be your messengers, I see not what we shall be able to do."

"Ay?" said Alan. "Ye're a man of small contrivance, David."

Thereupon he fell in a muse, looking in the embers of the fire; and presently, getting a piece of wood, he fashioned it in a cross, the four ends of which he blackened on the coals. Then he looked at me a little shyly.

"Could ye lend me my button?" says he. "It seems a strange thing to ask a gift again, but I own I am laith to cut another."

I gave him the button; whereupon he strung it on a strip of his great-coat which he had used to bind the cross; and tying in a little sprig of birch and another of fir, he looked upon his work with satisfaction.

"Now," said he, "there is a little clachan" (what is called a hamlet in the English) "not very far from Corryna-kiegh, and it has the name of Koalisnacoan. There, there are living many friends of mine whom I could trust with my life, and some that I am no just so sure of. Ye see, David, there will be money set upon our heads; James himsel' is to set money on them; and as for the Campbells, they would never spare siller where there was a Stewart to be hurt. If it was otherwise, I would go down to Koalisnacoan whatever, and trust my life into these people's hands as lightly as I would trust another with my glove."

"But being so?" said I.

"Being so," said he, "I would as lief they didnae see me. There's bad folk everywhere, and what's far worse, weak ones. So when it comes dark again, I will steal down into that clachan, and set this that I have been making in the window of a good friend of mine, John Breck Maccoll, a bouman of Appin's."

"With all my heart," says I; "and if he finds it, what is he to think?"

"Well," says Alan, "I wish he was a man of more penetration, for by my troth I am afraid he will make little enough of it! But this is what I have in my mind. This cross is something in the nature of the cross-tarrie, or fiery cross, which is the signal of gathering in our clans; yet he will know well enough the clan is not to rise, for there it is standing in his window, and no word with it. So he will say to himsel', The clan is not to rise, but there is something. Then he will see my button, and that was Duncan Stewart's. And then he will say to himsel', The son of Duncan is in the heather and has need of me."

"Well," said I, "it may be. But even supposing so, there is a good deal of heather between here and the Forth."

"And that is a very true word," says Alan. "But then John Breck will see the sprig of birch and the sprig of pine; and he will say to himsel' if he is a man of any penetration at all (which I misdoubt), Alan will be lying in a wood which is both of pines and birches. Then he will think to himsel', That is not so very rife hereabout; and then he will come and give us a look up in Corrynakiegh. And if he does not, David, the devil may fly away with him, for what I care; for he will no be worth the salt to his porridge."

"Eh, man," said I, drolling with him a little, "you're very ingenious! But would it not be simpler for you to write him a few words in black and white?"

"And that is an excellent observe, Mr. Balfour of Shaws," says Alan, drolling with me; "and it would certainly be much simpler for me to write to him, but it would be a sore

job for John Breck to read it. He would have to go to
school for two-three years; and it's possible we might be
wearied waiting on him."

So that night Alan carried down his fiery cross and set
it in the bouman's window. He was troubled when he came
back; for the dogs had barked and the folk run out from
their houses; and he thought he had heard a clatter of
arms and seen a red-coat come to one of the doors. On all
accounts, we lay the next day in the borders of the wood
and kept a close look-out; so that if it was John Breck
that came, we might be ready to guide him, and if it was the
red-coats, we should have time to get away.

About noon a man was to be spied, straggling up the open
side of the mountain in the sun, and looking round him as
he came, from under his hand. No sooner had Alan seen
him than he whistled; the man turned and came a little
toward us: then Alan would give another "peep!" and the
man would come still nearer; and so by the sound of
whistling, he was guided to the spot where we lay.

He was a ragged, wild, bearded man, about forty, grossly
disfigured with the smallpox, and looked both dull and
savage. Although his English was very bad and broken,
yet Alan (according to his very handsome use, whenever I
was by) would suffer him to speak no Gaelic. Perhaps the
strange language made him appear more backward than he
really was; but I thought he had little good-will to serve
us, and what he had was the child of terror.

Alan would have had him carry a message to James; but
the bouman would hear of no message. "She was forget it,"
he said in his screaming voice; and would either have a
letter or wash his hands of us.

I thought Alan would be graveled at that, for we lacked
the means of writing in the desert. But he was a man of
more resources than I knew; searched the wood until he
found a quill of a cushat-dove, which he shaped into a pen;
made himself a kind of ink with gunpowder from his horn
and water from the running stream; and tearing a corner
from his French military commission (which he carried in
his pocket, like a talisman to keep him from the gallows),
he sat down and wrote as follows:

"Dear Kinsman—Please send the money by the bearer to the place he kens of.

"Your affectionate cousin,
"A. S."

This he intrusted to the bouman, who promised to make what manner of speed he best could, and carried it off with him down the hill.

He was three full days gone, but about five in the evening of the third, we heard a whistling in the wood, which Alan answered; and presently the bouman came up the waterside, looking for us, right and left. He seemed less sulky than before, and indeed he was no doubt well pleased to have got to the end of such a dangerous commission.

He gave us the news of the country; that it was alive with red-coats; that arms were being found, and poor folk brought in trouble daily; and that James and some of his servants were already clapped in prison at Fort William, under strong suspicion of complicity. It seemed, it was noised on all sides that Alan Breck had fired the shot; and there was a bill issued for both him and me, with one hundred pounds reward.

This was all as bad as could be; and the little note the bouman had carried us from Mrs. Stewart was of a miserable sadness. In it she besought Alan not to let himself be captured, assuring him, if he fell in the hands of the troops, both he and James were no better than dead men. The money she had sent was all that she could beg or borrow, and she prayed Heaven we could be doing with it. Lastly, she said she inclosed us one of the bills in which we were described.

This we looked upon with great curiosity and not a little fear, partly as a man may look in a mirror, partly as he might look into the barrel of an enemy's gun to judge if it be truly aimed. Alan was advertised as "a small, pock-marked, active man of thirty-five or thereby, dressed in a feathered hat, a French side-coat of blue with silver buttons and lace a great deal tarnished, a red waist-coat and breeches of black shag;" and I as "a tall strong lad of about eighteen, wearing an old blue coat, very ragged, an old

Highland bonnet, a long homespun waist-coat, blue breeches; his legs bare; low-country shoes, wanting the toes; speaks like a Lowlander, and has no beard."

Alan was well enough pleased to see his finery so fully remembered and set down; only when he came to the word tarnish, he looked upon his lace like one a little mortified. As for myself, I thought I cut a miserable figure in the bill, and yet was well enough pleased too; for since I had changed these rags, the description had ceased to be a danger and become a source of safety.

"Alan," said I, "you should change your clothes."

"Na, troth!" said Alan, "I have nae others. A fine sight I would be if I went back to France in a bonnet!"

This put a second reflection in my mind: that if I were to separate from Alan and his tell-tale clothes, I should be safe against arrest, and might go openly about my business. Nor was this all; for suppose I was arrested when I was alone, there was little against me; but suppose I was taken in company with the reputed murderer, my case would begin to be grave. For generosity's sake, I dare not speak my mind upon this head; but I thought of it none the less.

I thought of it all the more, too, when the bouman brought out a green purse with four guineas in gold, and the best part of another in small change. True, it was more than I had. But then Alan, with less than five guineas, had to get as far as France; I, with my less than two, not beyond Queensferry; so that, taking things in their proportion, Alan's society was not only a peril to my life but a burden on my purse.

But there was no thought of the sort in the honest head of my companion. He believed he was serving, helping, and protecting me. And what could I do but hold my peace, and chafe, and take my chance of it?

"It's little enough," said Alan, putting the purse in his pocket, "but it'll do my business. And now, John Breck, if ye will hand me over my button, this gentleman and me will be for taking the road."

But the bouman, after feeling about in a hairy purse that hung in front of him in the Highland manner (though he wore otherwise the Lowland habit, with sea-trousers) began to roll his eyes strangely, and at last said, "Her nainsel will loss it," meaning he thought he had lost it.

"What!" cried Alan, "you will lose my button, that was my father's before me? Now, I will tell you what is in my mind, John Breck: it is in my mind this is the worst day's work that ever ye did since ye were born."

And as Alan spoke, he set his hands on his knees and looked at the bouman with a smiling mouth, and that dancing light in his eyes that meant mischief to his enemies.

Perhaps the bouman was honest enough; perhaps he had meant to cheat and then, finding himself alone with two of us in a desert place, cast back to honesty as being safer; at least, and all at once, he seemed to find the button and handed it to Alan.

"Well, and it is a good thing for the honor of the Maccolls," said Alan, and then to me, "Here is my button back again, and I thank you for parting with it, which is of a piece with all your friendships to me." Then he took the warmest parting of the bouman. "For," says he, "ye have done very well by me, and set your neck at a venture, and I will always give you the name of a good man."

Lastly, the bouman took himself off by one way; and Alan and I (getting our chattels together) struck into another to resume our flight.

CHAPTER XXII.

THE FLIGHT IN THE HEATHER: THE MUIR.

More than eleven hours of incessant, hard traveling brought us early in the morning to the end of a range of mountains. In front of us there lay a piece of low, broken, desert land, which we must now cross. The sun was not long up and shone straight in our eyes; a little, thin mist went up from the face of the moorland like a smoke; so that (as Alan said) there might have been twenty squadrons of dragoons there, and we none the wiser.

We sat down, therefore, in a howe of the hillside, till the

mist should have risen, and made ourselves a dish of drammach, and held a council of war.

"David," said Alan, "this is the kittle bit. Shall we lie here till it comes night, or shall we risk it and stave on ahead?"

"Well," said I, "I am tired indeed, but I could walk as far again, if that was all."

"Ay, but it isnae," said Alan, "nor yet the half. This is how we stand: Appin's fair death to us. To the south, it's all Campbells, and no to be thought of. To the north, well, there's no muckle to be gained by going north; neither for you, that wants to get to Queensferry, nor yet for me, that wants to get to France. Well, then we'll can strike east."

"East be it!" says I, quite cheerily; but I was thinking, in to myself: "O man, if you would only take one point of the compass and let me take any other, it would be the best for both of us."

"Well, then, east, ye see, we have the Muirs," said Alan. "Once there, David, its mere pitch-and-toss. Out on yon bald, naked, flat place, where can a body turn to? Let the red-coats come over a hill, they can spy you miles away; and the sorrow's in their horses' heels! they would soon ride you down. It's no good place, David; and I'm free to say, it's worse by daylight than by dark."

"Alan," said I, "hear my way of it. Appin's death for us; we have none too much money, nor yet meal; the longer they seek, the nearer they may guess where we are; it's all a risk; and I give my word to go ahead until we drop."

Alan was delighted. "There are whiles," said he, "when ye are altogether too canny and Whiggish to be company for a gentleman like me; but there come other whiles when ye show yoursel' a mettle spark; and it's then, David, that I love ye like a brother."

The mist rose and died away, and showed us that country lying as waste as the sea; only the moorfowl and the peewees crying upon it, and far over to the east, a herd of deer, moving like dots. Much of it was red heather; much of the rest broken up with bogs and hags and peaty pools; some had been burnt black in a heath-fire; and in another place there was quite a forest of dead firs, standing like skeletons. A wearier looking desert man never saw; but at least it was clear of troops, which was our point.

We went down accordingly into the waste, and began to make our toilsome and devious travel toward the eastern verge. There were the tops of mountains all round (you are to remember) from whence we might be spied at any moment; so it behooved us to keep in the hollow parts of the moor, and when these turned aside from our direction, to move upon its naked face with infinite care. Sometimes for half-an-hour together we must crawl from one heather-bush to another, as hunters do when they are hard upon the deer. It was a clear day again, with a blazing sun; the water in the brandy bottle was soon gone; and altogether, if I had guessed what it would be to crawl half the time upon my belly and to walk much of the rest stooping nearly to the knees, I should certainly have held back from such a killing enterprise.

Toiling and resting and toiling again, we wore away the morning; and about noon lay down in a thick bush of heather to sleep. Alan took the first watch; and it seemed to me I had scarce closed my eyes before I was shaken up to take the second. We had no clock to go by; and Alan stuck a sprig of heath in the ground to serve instead; so that as soon as the shadow of the bush should fall so far to the east, I might know to rouse him. But I was by this time so weary that I could have slept twelve hours at a stretch; I had the taste of sleep in my throat; my joints slept even when my mind was waking; the hot smell of the heather, and the drone of the wild bees, were like possets to me; and every now and again I would give a jump and find I had been dozing.

The last time I woke, I seemed to come back from farther away, and thought the sun had taken a great start in the Heavens. I looked at the sprig of heath, and at that I could have cried aloud; for I saw I had betrayed my trust. My head was nearly turned with fear and shame; and at what I saw, when I looked out around me on the muir, my heart was like dying in my body. For sure enough, a body of horse-soldiers had come down during my sleep, and were drawing near to us from the southeast, spread out in the shape of a fan and riding their horses to and fro in the deep parts of the heather.

When I waked Alan, he glanced first at the soldiers, then at the mark and the position of the sun, and knitted his brows with a sudden, quick look, both ugly and anxious, which was all the reproach I had of him.

"What are we to do now?" I asked.

"We'll have to play at being hares," said he. "Do ye see yon mountain?" pointing to one on the northeastern sky.

"Ay," said I.

"Well, then," says he, "let us strike for that. Its name is Ben Alder; it is a wild, desert mountain full of hills and hollows, and if we can win to it before the morn, we may do yet."

"But, Alan," cried I, "that will take us across the very coming of the soldiers!"

"I ken that fine," said he; "but if we are driven back on Appin, we are two dead men. So now, David man, be brisk!"

With that he began to run forward on his hands and knees with an incredible quickness, as though it were his natural way of going. All the time, too, he kept winding in and out in the lower parts of the moorland where we were the best concealed. Some of these had been burned or at least scathed with fire; and there rose in our faces (which were close to the ground) a blinding, choking dust as fine as smoke. The water was long out; and this posture of running on the hands and knees brings an overmastering weakness and weariness, so that the joints ache and the wrists faint under your weight.

Now and then, indeed, where was a big bush of heather, we lay awhile and panted, and putting aside the leaves, looked back at the dragoons. They had not spied us, for they held straight on; a half-troop, I think, covering about two miles of ground and beating it mighty thoroughly as they went. I had awakened just in time; a little later, and we must have fled in front of them, instead of escaping on one side. Even as it was, the least misfortune might betray us; and now and again, when a grouse rose out of the heather with a clap of wings, we lay as still as the dead and were afraid to breathe.

The aching and faintness of my body, the laboring of my throat and eyes in the continued smoke of dust and ashes, had soon grown to be so unbearable that I would gladly have given up. Nothing but the fear of Alan lent me enough of a false kind of courage to continue. As for himself (and you are to bear in mind that he was cumbered with a great-coat) he had first turned crimson, but as time went on, the redness began to be mingled with patches of white; his breath cried and whistled as it came; and his voice, when he whispered his observations in my ear during our halts, sounded like nothing human. Yet he seemed in no way dashed in spirits, nor did he at all abate in his activity; so that I was driven to marvel at the man's endurance.

At length, in the first gloaming of the night, we heard a trumpet sound, and looking back from among the heather, saw the troop beginning to collect. A little after, they had built a fire and camped for the night, about the middle of the waste.

At this I begged and besought that we might lie down and sleep.

"There shall be no sleep the night!" said Alan. "From now on, these weary dragoons of yours will keep the crown of the muirland, and none will get out of Appin but winged fowls. We got through in the nick of time, and shall we jeopard what we've gained? Na, na, when the day comes, it shall find you and me in a fast place on Ben Alder."

"Alan," I said, "it's not the want of will; it's the strength that I want. If I could, I would; but as sure as I'm alive, I cannot."

"Very well, then," said Alan. "I'll carry ye."

I looked to see if he were jesting; but no, the little man was in dead earnest; and the sight of so much resolution shamed me.

"Lead away!" said I. "I'll follow."

He gave me one look, as much to say, "Well done, David!" and off he set again at his top speed.

It grew cooler and even a little darker (but not much)

with the coming of the night. The sky was cloudless; it was still early in July, and pretty far north; in the darkest part of that night, you would have needed pretty good eyes to read, but for all that, I have often seen it darker in a winter midday. Heavy dew fell, and drenched the moor like rain; and this refreshed me for awhile. When we stopped to breathe, and I had time to see all about me the clearness and sweetness of the night, the shapes of the hills like things asleep, and the fire dwindling away behind us, like a bright spot in the midst of the moor, anger would come upon me in a clap that I must still drag myself in agony and eat the dust like a worm.

Day began to come in, after years, I thought; and by that time, we were past the greatest danger, and could walk upon our feet like men, instead of crawling like brutes. But, dear heart, have mercy! what a pair we must have made, going double like old grandfathers, stumbling like babes, and as white as dead folk. Never a word passed between us; each set his mouth and kept his eyes in front of him, and lifted up his foot and set it down again, like people lifting weights at a country play; all the while, with the moorfowl crying "peep!" in the heather, and the light coming slowly clearer in the east.

I say Alan did as I did: not that ever I looked at him, for I had enough ado to keep my feet; but because it is plain he must have been as stupid with weariness as myself, and looked as little where we were going, or we should not have walked into an ambush like blind men.

It fell in this way: We were going down a heathery brae, Alan leading and I following a pace or two behind, like a fiddler and his wife; when upon a sudden the heather gave a rustle, three or four ragged men leaped out, and the next moment we were lying on our backs each with a dirk at his throat.

I don't think I cared: the pain of this rough handling was quite swallowed up by the pains of which I was already full; and I was too glad to have stopped walking to mind about the dirk. I lay looking up in the face of the man that held me; and I mind his face was black with the sun and his eyes very light, but I was not afraid of him. I heard Alan and another whispering in the Gaelic; and what they said was all one to me.

Then the dirks were put up, our weapons were taken away, and we were set face to face, sitting in the heather.

"They are Cluny's men," said Alan. "We couldnae have fallen better. We're just to bide here with these, which are his out-sentries, till they can get word to the chief of my arrival."

Now Cluny Macpherson, the chief of the clan Vourich, had been one of the leaders of the great rebellion six years before; there was a price on his life; and I had supposed him long ago in France, with the rest of the heads of that desperate party. Even tired as I was, the surprise of what I heard half wakened me.

"What?" I cried. "Is Cluny still here?"

"Ay is he so!" said Alan. "Still in his own country and kept by his own clan. King George can do no more."

I think I would have asked farther, but Alan gave me the put-off. "I am rather wearied," he said, "and I would like fine to get a sleep." And without more words, he rolled on his face in a deep heather-bush, and seemed to sleep at once.

There was no such thing possible for me. You have heard grasshoppers whirring in the grass in the summer time? Well, I had no sooner closed my eyes, than my body, and above all my head, belly, and wrists, seemed to be filled with whirring grasshoppers; and I must open my eyes again at once, and tumble and toss, and sit up and lie down; and look at the sky which dazzled me, or at Cluny's wild and dirty sentries, peering out over the top of the brae and chattering to each other in the Gaelic.

That was all the rest I had, until the messenger returned; when, as it appeared that Cluny would be glad to receive us, we must get once more upon our feet and set forward. Alan was in excellent good spirits, much refreshed by his sleep, very hungry, and looking pleasantly forward to a dram and a dish of hot collops, of which, it seems, the messenger had brought him word. For my part, it made me sick to hear of eating. I had been dead-heavy before, and now I felt a kind of dreadful lightness, which would not suffer me to walk. I drifted like a gossamer; the ground seemed to me a cloud, the hills a feather-weight, the air to have a current, like a running burn, which carried me to and fro. With all that, a sort of horror and despair sat on my mind, so that I could have wept at my own helplessness.

I saw Alan knitting his brows at me, and supposed it was in anger; and that gave me a pang of light-headed fear, like what a child may have. I remember, too, that I was smiling, and could not stop smiling, hard as I tried; for I thought it was out of place at such a time. But my good companion had nothing in his mind but kindness; and the next moment, two of the gillies had me by the arms, and I began to be carried forward with great swiftness (or so it appeared to me, although I dare say it was slowly enough in truth) through a labyrinth of dreary glens and hollows and into the heart of that dismal mountain of Ben Alder.

CHAPTER XXIII.

CLUNY'S CAGE.

We came at last to the foot of an exceedingly steep wood, which scrambled up a scraggy hillside, and was crowned by a naked precipice.

"It's here," said one of the guides, and we struck up hill.

The trees clung upon the slope, like sailors on the shrouds of a ship; and their trunks were like the rounds of a ladder, by which we mounted.

Quite at the top, and just before the rocky face of the cliff sprang above the foliage, we found that strange house which was known in the country as "Cluny's Cage." The trunks of several trees had been wattled across, the intervals strengthened with stakes, and the ground behind this barricade leveled up with earth to make the floor. A tree, which grew out from the hillside, was the living center-beam of the roof. The walls were of wattle and covered with moss. The whole house had something of an egg shape;

and it half hung, half stood in that steep, hillside thicket, like a wasp's nest in a green hawthorn.

Within, it was large enough to shelter five or six persons with some comfort. A projection of the cliff had been cunningly employed to be the fireplace; and the smoke rising against the face of the rock, and being not dissimilar in color, readily escaped notice from below.

This was but one of Cluny's hiding-places; he had caves, besides, and underground chambers in several parts of his country; and following the reports of his scouts, he moved from one to another as the soldiers drew near or moved away. By this manner of living, and thanks to the affection of his clan, he had not only stayed all this time in safety, while so many others had fled or been taken and slain, but stayed four or five years longer, and only went to France at last by the express command of his master. There he soon died; and it's strange to reflect that he may have regretted his Cage upon Ben Alder.

When we came to the door, he was seated by his rock chimney, watching a gillie about some cookery. He was mighty plainly habited, with a knitted nightcap drawn over his ears, and smoked a foul cutty pipe. For all that he had the manners of a king, and it was quite a sight to see him rise out of his place to welcome us.

"Well, Mr. Stewart, come awa', sir!" said he, "and bring in your friend that as yet I dinna ken the name of."

"And how is yourself, Cluny?" said Alan. "I hope ye do brawly, sir. And I am proud to see ye, and to present to ye my friend the Laird of Shaws, Mr. David Balfour."

Alan never referred to my estate without a touch of a sneer, when we were alone; but with strangers, he rang the words out like a herald.

"Step in by, the both of ye, gentlemen," said Cluny. "I make ye welcome to my house, which is a queer, rude place for certain, but one where I have entertained a royal personage, Mr. Stewart—ye doubtless ken the personage I have in my eye. We'll take a dram for luck, and as soon as this handless man of mine has the collops ready, we'll dine and take a hand at the cartes as gentlemen should. My life is a bit driegh," says he, pouring out the brandy

"I see little company, and sit and twirl my thumbs, and mind
upon a great day that is gone by, and weary for another
great day that we all hope will be upon the road. And so
here's a toast to ye : The Restoration !"

Thereupon we all touched glasses and drank. I am sure I
wished no ill to King George; and if he had been there
himself in proper person, it's like he would have done as
I did. No sooner had I taken out the dram than I felt
hugely better, and could look on and listen, still a little
mistily perhaps, but no longer with the same groundless
horror and distress of mind.

It was certainly a strange place, and we had a strange
host. In his long hiding, Cluny had grown to have all manner
of precise habits, like those of an old maid. He had a
particular place, where no one else must sit; the Cage was
arranged in a particular way, which none must disturb;
cookery was one of his chief fancies, and even while he
was greeting us in, he kept an eye to the collops.

It appears, he sometimes visited or received visits from
his wife and one or two of his nearest friends, under the
cover of night; but for the most part lived quite alone, and
communicated only with his sentinels and the gillies that
waited on him in the Cage. The first thing in the morning,
one of them, who was a barber, came and shaved him, and
gave him the news of the country, of which he was im-
moderately greedy. There was no end to his questions; he
put them as earnestly as a child; and at some of the answers,
laughed out of all bounds of reason, and would break out
again laughing at the mere memory, hours after the barber
was gone.

To be sure, there might have been a purpose in his questions; for though he was thus sequestered, and like the other
landed gentlemen of Scotland, stripped by the late Act of
Parliament of legal powers, he still exercised a patriarchal
justice in his clan. Disputes were brought to him in his
hiding-hole to be decided; and the men of his country, who
would have snapped their fingers at the Court of Session,
laid aside revenge and paid down money at the bare word
of this forfeited and hunted outlaw. When he was angered,
which was often enough, he gave his commands and breathed

threats of punishment like any king; and his gillies trembled and crouched away from him like children before a hasty father. With each of them, as he entered, he ceremoniously shook hands, both parties touching their bonnets at the same time in a military manner. Altogether, I had a fair chance to see some of the inner workings of a Highland clan; and this with a proscribed, fugitive chief; his country conquered; the troops riding upon all sides in quest of him, sometimes within a mile of where he lay; and when the least of the ragged fellows whom he rated and threatened could have made a fortune by betraying him.

On that first day, as soon as the collops were ready, Cluny gave them with his own hand a squeeze of a lemon (for he was well supplied with luxuries) and bade us draw in to our meal.

I do not know if the collops were truly very good, but my heart rose against the very sight of them, and I could eat but little.

We were no sooner done eating, than Cluny brought out an old, thumbed, greasy pack of cards, such as you may find in a mean inn; and his eyes brightened in his face as he proposed that we should fall to playing.

Now, this was one of the things I had been brought up to eschew like disgrace; it being held by my father neither the part of a Christian not yet of a gentleman, to set his own livelihood and fish for that of others, on the cast of painted pasteboard. To be sure, I might have pleaded my fatigue, which was excuse enough; but I thought it behooved that I should bear a testimony. I must have got very red in the face, but I spoke steadily, and told them I had no call to be a judge of others, but for my own part, it was a matter in which I had no clearness.

Cluny stopped mingling the cards. "What in deil's name is this?" says he. "What kind of Whiggish, canting talk is this, for the house of Cluny Macpherson?"

"I will put my hand in the fire for Mr. Balfour," says Alan. "He is an honest and a mettle gentleman, and I would have ye bear in mind who says it. I bear a king's name," says he, cocking his hat; "and I and any that I call friend are company for the best. But the gentleman is tired, and should sleep; if he has no mind to the cartes, it will never hinder you and me. And I'm fit and willing, sir, to play ye any game that ye can name."

"Sir," says Cluny, "in this poor house of mine, I would have ye to ken that any gentleman may follow his pleasure. If your friend would like to stand on his head, he is welcome. And if either he, or you, or any other man, is not preceesely satisfied, I will be proud to step outside with him."

A strange heaviness had come over me; and I had scarce lain down upon a bed before I fell into a kind of trance in which I continued almost the whole time of our stay in the Cage. Sometimes I was broad awake and understood what passed; sometimes I only heard voices or men snoring, like the voice of a silly river; and the plaids upon the wall dwindled down and swelled out again, like firelight shadows on the roof. I must sometimes have spoken or cried out, for I remember I was now and then amazed at being answered; yet I was conscious of no particular nightmare, only of a general, black, abiding horror—a horror of the place I was in, and the bed I lay in, and the plaids on the wall, and the voices, and the fire, and myself.

The barber-gillie, who was a doctor, too, was called in to prescribe for me; but as he spoke in the Gaelic, I understood not a word of his opinion, and was too sick even to ask for a translation. I knew well enough I was ill, and that was all I cared about.

On the morning of the third day, when we had been forty-eight hours in the Cage, I awoke with a great relief of spirits, very weak and weary indeed, but seeing things of the right size and with their honest every-day appearance. I had a mind to eat, moreover; rose from bed of my own movement; and as soon as we had breakfasted, stepped to the entry of the Cage and sat down outside in the top of the wood. It was a gray day, with a cool, mild air; and I sat in a dream all morning, only disturbed by the passing by of Cluny's scouts and servants coming with provisions and reports; for as the coast was at that time clear, you might almost say he held court openly.

When I returned, Cluny and Alan were questioning a

gillie; and the chief turned about and spoke to me in the Gaelic.

"I have no Gaelic, sir," said I.

Everything I said or did had the power of annoying Cluny. "Your name has more sense than yourself, then," said he angrily; "for it's good Gaelic. But the point is this. My scout reports all clear in the south, and the question is have ye the strength to go?"

CHAPTER XXIV.

THE FLIGHT IN THE HEATHER: THE QUARREL.

Alan and I were put across Loch Errocht under cloud of night, and went down its eastern shore to another hiding-place near the head of Loch Rannoch, whither we were led by one of the gillies from the Cage. This fellow carried all our luggage and Alan's great-coat in the bargain, trotting along under the burthen, far less than the half of which used to weigh me to the ground, like a stout hill pony with a feather; yet he was a man that, in plain contest, I could have broken on my knee.

Doubtless it was a great relief to walk disencumbered; and perhaps without that relief, and the consequent sense of liberty and lightness, I could not have walked at all. I was but new risen from a bed of sickness, and there was nothing in the state of our affairs to hearten me for much exertion; traveling, as we did, over the most dismal deserts in Scotland, under a cloudy Heaven, and with divided hearts among the travelers.

For long, we said nothing; marching alongside or one behind the other, each with a set countenance; I, angry and proud, and drawing what strength I had from these two violent and sinful feelings: Alan angry and ashamed, ashamed that he had lost money, angry that I should take it so ill.

The thought of a separation ran always the stronger in my mind; and the more I approved of it, the more ashamed

I grew of my approval. It would be a fine, handsome, generous thing, indeed, for Alan to turn round and say to me: "Go, I am in the most danger, and my company only increases yours." But for me to turn to the friend who certainly loved me, and say to him: "You are in great danger, I am in but little; your friendship is a burden; go, take your risks and bear your hardships alone———" no, that was impossible; and even to think of it privily to myself, made my cheeks to burn.

And yet Alan had behaved like a child and (what is worse) a treacherous child. Wheedling my money from me while I lay once half-conscious was scarce better than theft; and yet here he was trudging by my side, without a penny to his name, and by what I could see, quite blithe to sponge upon the money he had driven me to beg. True I was ready to share it with him; but it made me rage to see him count upon my readiness.

These were the two things uppermost in my mind; and I could open my mouth upon neither without black ungenerosity. So I did the next worse, and said nothing, nor so much as looked once at my companion, save with the tail of my eye.

At last, upon the other side of Loch Errocht, going over a smooth, rushy place, where the walking was easy, he could bear it no longer, and came close to me.

"David," says he, "this is no way for two friends to take a small accident. I have to say that I'm sorry; and so that's said. And now if you have anything, ye'd better say it."

"O," says I, "I have nothing."

He seemed disconcerted, at which I was meanly pleased.

"No," said he, with a rather trembling voice, "but when I say I was to blame?"

"Why, of course, you were to blame," said I, coolly; "and you will bear me out that I have never reproached you."

"Never," says he; "but ye ken very well that ye've done worse. Are we to part? Ye said so once before. Are ye to say it again? There's hills and heather enough between here and the two seas, David; and I will own I'm no very keen to stay where I'm no wanted."

This pierced me like a sword, and seemed to lay bare my private disloyalty.

"Alan Breck!" I cried; and then: "Do you think I am one to turn my back on you in your chief need? You dursn't say it to my face. My whole conduct's there to give the lie to it. It's true, I fell asleep upon the Muir; but that was from weariness, and you do wrong to cast it up to me——"

"Which is what I never did," said Alan.

"But aside from that," I continued, "what have I done that you should even me to dogs by such a supposition? I never yet failed a friend, and it's not likely I'll begin with you. There are things between us that I can never forget, even if you can."

"I will only say this to ye, David," said Alan, very quietly, "that I have long been owing ye my life, and now I owe ye money. Ye should try to make that burden light for me."

This ought to have touched me, and in a manner it did, but the wrong manner. I felt I was behaving badly; and was now not only angry with Alan, but angry with myself in the bargain; and it made me the more cruel.

"You asked me to speak," said I. "Well, then, I will. You own yourself that you have done me a disservice; I have had to swallow an affront; I have never reproached you, I never named the thing till you did. And now you blame me," cried I, "because I cannae laugh and sing as if I was glad to be affronted. The next thing will be that I'm to go down upon my knees and thank you for it! Ye should think more of others, Alan Breck. If ye thought more of others, ye would perhaps speak less about yourself; and when a friend that likes you very well, has passed over an offense without a word, you would be blithe to let it lie, instead of making it a stick to break his back with. By your own way of it, it was you that was to blame; then it shouldnae be you to seek the quarrel."

"Aweel," said Alan, "say nae mair."

And we fell back into our former silence; and came to our journey's end and supped, and lay down to sleep, without another word.

The gillie put us across Loch Rannoch in the dusk of the next day, and gave us his opinion as to our best route. This was to get us up at once into the tops of the mountains: to go round by a circuit, turning the heads of Glen Lyon, Glen Lochay, and Glen Dochart, and come down upon the lowlands by Kippen and the upper waters of the Forth. Alan was little pleased with a route which led us through the country of his blood-foes, the Glenorchy Campbells. He objected that by turning to the east, we should come almost at once among the Athole Stewarts, a race of his own name and lineage, although following a different chief, and come besides by a far easier and swifter way to the place whither we were bound. But the gillie, who was indeed the chief man of Cluny's scouts, had good reasons to give him on all hands, naming the force of troops in every district, and alleging finally (as well as I could understand) that we should nowhere be so little troubled as in a country of the Campbells.

Alan gave way at last, but with only half a heart. "It's one of the dowiest countries in Scotland," said he. "There's naething there that I ken, but heath, and crows, and Campbells. But I see that ye're a man of some penetration; and be it as ye please!"

We set forth accordingly by this itinerary; and for the best part of three nights traveled on eerie mountains and among the well-heads of wild rivers; often buried in mist, almost continually blown and rained upon, and not once cheered by any glimpse of sunshine. By day, we lay and slept in the drenching heather; by night, incessantly clambered upon breakneck hills, and among rude crags. We often wandered; we were often so involved in fog, that we must lie quiet till it lightened. A fire was never to be thought of. Our only food was drammach and a portion of cold meat that we had carried from the Cage; and as for drink, Heaven knows we had no want of water.

This was a dreadful time, rendered the more dreadful by the gloom of the weather and the country. I was never warm; my teeth chattered in my head; I was troubled with a very sore throat, such as I had on the isle; I had a painful stitch in my side, which never left me; and when I slept in my wet bed, with the rain beating above and the mud oozing below me, it was to live over again in fancy the worst part of my adventures—to see the tower of Shaws lit by lightning, Ransome carried below on the men's backs, Shuan dying on the round-house floor, or Colin Campbell grasping at the bosom of his coat. From such broken slumbers, I would be aroused in the gloaming, to sit up in the same puddle where I had slept and sup cold drammach; the rain driving sharp in my face or running down my back in icy trickles; the mist enfolding us like as in a gloomy chamber—or perhaps, if the wind blew, falling suddenly apart and showing us the gulf of some dark valley where the streams were crying aloud.

During all these horrid wanderings, we had no familiarity, scarcely even that of speech. The truth is that I was sickening for my grave, which is my best excuse. But besides that I was of an unforgiving disposition from my birth, slow to take offense, slower to forget it, and now incensed both against my companion and myself. For the best part of two days, he was unweariedly kind; silent, indeed, but always ready to help, and always hoping (as I could very well see) that my displeasure would blow by. For the same length of time, I stayed in myself, nursing my anger, roughly refusing his services, and passing him over with my eyes as if he had been a bush or a stone.

The second night, or rather the peep of the third day, found us upon a very open hill, so that we could not follow our usual plan and lie down immediately to eat and sleep. Before we had reached a place of shelter, the gray had come pretty clear, for though it still rained, the clouds ran higher; and Alan, looking in my face, showed some marks of concern.

"Ye had better let me take your pack," said he, for perhaps the ninth time since we parted from the scout beside Loch Rannoch.

"I do very well, I thank you," said I, as cold as ice.

Alan flushed darkly. "I'll not offer it again," he said. "I'm not a patient man, David."

"I never said you were," said I, which was exactly the rude, silly speech of a boy of ten.

Alan made no answer at the time, but his conduct answered for him. Henceforth, it is to be thought, he quite forgave himself for the affair at Cluny's; cocked his hat again, walked jauntily, whistled airs, and looked at me upon one side with a provoking smile.

The third night we were to pass through the western end of the country of Balquidder. It came clear and cold, with a touch in the air like frost, and a northerly wind that blew the clouds away and made the stars bright. The streams were full, of course, and still made a great noise among the hills; but I observed that Alan thought no more upon the Kelpie and was in high good spirits. As for me, the change of weather came too late; I had lain in the mire so long that (as the Bible has it) my very clothes "abhorred me;" I was dead weary, deadly sick and full of pains and shiverings; the chill of the wind went through me, and the sound of it confused my ears. In this poor state, I had to bear from my companion something in the nature of a persecution. He spoke a good deal, and never without a taunt. "Whig" was the best name he had to give me. "Here," he would say, "here's a dub for ye to jump, my Whiggie! I ken you're a fine jumper!" And so on; all the time with a gibing voice and face.

I knew it was my own doing, and no one else's; but I was too miserable to repent. I felt I could drag myself but little farther; pretty soon, I must lie down and die on these wet mountains like a sheep or a fox, and my bones must whiten there like the bones of a beast. My head was light, perhaps; but I began to love the prospect, I began to glory in the thought of such a death, alone in the desert, with the wild eagles besieging my last moments. Alan would repent then, I thought; he would remember, when I was dead, how much he owed me, and the remembrance would be torture. So I went like a sick, silly, and bad-hearted schoolboy, feeding my anger against a fellowman, when I would have been better on my knees, crying on God for mercy. And at each of Alan's taunts I hugged myself. "Ah!" thinks I to myself, "I have a better taunt in readiness; when I lie down and die, you will feel it like a buffet in your face; ah, what a revenge! ah, how you will regret your ingratitude and cruelty!"

All the while I was growing worse and worse. Once I had fallen, my legs simply doubling under me, and this had struck Alan for the moment; but I was afoot so briskly, and set off again with such a natural manner, that he soon forgot the incident. Flushes of heat went over me, and then spasms of shuddering. The stitch in my side was hardly bearable. At last, I began to feel that I could trail myself no farther; and with that there came on me all at once the wish to have it out with Alan, let my anger blaze, and be done with my life in a more sudden manner. He had just called me "Whig." I stopped.

"Mr. Stewart," said I, in a voice that quivered like a fiddle string, "you are older than I am, and should know your manners. Do you think it either very wise or very witty to cast my politics in my teeth? I thought, where folk differed, it was the part of gentlemen to differ civilly; and if I did not, I may tell you I could find a better taunt than some of yours."

Alan had stopped opposite me, his hat cocked, his hands in his breeches pockets, his head a little to one side. He listened, smiling evilly, as I could see by the starlight; and when I had done he began to whistle a Jacobite air. It was the air made in mockery of General Cope's defeat at Preston Pans:—

"Hey, Johnnie Cope, are ye waukin' yet?
And are your drums a-beatin' yet?"

And it came in my mind that Alan, on the day of that battle, had been engaged upon the royal side.

"Why do ye take that air, Mr. Stewart?" said I. "Is that to remind me you have been beaten on both sides?"

The air stopped on Alan's lips. "David!" said he.

"But it's time these manners ceased," I continued; "and I mean you shall henceforth speak civilly of my king and my good friends the Campbells."

"I am a Stewart——" began Alan.

"O!" says I, "I ken ye bear a king's name. But you are to remember, since I have been in the Highlands, I have

seen a good many of those that bear it; and the best I can
say of them is this, that they would be none the worse of
washing."

"Do you know that you insult me?" said Alan, very low.

"I am sorry for that," said I, "for I am not done; and
if you distaste this sermon, I doubt the next will please you
as little. You have been chased in the field by the grown
men of my party; it seems a poor kind of pleasure to outface a boy. Both the Campbells and the Whigs have beaten
you; you have run before them like a hare. It behooves you
to speak of them as of your betters."

Alan stood quite still, the tails of his great-coat clapping
behind him in the wind.

"This is a pity," he said at last. "There are things said
that cannot be passed over."

"I never asked you to," said I. "I am as ready as yourself."

"Ready?" said he.

"Ready," I repeated. "I am no blower and boaster like
some that I could name. Come on!" And drawing my
sword, I fell on guard as Alan himself had taught me.

"David!" he cried. "Are ye daft? I cannae draw upon
ye, David. It's fair murder."

"That was your lookout when you insulted me," said I.

"It's the truth!" cried Alan, and he stood for a moment,
wringing his mouth in his hand like a man in sore perplexity. "It's the bare truth," he said, and drew his sword.
But before I could touch his blade with mine, he had
thrown it from him and fallen to the ground. "Na, na,"
he kept saying, "na, na—I cannae, I cannae."

At this the last of my anger oozed all out of me; and I
found myself only sick, and sorry, and blank, and wondering
at myself. I would have given the world to take back what
I had said; but a word once spoken, who can recapture
it? I minded me of all Alan's kindness and courage in
the past, how he had helped and cheered and borne with
me in our evil days; and then recalled my own insults, and
saw that I had lost forever that doughty friend. At the
same time, the sickness that hung upon me seemed to re-
double, and the pang in my side was like a sword for

sharpness. I thought I must have swooned where I stood.

This it was that gave me a thought. No apology could blot out what I had said; it was needless to think of one, none could cover the offense; but where an apology was vain, a mere cry for help might bring Alan back to my side. I put my pride away from me. "Alan!" I said; "if you cannae help me, I must just die here."

He started up sitting, and looked at me.

"It's true," said I. "I'm by with it. O, let me get into the bield of a house—I'll can die there easier." I had no need to pretend; whether I chose or not, I spoke in a weeping voice that would have melted a heart of stone.

"Can ye walk?" asked Alan.

"No," said I, "not without help. This last hour, my legs have been fainting under me; I've a stitch in my side like a red-hot iron; I cannae breathe right. If I die, ye'll can forgive me, Alan? In my heart, I liked ye fine—even when I was the angriest."

"Wheest, wheest!" cried Alan. "Dinnae say that! David, man, ye ken——" He shut his mouth upon a sob. "Let me get my arm about ye," he continued; "that's the way. Now lean upon me hard. Gude kens where there's a house! We're in Balwhidder, too; there should be no want of houses, no, nor friends' houses here. Do you gang easier so, Davie?"

"Ay," said I, "I can be doing this way;" and I pressed his arm with my hand.

Again he came near sobbing. "Davie," said he, "I'm no a right man at all; I have neither sense nor kindness; I couldnae remember ye were just a bairn, I couldnae see ye were dying on your feet; Davie, ye'll have to try and forgive me."

"O, man, let's say no more about it!" said I. "We're neither one of us to mend the other—that's the truth! We must just bear and forbear, man Alan! O, but my stitch is sore! Is there nae house?"

"I'll find a house to ye, David," he said, stoutly. "We'll follow down the burn, where there's bound to be houses. My poor man, will ye no be better on my back?"

"O, Alan," says I, "and me a good twelve inches taller?"

"Ye're no such a thing," cried Alan, with a start. "There may be a trifling matter of an inch or two; I'm no saying I'm just exactly what ye would call a tall man, whatever; and I dare say," he added, his voice tailing off in a laughable manner, "now when I come to think of it, I dare say ye'll be just about right. Ay, it'll be a foot, or near hand; or maybe even mair!"

It was sweet and laughable to hear Alan eat his words up in a fear of some fresh quarrel. I could have laughed, had not my stitch caught me so hard; but if I had laughed, I think I must have wept too.

"Alan," cried I, "what makes ye so good to me? what makes ye care for such a thankless fellow?"

"Deed, and I don't know," said Alan. "For just precisely what I thought I liked about ye, was that ye never quarreled—and now I like ye better!"

CHAPTER XXV.

IN BALQUIDDER.

At the door of the first house we came to, Alan knocked, which was no very safe enterprise in such a part of the Highlands as the Braes of Balquidder. No great clan held rule there; it was filled and disputed by small septs, and broken remnants, and what they call "chiefless folk," driven into the wild country about the springs of Forth and Teith by the advance of the Campbells. Here were Stewarts and Maclarens, which came to the same thing, for the Maclarens followed Alan's chief in war, and made but one clan with Appin.

Chance served us very well; for it was a household of Maclarens that we found, where Alan was not only welcome for his name's sake but known by reputation. Here, then, I was got to bed without delay, and a doctor fetched, who found me in a sorry plight. But whether because he was a very good doctor, or I a very young, strong man, I lay bedridden for no more than a week, and before a month I was able to take the road again with a good heart.

All this time Alan would not leave me; though I often pressed him, and indeed his foolhardiness in staying was a common subject of outcry with the two or three friends that were let into the secret. He hid by day in a hole of the braes under a little wood; and at night, when the coast was clear, would come into the house to visit me. I need not say if I was pleased to see him; Mrs. Maclaren, our hostess, thought nothing good enough for such a guest; and as Duncan Dhu (which was the name of our host) had a pair of pipes in his house and was much of a lover of music, the time of my recovery was quite a festival, and we commonly turned night into day.

The soldiers let us be; although once a party of two companies and some dragoons went by in the bottom of the valley, where I could see them through the window as I lay in bed. What was much more astonishing, no magistrate came near me, and there was no question put of whence I came or whither I was going; and in that time of excitement, I was as free of all inquiry as though I had lain in a desert. Yet my presence was known before I left to all the people in Balquidder and the adjacent parts; many coming about the house on visits, and these (after the custom of the country) spreading the news among their neighbors. The bills, too, had now been printed. There was one pinned near the foot of my bed, where I could read my own not very flattering portrait and, in larger characters, the amount of the blood-money that had been set upon my life. Duncan Dhu and the rest that knew that I had come there in Alan's company, could have entertained no doubt of who I was; and many others must have had their guess. For though I had changed my clothes, I could not change my age or person; and Lowland boys of eighteen were not so rife in these parts of the world, and above all about that time, that they could fail to put one thing with another and connect me with the bill. So it was, at least. Other folk keep a secret among two or three near friends, and somehow it leaks out; but among these clansmen, it is told to a whole countryside, and they will keep it for a century.

CHAPTER XXVI.

WE PASS THE FORTH.

The month, as I have said, was not yet out, but it was already far through August, and beautiful warm weather, with every sign of an early and great harvest, when I was pronounced able for my journey. Our money was now run to so low an ebb that we must think first of all on speed; for if we came not soon to Mr. Rankeillor's, or if when we came there he should fail to help me, we must surely starve. In Alan's view, besides, the hunt must have now greatly slackened; and the line of the Forth, and even Stirling Bridge, which is the main pass over that river, would be watched with little interest.

"It's a chief principle in military affairs," said he, "to go where ye are least expected. Forth is our trouble; ye ken the saying, 'Forth bridles the wild Hielandman.' Well, if we seek to creep round about the head of that river and come down by Kippen or Balfron, it's just precisely there that they'll be looking to lay hands on us. But if we stave on straight to the auld Brig' of Stirling, I'll lay my sword they let us pass unchallenged."

The first night, accordingly, we pushed to the house of a Maclaren in Strathire, a friend of Duncan's, where we slept the twenty-first of the month, and whence we set forth again about the fall of night to make another easy stage. The twenty-second we lay in a heather-bush on a hillside in Uam Var, within view of a herd of deer, the happiest ten hours of sleep in a fine, breathing sunshine and on bone-dry ground, that I have ever tasted. That night we struck Allan Water, and followed it down; and coming to the edge of the hills saw the whole Carse of Stirling underfoot, as flat as a pancake, with the town and castle on a hill in the midst of it, and the moon shining on the links of Forth.

"Now," said Alan, "I kenna if ye care, but ye're in your own land again. We passed the Hieland Line in the first hour; and now if we could but pass yon crooked water, we might cast our bonnets in the air."

In Allan Water, near by where it falls into the Forth, we found a little sandy islet, overgrown with burdock, butterbur, and the like low plants, that would just cover us if we lay flat. Here it was we made our camp, within plain view of Stirling Castle, whence we could hear the drums beat as some part of the garrison paraded. Shearers worked all day in a field on one side of the river, and we could hear the stones going on the hooks and the voices and even the words of the men talking. It behooved to lie close and keep silent. But the sand of the little isle was sun-warm, the green plants gave us shelter for our heads, we had food and drink in plenty; and to crown all, we were within sight of safety.

As soon as the shearers quit their work and the dusk began to fall, we waded ashore and struck for the Bridge of Stirling, keeping to the fields and under the field fences.

The bridge is close under the castle hill, an old, high, narrow bridge with pinnacles along the parapet; and you may conceive with how much interest I looked upon it, not only as a place famous in history, but as the very doors of salvation to Alan and myself. The moon was not yet up when we came there; a few lights shone along the front of the fortress, and lower down a few lighted windows in the town; but it was all mighty still, and there seemed to be no guard upon the passage.

I was for pushing straight across; but Alan was more wary.

"It looks unco quiet," said he; "but for all that we'll lie down here cannily behind a dyke, and make sure."

So we lay for about a quarter of an hour, whiles whispering, whiles lying still and hearing nothing earthly but the washing of the water on the piers. At last there came by an old, hobbling woman with a crutch stick; who first stopped a little, close to where we lay, and bemoaned herself and the long way she had traveled; and then set forth again up the steep spring of the bridge. The woman was so little, and the night still so dark, that we soon lost sight of her: only heard the sound of her steps, and her stick, and a cough that she had by fits, draw slowly farther away.

"She's bound to be across now," I whispered.

"Na," said Alan, "her foot still sounds hollow upon the bridge."

And just then—"Who goes?" cried a voice, and we heard the butt of a musket rattle on the stones. I must suppose the sentry had been sleeping, so that had we tried, we might have passed unseen; but he was awake now, and the chance forfeited.

"This'll never do," said Alan. "This'll never, never do for us, David."

And without another word, he began to crawl away through the fields; and a little after, being well out of eye-shot, got to his feet again, and struck along a road that led to the eastward. I could not conceive what he was doing; and indeed I was so sharply cut by the disappointment, that I was little likely to be pleased with anything. A moment back, and I had seen myself knocking at Mr. Rankeillor's door to claim my inheritance, like a hero in a ballad; and here was I back again, a wandering, hunted blackguard, on the wrong side of Forth.

"Well?" said I.

"Well," said Alan, "what would ye have? They're none such fools as I took them for. We have still the Forth to pass, Davie—weary fall the rains that fed and the hillsides that guided it!"

"And why go east?" said I.

"Ou, just upon the chance!" said he. "If we cannae pass the river, we'll have to see what we can do for the firth."

"There are fords upon the river, and none upon the firth," said I.

"To be sure there are fords, and a bridge forby," quoth Alan; "and of what service, when they are watched?"

"Well," said I, "but a river can be swum."

"By them that have the skill of it," returned he; "but

I have yet to hear that either you or me is much of a hand at that exercise; and for my own part, I swim like a stone."

"I'm not up to you in talking back, Alan," I said; "but I can see we're making bad worse. If it's hard to pass a river, it stands to reason it must be worse to pass a sea."

"But there's such a thing as a boat," says Alan, "or I'm the more deceived."

"Ay, and such a thing as money," says I. "But for us that have neither one nor other, they might just as well not have been invented."

"Ye think so?" said Alan.

"I do that," said I.

"David," says he, "ye're a man of small invention and less faith. But let me set my wits upon the hone, and if I cannae beg, borrow, nor steal a boat, I'll make one!"

"I think I see ye!" said I. "And what's more than all that: if ye pass a bridge, it can tell no tales; but if we pass the firth, there's the boat on the wrong side—somebody must have brought it—the countryside will all be in a bizz——"

"Man!" cried Alan, "if I make a boat, I'll make a body to take it back again! So deave me with no more of your nonsense, but walk (for that's what you've got to do) —and let Alan think for ye."

All night, then, we walked through the north side of the Carse under the high line of the Ochil mountains; and by Alloa and Clackmannan and Culross, all of which we avoided; and about ten in the morning, mighty hungry and tired, came to the little clachan of Limekilns. This is a place that sits near in by the waterside, and looks across the Hope to the town of Queensferry. Smoke went up from both of these, and from other villages and farms upon all hands. The fields were being reaped; two ships lay anchored, and boats were coming and going on the Hope. It was altogether a right pleasant sight to me; and I could not take my fill of gazing at these comfortable, green, cultivated hills and the busy people both of the field and sea.

For all that, there was Mr. Rankeillor's house on the

south shore, where I had no doubt wealth awaited me; and here was I upon the north, clad in poor enough attire of an outlandish fashion, with three silver shillings left to me of all my fortune, a price set upon my head, and an outlawed man for my sole company.

"O, Alan!" said I, "to think of it! Over there, there's all that heart could want waiting me; and the birds go over, and the boats go over—all that please can go, but just me only! O, man, but it's a heartbreak!"

In Limekilns we entered a small change-house, which we only knew to be a public by the wand over the door, and bought some bread and cheese from a good-looking lass that was the servant. This we carried with us in a bundle, meaning to sit and eat it in a bush of wood on the sea-shore, that we saw some third part of a mile in front. As we went, I kept looking across the water and sighing to myself; and though I took no heed of it, Alan had fallen into a muse. At last he stopped in the way.

"Did ye take heed of the lass we bought this of?" says he, tapping on the bread and cheese.

"To be sure," said I, "and a bonny lass she was."

"Ye thought that?" cries he. "Man David, that's good news."

"In the name of all that's wonderful, why so?" says I. "What good can that do?"

"Well," said Alan, with one of his droll looks, "I was rather in hopes it would maybe get us that boat."

"If it were the other way about, it would be liker it," said I.

"That's all that you ken, ye see," said Alan. "I don't want the lass to fall in love with ye, I want her to be sorry for ye, David; to which end, there is no manner of need that she should take you for a beauty. Let me see" (looking me curiously over). "I wish ye were a wee thing paler; but apart from that ye'll do fine for my purpose— ye have a fine, hang-dog, rag-and-tatter, clappermaclaw kind of a look to ye, as if ye had stolen the coat from a potato-bogle. Come; right about, and back to the change-house for that boat of ours."

I followed him laughing.

"David Balfour," said he, "ye're a very funny gentleman by your way of it, and this is a very funny employ for
ye, no doubt. For all that, if ye have any affection for my
neck (to say nothing of your own) ye will perhaps be kind
enough to take this matter responsibly. I am going to do
a bit of play-acting, the bottom ground of which is just
exactly as serious as the gallows for the pair of us. So
bear it, if ye please, in mind, and conduct yourself according."

"Well, well," said I, "have it as you will."

As we got near the clachan, he made me take his arm
and hang upon it like one almost helpless with weariness;
and by the time he pushed open the change-house door,
he seemed to be half carrying me. The maid appeared
surprised (as well she might be) at our speedy return; but
Alan had no words to spare for her in explanation, helped
me to a chair, called for a tass of brandy with which he fed
me in little sips, and then breaking up the bread and
cheese helped me to eat it like a nursery-lass; the whole
with that grave, concerned, affectionate countenance, that
might have imposed upon a judge. It was small wonder
if the maid were taken with the picture we presented, of a
poor, sick, overwrought lad and his most tender comrade.
She drew quite near, and stood leaning with her back on
the next table.

"What's like wrong with him?" said she at last.

Alan turned upon her, to my great wonder, with a kind
of fury. "Wrong?" cries he. "He's walked more hundreds
of miles than he has hairs upon his chin, and slept oftener
in wet heather than dry sheets. Wrong, quo' she? Wrong
enough, I would think! Wrong, indeed!" and he kept
grumbling to himself, as he fed me, like a man ill-pleased.

"He's young for the like of that," said the maid.

"Ower young," said Alan, with his back to her.

"He would be better riding," says she.

"And where could I get a horse for him?" cried Alan,
turning on her with the same appearance of fury. "Would
ye have me steal?"

I thought this roughness would have sent her off in
dudgeon, as indeed it closed her mouth for the time. But

my companion knew very well what he was doing; and
for as simple as he was in some things of life, had a great
fund of roguishness in such affairs as these.

"Ye neednae tell me," she said at last—"ye're gentry."

"Well," said Alan, softened a little (I believe against his
will) by this artless comment, "and suppose we were? did
ever you hear that gentrice put money in folk's pockets?"

She sighed at this, as if she were herself some disin-
herited great lady. "No," says she, "that's true indeed."

I was all this while chafing at the part I played, and
sitting tongue-tied between shame and merriment; but somehow at this I could hold in no longer, and bade Alan let
me be, for I was better already. My voice stuck in my
throat, for I ever hated to take part in lies; but my very
embarrassment helped on the plot, for the lass no doubt
set down my husky voice to sickness and fatigue.

"Has he nae friends?" said she, in a tearful voice.

"That has he so," cried Alan, "if we could but win to
them!—friends and rich friends, beds to lie in, food to eat,
doctors to see him—and here he must tramp in the dubs
and sleep in the heather like a beggarman."

"And why that?" says the lass.

"My dear," says Alan, "I cannae very safely say; but
I'll tell ye what I'll do instead," says he, "I'll whistle ye a
bit tune." And with that he leaned pretty far over the
table, and in a mere breath of a whistle, but with a wonderful pretty sentiment, gave her a few bars of "Charlie is my
darling."

"Wheest," says she, and looked over her shoulder to
the door.

"That's it," said Alan.

"And him so young!" cried the lass.

"He's old enough to——" and Alan struck his forefinger
on the back part of his neck, meaning that I was old enough
to lose my head.

"It would be a black shame," she cried, flushing high.

"It's what will be, though," said Alan, "unless we man-
age the better."

At this the lass turned and ran out of that part of the
house, leaving us alone together, Alan in high good humor

at the furthering of his schemes, and I in bitter dudgeon at being called a Jacobite and treated like a child.

"Alan," I cried, "I can stand no more of this."

"Ye'll have to sit it then, Davie," said he. "For if ye upset the pot now, ye may scrape your own life out of the fire, but Alan Breck is a dead man."

This was so true that I could only groan; and even my groan served Alan's purpose, for it was overheard by the lass as she came flying in again with a dish of white puddings and a bottle of strong ale.

"Poor lamb!" says she, and had no sooner set the meat before us, than she touched me on the shoulder with a little friendly touch, as much as to bid me cheer up. Then she told us to fall to, and there would be no more to pay; for the inn was her own, or at least her father's, and he was gone for the day to Pittencrieff. We waited for no second bidding, for bread and cheese is but cold comfort, and the puddings smelt excellently well; and while we sat and ate, she took up that same place by the next table, looking on, and thinking, and frowning to herself, and drawing the string of her apron through her hand.

"I'm thinking ye have rather a long tongue," she said at last to Alan.

"Ay," said Alan; "but ye see I ken the folk I speak to."

"I would never betray ye," said she, "if ye mean that."

"No," said he, "ye're not that kind. But I'll tell ye what ye would do, ye would help."

"I couldnae," said she, shaking her head. "Na, I couldnae."

"No," said he, "but if ye could?"

She answered him nothing.

"Look here, my lass," said Alan, "there are boats in the kingdom of Fife, for I saw two (no less) upon the beach, as I came in by your town's end. Now if we could have the use of a boat to pass under cloud of night into Lothian, and some secret, decent kind of a man to bring that boat back again and keep his counsel, there would be two souls saved—mine to all likelihood—his to a dead surety. If we lack that boat, we have but three shillings left in this wide world; and where to go, and how to do, and what

other place there is for us except the chains of a gibbet—
I give you my naked word, I kenna! Shall we go wanting, lassie? Are ye to lie in your warm bed and think
upon us, when the wind gowls in the chimney and the rain
tirls on the roof? Are ye to eat your meat by the cheeks
of a red fire, and think upon this poor sick lad of mine,
biting his finger-ends on a blae muir for cauld and hunger?
Sick or sound, he must aye be moving; with the death-
grapple at his throat, he must aye be trailing in the rain
on the long roads; and when he gants his last on a rickle
of cauld stanes, there will be nae friends near him but
only me and God."

At this appeal, I could see the lass was in great trouble
of mind, being tempted to help us, and yet in some fear
she might be helping malefactors; and so now I determined to step in myself and to allay her scruples with a
portion of the truth.

"Did you ever hear," said I, "of Mr. Rankeillor of the
Queensferry?"

"Rankeillor the writer?" said she. "I dare say that!"

"Well," said I, "it's to his door that I am bound, so you
may judge by that if I am an ill-doer; and I will tell you
more, that though I am indeed, by a dreadful error, in
some peril of my life, King George has no truer friend in
all Scotland than myself."

Her face cleared up mightily at this, although Alan's
darkened.

"That's more than I would ask," said she. "Mr. Rankeillor is a kennt man." And she bade us finish our meat,
get clear of the clachan as soon as might be, and lie close
in the bit wood on the sea-beach. "And ye can trust
me," says she, "I'll find some means to put you over."

At this we waited for no more, but shook hands with
her upon the bargain, made short work of the puddings,
and set forth again from Limekilns as far as to the wood.

The day came to an end with the same brightness; the
night fell quiet and clear; lights came out in houses and
hamlets and then, one after another, began to be put
out; but it was past eleven, and we were long since strangely
tortured with anxieties, before we heard the grinding of

oars upon the rowing-pins. At that we looked out and saw the lass herself coming rowing to us in a boat. She had trusted no one with our affairs, not even her sweetheart, if she had one; but as soon as her father was asleep, had left the house by a window, stolen a neighbor's boat, and come to our assistance single-handed.

I was abashed how to find expression for my thanks; but she was no less abashed at the thought of hearing them; begged us to lose no time and to hold our peace, saying (very properly) that the heart of our matter was in haste and silence; and so, what with one thing and another, she had set us on the Lothian shore not far from Carriden, had shaken hands with us, and was out again at sea and rowing for Limekilns, before there was one word said either of her service or our gratitude.

Even after she was gone we had nothing to say, as indeed nothing was enough for such a kindness. Only Alan stood a great while upon the shore shaking his head.

"It is a very fine lass," he said at last. "David, it is a very fine lass." And a matter of an hour later, as we were lying in a den on the seashore and I had been already dozing, he broke out again in commendations of her character. For my part, I could say nothing, she was so simple a creature that my heart smote me both with remorse and fear; remorse, because we had traded upon her ignorance; and fear, lest we should have any way involved her in the dangers of our situation.

CHAPTER XXVII.

I COME TO MR. RANKEILLOR.

The next day it was agreed that Alan should fend for himself till sunset; but as soon as it began to grow dark, he should lie in the fields by the roadside near to Newhalls, and stir for naught until he heard me whistling. At first, I proposed I should give him for signal the "Bonnie House

of Airlie," which was a favorite of mine; but he objected
that as the piece was very commonly known, any ploughman might whistle it by accident; and taught me instead
a little fragment of a Highland air, which has run in my
head from that day to this, and will likely run in my head
when I lie dying. Every time it comes to me it takes me
off to that last day of my uncertainty, with Alan sitting up
in the bottom of the den, whistling and beating the measure with a finger, and the gray of the dawn coming on his
face.

I was in the long street of Queensferry before the sun
was up. It was a fairly built burgh, the houses of good
stone, many slated; the town-hall not so fine, I thought, as
that of Peebles, nor yet the street so noble; but take it altogether, it put me to shame for my foul tatters.

As the morning went on, and the fires began to be
kindled, and the windows to open, and the people to appear
out of the houses, my concern and despondency grew ever
the blacker. I saw now that I had no grounds so stand
upon; and no clear proof of my rights, nor so much as
of my own identity. If it was all a bubble, I was indeed
sorely cheated and left in a sore pass. Even if things were
as I conceived, it would in all likelihood take time to
establish my contentions; and what time had I to spare
with three shillings in my pocket, and a condemned, hunted
man upon my hands to ship out of the country? Truly,
if my hope broke with me, it might come to the gallows
yet for both of us. And as I continued to walk up and
down, and saw people look askance at me upon the street
or out of windows, and nudging or speaking one to another with smiles, I began to take fresh apprehension; that
it might be no easy matter even to come to speech of the
lawyer, far less to convince him of my story.

For the life of me I could not muster up the courage to
address any of these reputable burghers; I thought shame
even to speak with them in such a pickle of rags and dirt;
and if I had asked for the house of such a man as Mr.
Rankeillor, I supposed they would have burst out laughing in my face. So I went up and down, and through
the street, and down to the harbor-side like a dog that has

lost its master, with a strange gnawing in my inwards, and every now and then a movement of despair. It grew to be high day at last, perhaps nine in the forenoon; and I was worn with these wanderings, and chanced to have stopped in front of a very good house on the landward side, a house with beautiful, clear glass windows, flowering knots upon the sills, the walls new-harled, and a chase-dog sitting yawning on the step like one that was at home. Well, I was even envying this dumb brute, when the door fell open and there issued forth a little shrewd, ruddy, kindly consequential man in a well-powdered wig and spectacles. I was in such a plight that no one set eyes on me once but he looked at me again; and this gentleman, as it proved, was so much struck with my poor appearance that he came straight up to me and asked me what I did.

I told him I was come to the Queensferry on business, and taking heart of grace, asked him to direct me to the house of Mr. Rankeillor.

"Why," said he, "that is his house that I have just come out of; and for a rather singular chance, I am that very man."

"Then, sir," said I, "I have to beg the favor of an interview."

"I do not know your name," said he, "nor yet your face."

"My name is David Balfour," said I.

"David Balfour?" he repeated, in rather a high tone, like one surprised. "And where have you come from, Mr. David Balfour?" he asked, looking at me pretty dryly in the face.

"I have come from a great many strange places, sir," said I; "but I think it would be as well to tell you where and how in a more private manner."

He seemed to muse awhile, holding his lip in his hand, and looking now at me and now upon the causeway of the street.

"Yes," says he, "that will be the best, no doubt." And he led me back with him into his house, cried out to some one whom I could not see that he would be engaged all

morning, and brought me into a little dusty chamber full
of books and documents. Here he sat down, and bade
me be seated; though I thought he looked a little rue-
fully from his clean chair to my muddy rags. "And now,"
says he, "if you have any business, pray be brief and come
swiftly to the point. *Nec germino bellum Trojanum orditur
ab ovo*—do you understand that?" says he, with a keen look.

"I will even do as Horace says, sir," I answered, smiling, "and carry you *in medias res*." He nodded as if he
was well pleased, and indeed his scrap of Latin had been
set to test me. For all that, and though I was somewhat
encouraged, the blood came in my face when I added:
"I have reason to believe myself some rights on the estate
of Shaws."

He got a paper book out of a drawer and set it before
him open. "Well?" said he.

But I had shot my bolt and sat speechless.

"Come, come, Mr. Balfour," said he, "you must continue. Where were you born?"

"In Essendean, sir," said I, "in the year 1734, the 12th
of March."

He seemed to follow this statement in his paper book;
but what that meant I knew not. "Your father and
mother?" said he.

"My father was Alexander Balfour, schoolmaster of that
place," said I, "and my mother Grace Pitarrow; I think
her people were from Angus."

"Have you any papers proving your identity?" asked Mr.
Rankeillor.

"No, sir," said I, "but they are in the hands of Mr. Campbell, the minister, and could be readily produced. Mr.
Campbell, too, would give me his word; and for that matter, I do not think my uncle would deny me."

"Meaning Mr. Ebenezer Balfour?" says he.

"The same," said I.

"Whom you have seen?" he asked.

"By whom I was received in his own house," I answered.

"Did you ever meet a man of the name of Hoseason?"
asked Mr. Rankeillor.

"I did so, sir, for my sins," said I; "for it was by his

means and the procurement of my uncle, that I was kidnapped within sight of this town, carried to sea, suffered shipwreck and a hundred other hardships, and stand before you to-day in this poor accoutrement."

"You say you were shipwrecked," said Rankeillor; "where was that?"

"Off the south end of the Isle of Mull," said I. "The name of the isle on which I was cast up is the Island Earraid."

"Ah!" said he smiling, "you are deeper than me in the geography. But so far, I may tell you, this agrees pretty exactly with other information that I hold. But, you say you were kidnapped; in what sense?"

"In the plain meaning of the word, sir," said I. "I was on my way to your house, when I was trepanned on board the brig, cruelly struck down, thrown below, and knew no more of anything till we were far at sea. I was destined for the plantations; a fate that, in God's providence, I have escaped."

"The brig was lost on June the 27th," says he, looking in his book, "and we are now at August the 24th. Here is a considerable hiatus, Mr. Balfour, of near upon two months. It has already caused a vast amount of trouble to your friends; and I own I shall not be very well contented until it is set right."

"Indeed, sir," said I, "these months are very easily filled up; but yet before I told my story, I would be glad to know that I was talking to a friend."

"This is to argue in a circle," said the lawyer. "I cannot be convinced till I have heard you. I cannot be your friend until I am properly informed. If you were more trustful, it would better befit your time of life. And you know, Mr. Balfour, we have a proverb in the country that evil-doers are aye evil-dreaders."

"You are not to forget, sir," said I, "that I have already suffered by my trustfulness; and was shipped off to be a slave by the very man that (if I rightly understand) is your employer."

All this while I had been gaining ground with Mr. Rankeillor, and in proportion as I gained ground, gaining confidence. But at this sally, which I made with something of a smile myself, he fairly laughed aloud.

"No, no," said he, "it is not so bad as that. *Fui, non sum.* I was indeed your uncle's man of business; but while you (*imberbis juvenis custode remoto*) were gallivanting in the west, a good deal of water has run under the bridges; and if your ears did not sing, it was not for lack of being talked about. On the very day of your sea disaster, Mr. Campbell stalked into my office, demanding you from all the winds. I had never heard of your existence; but I had known your father; and from matters in my competence (to be touched upon hereafter) I was disposed to fear the worst. Mr. Ebenezer admitted having seen you; declared (what seemed improbable) that he had given you considerable sums; and that you had started for the continent of Europe, intending to fulfill your education, which was probable and praiseworthy. Interrogated how you had come to send no word to Mr. Campbell, he deponed that you had expressed a great desire to break with your past life. Farther interrogated where you now were, protested ignorance, but believed you were in Leyden. That is a close sum of his replies. I am not exactly sure that any one believed him," continued Mr. Rankeillor with a smile; "and in particular he so much disrelished some expressions of mine that (in a word) he showed me to the door. We were then at a full stand; for whatever shrewd suspicions we might entertain, we had no shadow of probation. In the very article, comes Captain Hoseason with the story of your drowning; whereupon all fell through; with no consequences but concern to Mr. Campbell, injury to my pocket, and another blot upon your uncle's character, which could very ill afford it. And now, Mr. Balfour," said he, "you understand the whole process of these matters, and can judge for yourself to what extent I may be trusted."

Indeed he was more pedantic than I can represent him, and placed more scraps of Latin in his speech; but it was all uttered with a fine geniality of eye and manner which went far to conquer my distrust. Moreover, I could see he now treated me as if I was myself beyond a doubt; so that first point of my identity seemed fully granted.

"Sir," said I, "if I tell you my story, I must commit a friend's life to your discretion. Pass me your word it shall be sacred; and for what touches myself, I will ask no better guarantee than just your face."

He passed me his word very seriously. "But," said he, "these are rather alarming prolocutions; and if there are in your story any little jostles to the law, I would beg you to bear in mind that I am a lawyer, and pass lightly."

Thereupon I told him my story from the first, he listening with his spectacles thrust up and his eyes closed, so that I sometimes feared he was asleep. But no such matter! he heard every word (as I found afterward) with such quickness of hearing and precision of memory as often surprised me. Even strange, outlandish Gaelic names, heard for that time only, he remembered and would, remind me of years after. Yet when I called Alan Breck in full, we had an odd scene. The name of Alan had of course rung through Scotland, with the news of the Appin murder and the offer of the reward; and it had no sooner escaped me than the lawyer moved in his seat and opened his eyes.

"I would name no unnecessary names, Mr. Balfour," said he; "above all of Highlanders, many of whom are obnoxious to the law."

"Well, it might have been better not," said I; "but since I have let it slip, I may as well continue."

"Not at all," said Mr. Rankeillor. "I am somewhat dull of hearing, as you may have remarked; and I am far from sure I caught the name exactly. We will call your friend, if you please, Mr. Thomson—that there may be no reflections. And in future, I would take some such way with any Highlander than you may have to mention—dead or alive."

By this, I saw he must have heard the name all too clearly and had already guessed I might be coming to the murder. If he chose to play this part of ignorance, it was no matter of mine; so I smiled, said it was no very Highland sounding name, and consented. Through all the rest of my story Alan was Mr. Thomson; which amused me the more, as it was a piece of policy after his own heart. James Stewart, in like manner, was mentioned un-

der the style of Mr. Thomson's kinsman; Colin Campbell
passed as a Mr. Glen; and to Cluny, when I came to that
part of my tale, I gave the name of "Mr. Jameson, a Highland chief." It was truly the most open farce, and I wondered that the lawyer should care to keep it up; but after
all it was quite in the taste of that age, when there were
two parties in the state, and quiet persons, with no very
high opinions of their own, sought out every cranny to
avoid offense to either.

"Well, well," said the lawyer, when I had quite done,
"this is a great epic, a great Odyssey of yours. You must
tell it, sir, in a sound Latinity when your scholarship is
riper; or in English, if you please, though for my part I
prefer the stronger tongue. You have rolled much; *quae
regio in terris*—what parish in Scotland (to make a homely
translation) has not been filled with your wanderings?
You have shown besides a singular aptitude for getting
into false positions; and, yes, upon the whole, for behaving well in them. This Mr. Thomson seems to me a gentleman of some choice qualities, though perhaps a trifle bloody-
minded. It would please me none the worse, if (with
all his merits) he were soused in the North Sea; for the
man, Mr. David, is a sore embarrassment. But you are
doubtless quite right to adhere to him; indubitably, he ad-
hered to you. It comes—we may say—he was your true
companion; nor less, *paribus curis vestigai figit,* for I dare
say you would both take an orra thought upon the gallows.
Well, well, these days are fortunately by; and I think
(speaking humanly) that you are near the end of your
troubles."

He rose, called over the stair to lay another plate, for
Mr. Balfour would stay to dinner, and led me into a bedroom in the upper part of the house. Here he set before
me water and soap and a comb; and laid out some clothes
that belonged to his son; and here, with another apposite tag,
he left me to my toilet.

CHAPTER XXVIII.

I GO IN QUEST OF MY INHERITANCE.

Here I made what change I could in my appearance; and blithe I was to look in the glass and find the beggar-man a thing of the past, and David Balfour come to life again. And yet I was ashamed of the change, too, and above all, of the borrowed clothes. When I had done, Mr. Rankeillor caught me on the stair, and made me his compliments, and had me again into the cabinet.

"Sit ye down, Mr. David," said he, "and now that you are looking a little more like yourself, let me see if I can find you any news. You will be wondering, no doubt, about your father and your uncle? To be sure, it is a singular tale; and the explanation is one that I blush to have to offer you. For," says he, really with embarrassment, "the matter hinges on a love affair."

"Truly," said I, "I cannot very well join that notion with my uncle."

"But your uncle, Mr. David, was not always old," replied the lawyer, "and what may perhaps surprise you more, not always ugly. He had a fine, gallant air; people stood in their doors to look after him, as he went by upon a mettle horse. I have seen it with these eyes, and I ingenuously confess, not altogether without envy; for I was a plain lad myself and a plain man's son; and in those days, it was a case of *Odi te, qui bellus es, Sabelle.*"

"It sounds like a dream," said I.

"Ay, ay," said the lawyer, "that is how it is with youth and age. Nor was that all, but he had a spirit of his own that seemed to promise great things in the future. In 1715, what must he do but run away to join the rebels? It was your father that pursued him, found him in a ditch, and brought him back *multum gemeus;* to the mirth of the whole country. However, *majora canamus*—the two lads fell in love, and that with the same lady. Mr. Ebenezer, who was the admired and the beloved, and the spoiled one, made, no doubt, mighty certain of the victory; and when he found he had deceived himself, screamed like a peacock. The whole country heard of it; now he lay sick at home, with his silly family standing round the bed in tears; now he rode from public-house to public-house and shouted his sorrows into the lug of Tom, Dick, and Harry. Your father, Mr. David, was a kind gentleman; but he was weak, dolefully weak; took all this folly with a long countenance; and one day—by your leave!—resigned the lady. She was no such fool, however; it's from her you must inherit your excellent good sense; and she refused to be bandied from one to another. Both got upon their knees to her; and the upshot of the matter for that while was that she showed both of them the door. That was in August; dear me! the same year I came from college. The scene must have been highly farcical."

I thought myself it was a silly business, but I could not forget my father had a hand in it. "Surely, sir, it had some note of tragedy," said I.

"Why, no, sir, not at all," returned the lawyer. "For tragedy implies some ponderable matter in dispute, some *dignus vindice nodus;* and this piece of work was all about the petulance of a young ass that had been spoiled, and wanted nothing so much as to be tied up and soundly belted. However, that was not your father's view; and the end of it was, that from concession to concession on your father's part, and from one height to another of squalling, sentimental selfishness upon your uncle's, they came at last to drive a sort of bargain, from whose ill-results you have recently been smarting. The one man took the lady, the other the estate. Now, Mr. David, they talk a great deal of charity and generosity; but in this disputable state of life, I often think the happiest consequences seem to flow when a gentleman consults his lawyer and takes all the law allows him. Anyhow, this piece of Quixotry upon your father's part, as it was unjust in itself, has brought forth a monstrous family of injustices. Your father and mother lived and died poor folk; you were poorly reared; and in the meanwhile, what a time it has been for the poor tenants on the estate of Shaws! And I might add (if it

was a matter I cared much about) what a time for Mr.
Ebenezer!"

"And yet that is certainly the strangest part of all,"
said I, "that a man's nature should thus change."

"True," said Mr. Rankeillor. "And yet I imagine it was
natural enough. He could not think that he had played
a handsome part. Those who knew the story gave him
the cold shoulder; those who knew it not, seeing one
brother disappear, and the other succeed in the estate, raised
a cry of murder; so that upon all sides, he found himself
evited. Money was all he got by his bargain; well, he
came to think the more of money. He was selfish when
he was young, he is selfish now that he is old; and the
latter end of all these pretty matters and fine feelings you
have seen for yourself."

"Well, sir," said I, "and in all this, what is my position?"

"The estate is yours beyond a doubt," replied the lawyer.
"It matters nothing what your father signed, you are the
heir of entail. But your uncle is a man to fight the in-
defensible; and it would be likely your identity that he
would call in question. A lawsuit is always expensive,
and a family lawsuit always scandalous; besides which,
if any of your doings with your friend Mr. Thomson were
to come out, we might find that we had burned our fingers.
The kidnapping, to be sure, would be a court card upon
our side, if we could only prove it. But it may be difficult
to prove; and my advice (upon the whole) is to make a
very easy bargain with your uncle, perhaps even leaving
him at Shaws where he has taken root for a quarter of
a century, and contenting yourself in the meanwhile with a
fair provision."

"The great affair," I asked, "is to bring home to him the
kidnapping?"

"Surely," said Mr. Rankeillor, "and if possible, out of
court. For mark you here, Mr. David, we could no doubt
find some men of the *Covenant* who would swear to you
reclusion; but once they were in the box we could no
longer check their testimony, and some word of your friend
Mr. Thomson must certainly crop out. Which (from what
you have let fall) I cannot think to be desirable."

"Well, sir," said I, "here is my way of it." And I opened
my plot to him.

"But this would seem to involve my meeting the man
Thomson?" says he, when I had done.

"I think so, indeed, sir," said I.

"Dear doctor!" cries he, rubbing his brow. "Dear doctor! No, Mr. David, I am afraid your scheme is inad-
missible. I say nothing against your friend Mr. Thomson; I know nothing against him, and if I did—mark this,
Mr. David!—it would be my duty to lay hands on him.
Now I put it to you: is it wise to meet? He may have
matters to his charge. He may not have told you all.
His name may not be even Thomson!" cries the lawyer,
twinkling; "for some of these fellows will pick up names
by the roadside as another would gather haws."

"You must be the judge, sir," said I.

But it was clear my plan had taken hold upon his fancy,
for he kept musing to himself till we were called to dinner
and the company of Mrs. Rankeillor; and that lady had
scarce left us again to ourselves and a bottle of wine, ere
he was back harping on my proposal. When and where
was I to meet my friend Mr. Thomson; was I sure of Mr.
T.'s discretion; supposing we could catch the old fox
tripping, would I consent to such and such a term of an
agreement—these and the like questions he kept asking
at long intervals, while he thoughtfully rolled his wine
upon his tongue. When I had answered all of them,
seemingly to his contentment, he fell into a still deeper
muse, even the claret being now forgotten. Then he got
a sheet of paper and a pencil, and set to work writing and
weighing every word; and at last touched a bell and had
his clerk into the chamber.

"Torrance," said he, "I must have this written out fair
against to-night; and when it is done, you will be so kind
as put on your hat and be ready to come along with this
gentleman and me, for you will probably be wanted as a
witness."

"What, sir," cried I, as soon as the clerk was gone, "are
you to venture it?"

"Why, so it would appear," says he, filling his glass.

"But let us speak no more of business. The very sight of Torrance brings in my head a little, droll matter of some years ago, when I had made a tryst with the poor oaf at the cross of Edinburgh. Each had gone his proper errand; and when it came four o'clock, Torrance had been taking a glass and did not know his master, and I, who had forgot my spectacles, was so blind without them, that I give you my word I did not know my own clerk." And thereupon he laughed heartily.

Toward the time I had appointed with Alan, we set out from the house, Mr. Rankeillor and I arm in arm and Torrance following behind with the deed in his pocket and a covered basket in his hand. All through the town, the lawyer was bowing right and left, and continually being buttonholed by gentlemen on matters of burgh or private business; and I could see he was one greatly looked up to in the country. At last we were clear of the houses, and began to go along the side of the haven and toward the Hawes Inn and the ferry pier, the scene of my misfortune. I could not look upon the place without emotion, recalling how many that had been there with me that day were now no more: Ransome taken, I could hope, from the evil to come; Shuan passed where I dare not follow him; and the poor souls that had gone down with the brig in her last plunge. All these, and the brig herself, I had outlived; and come through these hardships and fearful perils without a scathe. My only thought should have been of gratitude; and yet I could not behold the place without sorrow for others and a chill of recollected fear.

I was so thinking when, upon a sudden, Mr. Rankeillor cried out, clapped his hand to his pockets, and began to laugh.

"Why," he cries, "if this be not a farcical adventure! After all that I said, I have forgot my glasses!"

At that, of course, I understood the purpose of his anecdote, and knew that if he had left his spectacles at home it had been done on purpose, so that he might have the benefit of Alan's help without the awkwardness of recognizing him. And indeed it was well thought upon; for now (suppose things to go the very worst) how could Rankeillor swear to my friend's identity, or how be made to bear damaging evidence against myself? For all that, he had been a long while in finding out his want, and had spoken to and recognized a good few persons as we came through the town; and I had little doubt myself that he saw reasonably well.

As soon as we were past the Hawes (where I recognized the landlord smoking his pipe in the door, and was amazed to see him look no older) Mr. Rankeillor changed the order of march, walking behind with Torrance and sending me forward in the manner of a scout. I went up the hill, whistling from time to time my Gaelic air; and at length I had the pleasure to hear it answered and to see Alan rise from behind a bush. He was somewhat dashed in spirits, having passed a long day alone skulking in the county, and made but a poor meal in an alehouse near Dundas. But at the mere sight of my clothes, he began to brighten up; and as soon as I had told him in what a forward state our matters were, and the part I looked to him to play in what remained, he sprang into a new man.

"And that is a very good notion of yours," says he; "and I dare to say that you could lay your hands upon no better man to put it through, than Alan Breck. It is not a thing (mark ye) that any one could do, but takes a gentleman of penetration. But it sticks in my head your lawyer-man will be somewhat wearying to see me," says Alan.

Accordingly, I cried and waved on Mr. Rankeillor, who came up alone and was presented to my friend, Mr. Thomson.

"Mr. Thomson, I am pleased to meet you," said he. "But I have forgotten my glasses; and our friend, Mr. David here" (clapping me on the shoulder) "will tell you that I am little better than blind, and that you must not be surprised if I pass you by to-morrow."

This he said, thinking that Alan would be pleased; but the Highlandman's vanity was ready to startle at a less matter than that.

"Why, sir," said he stiffly, "I would say it mattered the

less as we are met here for a particular end, to see justice
done to Mr. Balfour; and by what I can see, not very
likely to have much else in common. But I accept your
apology, which was a very proper one to make."

"And that is more than I could look for, Mr. Thomson," said Rankeillor, heartily. "And now as you and
I are the chief actors in this enterprise, I think we should
come into a nice agreement; to which end, I propose that
you should lend me your arm, for (what with the dusk and
the want of my glasses) I am not very clear as to the path;
and as for you, Mr. David, you will find Torrance a
pleasant kind of body to speak with. Only let me remind
you, it's quite needless he should hear more of your adventures or those of—ahem—Mr. Thomson."

Accordingly, these two went on ahead in very close talk,
and Torrance and I brought up the rear.

Night was quite come when we came in view of the
house of Shaws. Ten had been gone some time; it was
dark and mild, with a pleasant, rustling wind in the southwest that covered the sound of our approach; and as we
drew near we saw no glimmer of light in any portion of
the building. It seemed my uncle was already in bed,
which was indeed the best thing for our arrangements.
We made our last whispered consultations some fifty yards
away; and then the lawyer and Torrance and I crept
quietly up and crouched beside the corner of the house;
and as soon as we were in our places, Alan strode to the
door without concealment and began to knock.

CHAPTER XXIX.

I AM COME INTO MY KINGDOM.

For some time Alan volleyed upon the door, and his
knocking only roused the echoes of the house and neighborhood. At last, however, I could hear the noise of a
window gently thrust up, and knew that my uncle had

come to his observatory. By what light there was, he would see Alan standing, like a dark shadow, on the steps; the three witnesses were hidden quite out of his view; so that, in what he saw, there was nothing to alarm an honest man in his own house. For all that, he studied his visitor awhile in silence, and when he spoke his voice had a quaver of misgiving.

"What's this?" says he. "This is nae kind of time of night for decent folk; and I hae nae dealings wi' night-hawks. What brings ye here? I have a blunderbush."

"Is that yoursel', Mr. Balfour?" returned Alan, stepping back and looking up in the darkness. "Have a care of that blunderbuss; they're nasty things to burst."

"What brings ye here? and whae are ye?" says my uncle, angrily.

"I have no manner of inclination to rowt out my name to the countryside," said Alan; "but what brings me here is another story, being more of your affairs than mine; and if ye're sure it's what ye would like, I'll set it to a tune and sing it to you."

"And what is't?" asked my uncle.

"David," said Alan.

"What was that?" cried my uncle, in a mighty changed voice.

"Shall I give ye the rest of the name then?" said Alan.

There was a pause; and then, "I'm thinking I'll better let ye in," says my uncle, doubtfully.

"I dare say that," said Alan; "but the point is, would I go? Now I will tell you what I am thinking. I am thinking that it is here upon this doorstep that we must confer undo the fastenings, repenting (I dare say) and taken with whatever; for I would have you to understand that I am as stiff-necked as yoursel', and a gentleman of better family."

This change of note disconcerted Ebenezer; he was a little while digesting it; and then says he, "Weel, weel, what must be must," and shut the window. But it took him a long time to get downstairs, and a still longer to undo the fastenings, repenting (I dare say) and taken with fresh claps of fear at every second step and every bolt and bar. At last, however, we heard the creak of the hinges, and it seems my uncle slipped gingerly out and (seeing that Alan had stepped back a pace or two) sat him down on the top doorstep with the blunderbuss ready in his hands.

"And now," says he, "mind I have my blunderbush, and if ye take a step nearer ye're as good as deid."

"And a very civil speech," says Alan, "to be sure."

"Na," says my uncle, "but this no a very chancy kind of a proceeding, and I am bound to be prepared. And now that we understand each other, ye'll can name your business."

"Why," says Alan, "you that are a man of so much understanding, will doubtless have perceived that I am a Hieland gentleman. My name has nae business in my story; but the country of my friends is no very far from the Isle of Mull, of which ye will have heard. It seems there was a ship lost in those parts; and the next day a gentleman of my family was seeking wreck-wood for his fire along the sands, when he came upon a lad that was half drowned. Well, he brought him to; and he and some other gentlemen took and clapped him in an auld, ruined castle, where from that day to this he has been a great expense to my friends. My friends are a wee wild-like, and not so particular about the law as some that I could name; and finding that the lad owned some decent folk, and was your born nephew, Mr. Balfour, they asked me to give ye a bit call and to confer upon the matter. And I may tell ye at the off-go, unless we can agree upon some terms, ye are little likely to set eyes upon him. For my friends," added Alan, simply, "are no very well off."

My uncle cleared his throat. "I'm no very caring," says he. "He was nae a good lad at the best of it, and I've nae call to interfere."

"Ay, ay," said Alan, "I see what ye would be at: pretending ye don't care, to make the ransom smaller."

"Na," said my uncle, "it's the mere truth. I take nae manner of interest in the lad, and I'll pay nae ransom, and ye can make a kirk and a mill of him for what I care."

"Hoot, sir," says Alan. "Blood's thicker than water, in

the deil's name! Ye cannae desert your brother's son for the fair shame of it; and if ye did, and it came to be kennt, ye wouldnae be very popular in your countryside, or I'm the more deceived."

"I'm no just very popular the way it is," returned Ebenezer; "and I dinnae see how it would come to be kennt. No by me, onyway; nor yet by you or your friends. So that's idle talk, my buckie," says he.

"Then it'll have to be David that tells it," said Alan.

"How that?" says my uncle, sharply.

"Ou, just this way," says Alan. "My friends would doubtless keep your nephew as long as there was any likelihood of siller to be made of it, but if there was nane, I am clearly of opinion they would let him gang where he pleased, and be damned to him!"

"Ay, but I'm no very caring about that either," said my uncle. "I wouldnae be muckle made up with that."

"I was thinking that," said Alan.

"And what for why?" asked Ebenezer.

"Why, Mr. Balfour," replied Alan, "by all that I could hear, there were two ways of it: either ye liked David and would pay to get him back; or else ye had very good reasons for not wanting him, and would pay for us to keep him. It seems it's not the first; well then, it's the second; and blythe am I to ken it, for it should be a pretty penny in my pocket and the pockets of my friends."

"I dinnae follow ye there," said my uncle.

"No?" said Alan. "Well, see here: you dinnae want the lad back; well, what do ye want done with him, and how much will ye pay?"

My uncle made no answer, but shifted uneasily on his seat.

"Come, sir," cried Alan. "I would have ye to ken that I am a gentleman; I bear a king's name; I am nae rider to kick my shanks at your hall door. Either give me an answer in civility, and that out of hand; or by the top of Glencoe, I will run three feet of iron through your vitals."

"Eh, man," cried my uncle, scrambling to his feet, "give me a meenit! What's like wrong with ye? I'm just a plain man, and nae dancing-master; and I'm trying to be as ceevil as it's morally possible. As for that wild talk, it's fair disrepitable. Vitals, says you! and where would I be with my blunderbush?" he snarled.

"Powder and your auld hands are but as the snail to the swallow against the bright steel in the hands of Alan," said the other. "Before your jottering finger could find the trigger, the hilt would dirl on your breastbane."

"Eh, man, whae's denying it?" said my uncle. "Pit it as ye please, hae't your ain way; I'll do naething to cross ye. Just tell me what like ye'll be wanting, and ye'll see that we'll can agree fine."

"Troth, sir," said Alan, "I ask for nothing but plain dealing. In two words: do ye want the lad killed or kept?"

"O, sirs!" cried Ebenezer. "O, sirs, me! that's no kind of language!"

"Killed or kept?" repeated Alan.

"O keepit, keepit!" wailed my uncle. "We'll have nae bloodshed, if you please."

"Well," says Alan, "as ye please; that'll be the dearer."

"The dearer!" cries Ebenezer. "Would ye fyle your hands wi' crime?"

"Hoot!" said Alan, "they're baith crime, whatever! And the killing's easier, and quicker, and surer. Keeping the lad'll be a troublesome job, a fashious, kittle business."

"I'll have him keepit, though," returned my uncle. "I never had naething to do with anything morally wrong; and I'm no gaun to begin to pleasure a wild Hielandman."

"Ye're unco scrupulous," sneered Alan.

"I'm a man o' principle," said Ebenezer simply; "and if I have to pay for it, I'll have to pay for it. And besides," says he, "ye forget the lad's my brother's son."

"Well, well," said Alan, "and now about the price. It's no very easy for me to set a name upon it; I would first have to ken some small matters. I would have to ken, for instance, what ye gave Hoseason at the first off-go?"

"Hoseason?" cries my uncle, struck aback. "What for?"

"For kidnapping David," says Alan.

"It's a lee, it's a black lee!" cried my uncle. "He was never kidnapped. He leed in his throat that tauld ye that. Kidnapped? He never was!"

"That's no fault of mine nor yet of yours," said Alan; "nor yet of Hoseason's, if he's a man that can be trusted."

"What do ye mean?" cried Ebenezer; "did Hoseason tell ye?"

"Why, ye donnered auld runt, how else would I ken?" cried Alan. "Hoseason and I are partners; we gang shares; so ye can see for yoursel' what good ye can do leeing. And I must plainly say ye drove a fool's bargain when ye let a man like the sailor-man so far forward in your private matters. But that's past praying for; and ye must lie on your bed the way ye made it. And the point in hand is just this: what did ye pay him?"

"Has he tauld ye himsel'?" asked my uncle.

"That's my concern," said Alan.

"Weel," said my uncle, "I dinnae care what he said, he leed, and the solemn God's truth is this, that I gave him twenty pound. But I'll be perfec'ly honest with ye: forby that, he was to have the selling of the lad in Caroliny, whilk would be as muckle mair, but no from my pocket, ye see."

"Thank you, Mr. Thomson. That will do excellently well," said the lawyer, stepping forward; and then mighty civilly, "Good-evening, Mr. Balfour," said he.

And, "Good-evening, Uncle Ebenezer," said I.

And, "It's a braw nicht, Mr. Balfour," added Torrance.

Never a word said my uncle, neither black nor white; but just sat where he was on the top doorstep and stared upon us like a man turned to stone. Alan filched away his blunderbuss; and the lawyer, taking him by the arm, plucked him up from the doorstep, led him into the kitchen, whither we all followed, and set him down in a chair beside the hearth, where the fire was out and only a rushlight burning.

"Come, come, Mr. Ebenezer," said the lawyer, "you must not be down-hearted, for I promise you we shall make easy terms. In the meanwhile give us the cellar key, and Torrance shall draw us a bottle of your father's wine in honor of the event." Then, turning to me and taking me by the hand, "Mr. David," says he, "I wish you all joy in your good fortune, which I believe to be deserved." And then to Alan, with a spice of drollery, "Mr. Thomson, I pay you my compliment; it was most artfully conducted; but in one point you somewhat outran my comprehension. Do I understand your name to be James? or Charles? or is it George, perhaps."

"And why should it be any of the three, sir?" quoth Alan, drawing himself up, like one who smelt an offense.

"Only, sir, that you mentioned a king's name," replied Rankeillor; "and as there has never yet been a King Thomas, or his fame at least has never come my way, I judged you must refer to that you had in baptism."

This was just the stab that Alan would feel keenest, and I am free to confess he took it very ill. Not a word would he answer, but stepped off to the far end of the kitchen, and sat down and sulked; and it was not till I stepped after him, and gave him my hand, and thanked him by title as the chief spring of my success, that he began to smile a bit, and was at last prevailed upon to join our party.

By that time we had the fire lighted, and a bottle of wine uncorked; a good supper came out of the basket, to which Torrance and I and Alan set ourselves down; while the lawyer and my uncle passed into the next chamber to consult. They stayed there closeted about an hour; at the end of which period they had come to a good understanding, and my uncle and I set our hands to the agreement in a formal manner. By the terms of this, my uncle was confirmed for life in the possession of the house and lands; and bound himself to satisfy Rankeillor as to his intromissions, and to pay me two clear thirds of the yearly income.

CHAPTER XXX.

GOOD-BYE.

So far as I was concerned myself, I had come to port; but I had still Alan, to whom I was so much beholden, on my hands; and I felt besides a heavy charge in the matter of the murder and James of the Glens. On both these heads I unbosomed to Rankeillor the next morning, walking to and fro about six of the clock before the house of Shaws, and with nothing in view but the fields and woods that had been my ancestors and were now mine. Even as I spoke on these grave subjects, my eye would take a glad bit of a run over the prospect, and my heart jump with pride.

About my clear duty to my friend, the lawyer had no doubt; I must help him out of the country at whatever risk; but in the case of James, he was of a different mind. "Mr. Thomson," says he, "is one thing, Mr. Thomson's kinsman quite another. I know little of the facts, but I gather that a great noble (whom we will call, if you like, the D. of A.) has some concern and is even supposed to feel some animosity in the matter. The D. of A. is doubtless an excellent nobleman; but, Mr. David, *timeo qui nocere deos*. If you interfere to balk his vengeance, you should remember there is one way to shut your testimony out; and that is to put you in the dock. There, you would be in the same pickle as Mr. Thomson's kinsman. You will object that you are innocent; well, but so is he. And to be tried for your life before a Highland jury, on a Highland quarrel, and with a Highland judge upon the bench, would be a brief transition to the gallows."

Now I had made all these reasonings before and found no very good reply to them; so I put on all the simplicity I could. "In that case, sir," said I, "I would just have to be hanged—would I not?"

"My dear boy," cries he, "go in God's name, and do what you think is right. It is a poor thought that at my time of life I should be advising you to choose the safe and shameful; and I take it back with an apology. Go and do your duty; and be hanged, if you must, like a gentleman. There are worse things in the world than to be hanged."

"Not many, sir," said I, smiling.

"Why, yes, sir," he cried, "very many. And it would be ten times better for your uncle (to go no further afield) if he were dangling decently upon a gibbet."

Thereupon he turned into the house (still in a great fervor of mind, so that I saw I had pleased him heartily) and there he wrote me two letters, making his comments on them as he wrote.

"This," says he, "is to my bankers, the British Linen Company, placing a credit to your name. Consult Mr. Thomson; he will know of ways; and you, with this credit, can supply the means. I trust you will be a good husband of your money; but in the affair of a friend like Mr. Thomson, I would be even prodigal. Then, for his kinsman, there is no better way than that you should seek the Advocate, tell him your tale, and offer testimony; whether he may take it or not, is quite another matter, and will turn on the D. of A. Now that you may reach the Lord Advocate well recommended, I give you here a letter to a namesake of your own, the learned Mr. Balfour of Pilrig, a man whom I esteem. It will look better that you should be presented by one of your own name; and the laird of Pilrig is much looked up to in the Faculty and stands well with Lord Advocate Grant. I would not trouble him, if I were you, with any particulars; and (do you know?) I think it would be needless to refer to Mr. Thomson. Form yourself upon the laird, he is a good model; when you deal with the Advocate, be discreet; and in all these matters, may the Lord guide you, Mr. David!"

In the meanwhile Alan and I went slowly forward upon our way, having little heart either to walk or speak. The same thought was uppermost in both, that we were near the time of our parting; and remembrance of all the by-gone days sat upon us sorely. We talked indeed of what should be done; and it was resolved that Alan should keep to the country, biding now here, now there, but coming once in a day to a particular place where I might be able to communicate with him, either in my own person or by messenger. In the meanwhile, I was to seek out a law-yer, who was an Appin Stewart, and a man therefore to be wholly trusted; and it should be his part to find a ship and to arrange for Alan's safe embarkation.

We came by way over the hill of Corstorphine; and when we got near to the place called Rest-and-be-Thank-ful, and looked down on Corstorphine bogs and over to the city and the castle on the hill, we both stopped, for we both knew, without a word said, that we had come to where our ways parted. Here he repeated to me once again what had been agreed upon between us: the address of the lawyer, the daily hour at which Alan might be found, and the signals that were to be made by any that came seeking him. Then I gave what money I had (a guinea or two of Rankeillor's), so that he should not starve in the meanwhile; and then we stood a space, and looked over at Edinburgh in silence.

"Well, good-bye," said Alan, and held out his left hand.

"Good-bye," said I, and gave the hand a little grasp, and went off down the hill.

It was coming near noon, when I passed in by the West Kirk and the Grassmarket into the streets of the capital. The huge height of the buildings, running up to ten and fifteen stories, the narrow arched entries that continually vomited passengers, the wares of the merchants in their windows, the hubbub and endless stir, the foul smells and the fine clothes, and a hundred other particulars too small to mention, struck me into a kind of stupor of surprise, so that I let the crowd carry me to and fro; and yet all the time what I was thinking of was Alan at Rest-and-be-Thankful; and all the time there was a cold gnawing in my inside like a remorse for something wrong.

The hand of Providence brought me in my drifting to the very doors of the British Linen Company's bank.

(Just there, with his hand upon his fortune, the present editor inclines for the time to say farewell to David. How Alan escaped, and what was done about the murder, with a variety of other delectable particulars, may be some day set forth. That is a thing, however, that hinges on the public fancy. The editor has a great kindness for both Alan and David, and would gladly spend much of his life in their society; but in this he may find himself to stand alone. In the fear of which, and lest any one should complain of scurvy usage, he hastens to protest that all went well with both, in the limited and human sense of the word "well;" that whatever befell them, it was not dishonor, and whatever failed them, they were not found wanting to themselves.)